Redemption

By Karen Salamone-Jourdan

Edited by David Trousdale and Selina Lamken. Formatting, Cover Art, and Graphics by True Beginnings Publishing. All Illustrations, Cover Art, and text is Copyright Protected by My Original Works. Reference #63655.

ISBN-13: 978-0615875927
ISBN-10: 0615875920

Ordering Information:
Quantity sales. Special discounts are available on quantity purchases by corporations, associations, and others. For details, contact the Author at the address above.

To order additional copies of this book, please visit:
https://www.createspace.com/4416500

First Printing, 2013.

For Mom and Dad

I love and appreciate you beyond measure

To my children, Kelly and Katie, and my daughter-in-law, Nancy and future son-in-law, David Michael Trousdale. Thanks for the laughs, guys.

To my family and friends who made sure I stayed on track. Thank you.

To Selina Ahnert Lamken who took my vision for my cover and made it a reality. Thank you.

Finally, to my readers. Thank you for being so very patient.

Happy Reading Everyone!

Prologue

*L*egend said vampires didn't dream. The woman on the bed begged to differ. She dreamed the same dream, and she should know. She had it every day, but this time it was different. The images were clearer, sharper, and this time she knew. She would see it through to the end. Finally, she would see the face of the creature responsible for destroying her life.

Up until now, she had been successful in blocking his image. She didn't want to know what he looked like.

That time was over. She would allow herself to experience it all. She would relive it all, no matter what the cost.

Once again, she experienced the sweltering streets, the wild crowd. She heard the taunts from a thousand throats as the three condemned men were paraded through the street.

The blazing sun beat through her robes, made of the finest lawn. The heat made her feel hot, sticky and irritable.

She should not have come. Sheer curiosity bade her slip from her stepfather's house and make her way to the heart of the city.

Such a fuss, she thought, over three condemned men. What did they have to do with her? Why had she come?

Then, they were abreast of her, and the one in the middle fell. A snide laugh escaped her carefully rouged lips as He struggled to his feet. His eyes met her own, and she looked away, not daring to look at Him until he passed. Then she watched his back as He made his way through the crowded streets, staggering under the unbearable weight.

She turned to go. She needed to get home and get home quickly, before she was missed.

The attack happened so quickly. Clasped in a vice-like grip, she could not catch her breath or scream for help. He lifted her off her feet and dragged her into the shadowy doorway of a hovel.

The stench made her want to gag. So did her fear. How dare he touch her like this! He had no right! She would have him killed for touching her. She would see to it his death would be slow and painful.

Why oh why had she slipped from the protective gaze of Abram, her most trusted bodyguard? She should have remained at home, tending her two small sons and seeing to her husband's needs. Now, it was too late.

She was turned to face her attacker. She raised her hand, her fingers curved like talons to claw his evilly beautiful face, but he easily overcame her pathetic attempts. He laughed at her. He dared laugh at her! Did he not know who she was? She was the daughter of a king! She was the step-daughter of a king! He would pay for this outrage!

Looking into his deep eyes, now blazing red, she had only a moment to realize how perfect his appearance was.

Pale skin, as fine marble, covered sculpted cheekbones. Eyebrows slanted over those blazing eyes, giving him a forbidding look. His un-naturally ruby lips gave her a smile that chilled her.

His wide shoulders covered by fine black robes, gave truth to his strength and she could feel his thighs, tight against her and rock hard.

The smile widened into a grin and she could see white even teeth, and then watched in horrible fascination as the canines lengthened and sharpened.

He wanted her to see what he was. Wanted her fear the way some want food and water.

She fought in earnest, terrified, but her puny strength was no match for his.

He lowered his head and she felt his lips on her throat. Felt those lips part and felt his teeth on her skin.

The pain, as he bit, was unbearable and her head lolled back. Her bones and muscles felt on fire and she could feel the loss of herself. As her legs gave way, he held her still.

She was dying. She could feel her heart flutter in her chest and she knew she was dying, but just as the darkness began to wrap itself around her, she felt something sickly sweet and coppery forced down her throat. She wanted to spit it out, but was too weak even for that small reaction.

He worked her throat, forcing her to swallow his blood, laughing as she remained in his arms, powerless to do anything but what he wanted.

The pain increased tenfold before the darkness came to her. When it did, it was blessed relief.

This was not the end of it. Once again, she saw herself rise from her mourning couch. Slipping from her death chamber, where she had been laid after Abram found her in the street. She had heard the weeping of her two young sons. She heard the pitiful wails of her mother when Abram laid her to rest. She wanted to reach out and console, but she could not move.

To all of them, she was dead.

Now, rising from this bed of death, she was hungry. Abram stood watch, just as he always did.

Once again, she saw the horror on his face as she came to him, touched his shoulder and turned him to face her.

Wrapping him in an embrace, she made him just like her.

She would always need Abram, for she trusted no other. Nothing else mattered to her. She needed Abram, so she sired him, just as she herself had been sired.

She forced him, just as she was forced, to drink her blood as he lay in her arms, dying.

In the dream, she again saw herself drag his body and hide it until his awakening.

Returning to her death couch, she rested herself and waited.

She watched as she and Abram slipped from the palace the following night,

Thinking on the past years, she felt a charge in the air. The atmosphere around her felt different.

Something is coming, she told herself in her dream. The time of reckoning.

Chapter 1

J ulie King's eyes snapped open. The dregs of the dream still on her, she felt her opulent surroundings crowd her. She needed peace and solitude. There was just one place she could find those things.

Whipping aside the heavy, deep ruby drapes, she saw the rain beat on her window with tiny fists. Perfect! Nothing like a good storm to clear one's mind.

Dressing quickly in a black sweater and jeans, she drew fine leather boots on her slim feet and grabbing her leather duster, the same hue as her outfit, bolted for the door.

Julie entered the kitchen just as Abram, her bodyguard, friend and manservant, emerged from his own room. His piercing black eyes bored into her almond brown orbs.

Abram raised his bushy eyebrows and was disturbed when she hustled past him, growling, "Leave me alone!"

Emma Logham, Julie's housekeeper, raised her eyebrows as well, as the mistress of the house slammed the door behind her. Moments later, they heard her gun the engine as she tore from the garage, barely giving the doors time to open.

"Well, she's in a fine mood, today," Emma commented, mostly to herself, causing Abram to pause.

He liked this housekeeper. He liked her plump cheerfulness and twinkling blue eyes. Because he liked her, he made it a point to stay away from her. Now though, he stood next to her, while she submerged her hands in soapy water.

"She's been edgy lately, as have I." His voice was a pleasant rumble and Emma's cheeks pinked. She may be old, but she sure wasn't dead and Abram appealed to her.

"I've noticed. Is there something I can do?" Emma continued her work with hands that trembled slightly.

"There's nothing." He paused, studying her. She had an agile mind. Just how agile that mind was, remained to be seen.

Abram also felt a change in the atmosphere around him, and he knew his mistress felt it, too.

His dreams were dark and disturbing, and the urge to hunt, bite and kill was strong. Only his superior willpower kept him from running through the city streets, as he did in the old days, and feeding on hapless humans. His willpower, his soldier's discipline and his healthy fear of his mistress.

He knew she could end him just as she had sired him.

Still, he liked this housekeeper, with her cheerful ways and sweet demeanor. He needed to warn her.

"Missus Logham," he began but she stopped him.

"Emma... just call me Emma."

Abram flashed a rare smile. "Emma then. There is, I believe, going to come a day, and I believe it will be very soon, that I will come into this kitchen and tell you to leave. You must do so. I tell you this because I like you. I believe you are a good person and I tell you this to protect you. Something is coming. Something evil." He felt restless, uneasy.

To his utter shock and dismay, the feisty woman shook her head at him and looked him straight in the eye.

"I think not, Abram." Her voice was firm and almost motherly.

"I'm not the sort to cut and run. That girl,' she pointed a wet finger toward the door, "That girl gave me a shot when no one else would. You've both been more than decent to me, so no, Abram. I'm not gonna run." She gave him a saucy grin then and then added, "Now get out of my kitchen."

Going back to her dishes, her parting shot to Abram, as he headed out of the room, stopped him dead in his tracks.

"By the way, Abram. I know about the two of you."

The woman walked along the beach, soaking in the peace and solitude. She reveled in the storm buffeting the beach.

Wind, wild and wet, whipped her hair across her face like a thick, dense, black veil.

One of the things Julie loved about walking along this particular stretch of sand was the cool breeze coming from Lake Michigan. In summer, it cooled the air, making the hot, humid summers tolerable. She would wait until sundown and the beach goers would be gone and then walk along what she considered to be her stretch of beach.

Now though, it was late October. An odd time to be walking on Bradford Beach, but Julie enjoyed the solitude. She reveled in the waves crashing on the breakwater and the untamed storm breaking around her.

This storm was just what she needed.

She raised her head and sniffed the air. Something is in the wind, she thought, and knew whatever it was would be powerful and it would be coming for her.

Walking along, lost in thought, she slowly realized someone was watching her; and the notion caused her to pause as she scanned her surroundings.

She did not sense any threat, but Julie knew someone watched her, intensely.

She stopped and looked at the high-rise apartment building across from the beach.

Slowly and carefully, she scanned each window, searching until she found the watcher.

He stood at the window, staring intently down at her. Even from this distance, she could see the man behind the glass, thanks to her keen eyesight, a benefit of her 'condition.'

Julie faced him directly, taking in this possible threat.

This is a big man, she thought, and comfortable in his skin. She studied the wavy sandy hair, intense gray eyes, and the sweet expression on his face. Of course, she could not know if he could actually see her, but it seemed he stared directly into her eyes.

Odd, she thought, he is not like me, so how can this be? How can he see me? What does he know of me? She had more questions and no answers and that frustrated her, just as it brought a bubble of fear.

She was alone, possibly defenseless. Perhaps she had made a mistake coming here, after all.

Turning on her heel, she walked quickly down the beach, heading in the direction of the large shopping mall where she left her car. If this man was a threat, then Abram needed to know.

Julie walked swiftly toward her car, then stopped abruptly.

The creature, as she always thought of him, leaned against her vehicle, looking evil and elegant, just as he had been in her dream, and Julie hated him with every fiber of her being. Here stood the being responsible for making her what she was.

"What do you want?" Her eyes gleamed red as she spat out the words. "Get away from my car! Get away from me!"

His laughter was not pleasant. It was low, slimy, and evil, just as she remembered.

"I want what I've always wanted, my dear. I have come for you. It's time."

He reached for her and she viciously slapped at his long elegant hand. She remembered all too well how hurtful those hands could be.

She glared into his handsome face. He had the sensuous look of a wicked angel.

His hair, so black it shimmered blue, giving one the impression it had pulled every ounce of color from his pale face.

His skin resembled fine Italian marble. It was the eyes, though. One could get lost in those eyes, she thought, and surely lose their soul. Was not she the perfect example?

His very beauty was frightening, and sensing it, he reveled in Julie's fear, thinking he had the upper hand.

"Get away from me, " she spat out.

With sheer willpower, she forced herself not to tremble. She would not give him that satisfaction.

His smile turned to a sneer. "Oh yes, my dear. I will have you. I have waited a very long time for you. You will come to me and of your own free will."

"You can wait another two thousand years. You can wait for all eternity for all I care. I will never come to you. Not now, not ever! I loathe you. I detest you! If ever I can find a way to destroy you, I will. I promise you that!" She hissed at him like a spitting cat.

Because she was the only person who could destroy him, his rage gnawed at him like a hungry thing. How dare she! He would teach this ungrateful bitch who was master here! Hadn't he given her a wonderful gift? Wasn't he about to bestow on her another? Ungrateful little wretch, he thought. He would teach her who was master here.

If she did not want to be part of the plans he had for her, then he would end her, here and now.

Livid, he snaked out a hand, reaching for her throat. He would kill her on the spot and find another to take her place. It was his right, his prerogative.

Feeling those powerful hands on her, knowing he could kill her with a flick of a wrist, her fingers curved into talons and she elongated her canines, prepared to do battle with this creature. She would not go down without a fight.

He bared his own sharp little weapons, intent on tearing out her throat and twisting that beautiful head from her shoulders, but before he could act however, a noise coming from the far side of her small sporty car drew his attention.

It would not do to have a witness. He would, of course, kill whoever it was with the bad luck to interrupt him. It didn't matter to him. What was another pitiful life to him? Mortals were of no consequence to him.

However, seeing just who the intruder was gave him pause.

"Hello, Hunter. I should have known you'd show up to save the day," he ground out.

In his ire, he gave Julie a small shake, letting her taste his power.

The other man walked around the car, placing his body between the two combatants.

The creature shrank back, shielding his eyes with his free hand.

"We have a pact, my friend." The interloper said, calmly. "One you were about to break. That's not exactly playing fair," He said with a wide smile. "Tell me. What name have you chosen for this time and place?"

"Lance. Lance Ebon. I thought it rather suited me."

The hunter's smile became wider. "Nice play on words. The black spear. Very fitting. However, getting back to our original conversation, you cannot touch her. That is the agreement. Of course, you knew that, did you not? You weren't about to destroy your creation, were you?" The hunter chuckled. "No, of course you weren't."

The hunter had him and Lance didn't like it.

So sure of his power was he, so certain the woman would come to him, he agreed to that damn pact eons ago.   Now, for the time being, he was stuck with it.

Silently vowing his revenge on both, he turned and stalked away.

Julie turned and stared at her savior. She knew she had been moments from destruction. Her incredible strength was nothing compared to the creature walking away.

It hurt her to look at this person standing before her, but she forced herself to look into his calm eyes. Eyes that swirled with different colors and radiated an inner goodness she never understood.

His hair, worn long and curling about his shoulders, gleamed in the dim garage light. Those pure white locks gleamed golden. His entire body radiated that glow. She envied him.

His face, so serene and gentle, was too beautiful for words. She took in the gentle blush on high cheekbones and the full lips that even now curled with an amused, gentle and accepting smile. His wide shoulders and trim and toned body was clad in an elegant suit of slate gray.

He certainly knows how to dress, she thought, but then he has always looked so elegant, so perfect.

Still, she stared into his open, beautiful face and wondered about him, forcing herself not to shy away as Lance had done…

He was aware of what Julie had been, what she was now, yet she found no judgment in him. There was only a kind of beautiful acceptance along with a sense of waiting, and it hurt her. She felt unworthy.

"So, Hunter, you're here. You saved me from him, but still, you have no words for me. Nothing to guide me that I may save myself from this existence."

Hunter gave a small shrug.

"This much I can tell you. Seek the man you saw today. The one you saw in the window. He is part of your destiny. You must seek the man and one other. Learn from them, child. Perhaps then you will know what you must do."

"That's all you can tell me?" she hissed, "How very cryptic of you. Always, you are cryptic. You're of no help to me at all."

He turned and began to walk away.

"I saved you from certain destruction, child. That's enough for one day," he tossed over his shoulder as he made his way out of the parking garage.

Furious, Julie slammed her fist on the roof of her car. She had so much to deal with. First, she confronted the creature whom she loathed and now this hunter.

That was something else she found annoying. For eons, the hunter always showed himself, waiting and watching.

It was she who named him the hunter, because she felt he was always seeking her out, hunting for her. Never, though, in all this time had he ever murmured his name. Who was he? Why did he always seek her out, and then do nothing? Well, she decided, before this thing is through she would find out who he truly was.

Now though, she must go home. She had to speak with Abram and set him on a task.

Climbing into her vehicle, she brought the engine to life and roared out of the parking garage.

Damien Crist stood at his window, watching the woman down on the beach. From this height, fourteen floors up, he couldn't really make out her features. Oh, he did enjoy watching the wind whip those fabulous curls around her head, but he couldn't make out her features.

Still, something tugged at him. It was a sort of drawing deep in his soul. He wondered who she was. He also wondered if they were destined to meet. He rather thought so.

He watched as she came to a standstill, then turned and faced his building head-on. She couldn't see him, he told himself. Of course, she couldn't really see him. Why then, he wondered, did it feel as if she was staring straight into his eyes? Why did he sense this unease coming from her?

Interesting questions, he thought. He also knew the answers would be just as intriguing.

He wanted to reach out to her, tell her she had nothing to fear from him, but that was impossible. Still, fate had a way of working things out, he told himself. If she is truly his destiny, then fate would see to it they met. He continued to watch until she turned on her heel and walked back to the parking garage.

Hearing a noise behind him, Damien turned and watched his friend, Steve Worthington, enter the room bearing a tray with two steaming mugs.

"Come sit down, Damien. It's been ages since we've seen each other. I'm glad I decided to take a nice little side-trip before heading for New York."

Damien grinned. "My mother is thrilled to death you're here. Moreover, a word to the wise, you had better plan to spend at least one evening with her. She's bragging all over Wisconsin how she gave you your first big break."

Steve laughed. "Actually, big guy, she did."

Damien studied his friend. After living in Italy for the past two years, studying under the best designers, Steve had panache to him. The poor little frightened boy, whom Damien protected while they were growing up, was gone. In his place was a self-assured young man.

Steve was dressed elegantly in black. His sweater was of the softest mohair and his pants, tailored to fit his slight frame, suited him.

Mahogany brown hair waved around his sweet face, offsetting eyes the color of a fine emerald. When he smiled, he flashed an adorable dimple next to his generous mouth.

He could have had his pick of any female on the planet. Sadly, for the female sex, Steve was also gay.

"I'll never forget that night, Damien. Her dress for that dinner was a mess. I don't know what that woman was thinking. You know... the dressmaker your mom used. She totally ruined that outfit. There stood your poor mom, crying in the middle of the room, glaring at the dress and then stalking over and pulling every outfit out of her closet. She was in a tizzy."

"Yep, that's my mom." Damien smiled. "But, you came in and saved the day."

Steve waved that away, then sat and contemplated it. "Maybe I did."

"Yeah, but you had some fast explaining to do when dad walked in and caught you pinning stuff to her body and she, standing there in her underwear."

Steve dimpled at the thought. "Your mother handled that beautifully. Your dad was amazed after I added bits and pieces to a potentially wreck of a gown and made her something new and exciting. He was particularly pleased I managed to save him oodles of money, not to mention the wear and tear on his nerves since she didn't have 'a thing to wear!'"

Steven grinned. "And he was so thrilled, he paid for my school." Steve shook his head. "When you think about it, your family believed in me before anyone else did. Therefore, your mother IS correct. She DID give me my first big break and I will be eternally grateful."

Damien sipped his coffee. The two men settled into easy conversation. It seemed as if Steve had never been away.

"What's the matter, ol' pal? You look a tad peaked. Not coming down with something, are you?" Steve studied Damien's face with mildly concerned eyes.

"I don't know, Steve. I don't want to get into that, right now. I'm just going to sit here, drink my coffee and catch up with you. Anything else can wait."

Oh-oh, Steve thought. He knew what that meant.

Ever since they were kids, he knew about Damien's special gift, and Steven had seen Damien go into his visions more than once. To say the experience was upsetting was putting it mildly.

The two men spent the evening catching up about major and minor events in their lives.

Steve's broken heart over a young Italian who decided he wanted someone older... or in other words... richer.

They talked about Damien's broken heart when his fiancée walked in while he was in the throes of a particularly nasty vision and ran out of the room and out of his life.

Damien caught Steven up on family news. Steven, who didn't have family, caught Damien up on his life for the past two years, studying dress design.

"Now you're going to have your own show, Stevie! That's great news!"

"Yeah, well, the masters thought it was time for me to spread my gossamer wings. They're fronting me the money, but my collection will stand on its own, or it will fail. Then, I'll know."

If Steve was nervous, he didn't show it. Like so many things, he took this in stride, as well.

"So! Are we staying in for dinner, and if so, what do you have in your freezer?"

Damien grinned, showing perfect white teeth. "Plenty of frozen pizzas in there. Usually I just send out for something. I have every delivery place in a fifty-mile radius on speed-dial. Take your pick. There's also a decent restaurant in the building. We can send down for something from them, as well."

Steve sat back, cocked his head, and peered at Damien.

"You know, boy-o. You've managed to have the best of all worlds in this building. I hear the one you built for the masses is just as nice. I heard it's even kid friendly."

Damien shrugged. "It's almost the same as this one. Large, open concept living, dining and kitchen space. Plenty of counter space, too. Attractive built-ins. They're two and three bedrooms, just like this building, but the rooms are smaller, more compact. Still, we didn't skimp on the closets and yeah, it was important to make them kid friendly. Most of my tenants have a kid or two. We wanted to keep the rent down, so rather than cut back on materials we just made the units smaller. The folks living there seem to like it. There's outdoor play space, a pool in the building, and a grocery store. No restaurant, though, but it's located close to many restaurants in the area, so that's all right. Fireplaces are smaller, too. They all run on gas, are efficient, and give each of the apartment homes a nice feel."

"Rich kid with a heart," Steve said, smiling, "I always knew you'd do something exceptional. Any tenant problems?"

Damien shook his head. "It's funny. Everyone warned me about how the tenants would wreck the place. We've yet to have any problems. It's like, you know, give them a decent place to live, help them find a job if they need it and they go out of their way to not take advantage. I like proving the nay-sayers wrong."

The two men talked into the evening, and after Steve gave a couple of huge yawns, Damien suggested his friend turn in.

"You had a long trip. You've gotta be on Italian time, yet. C'mon. I'll show you where everything is. We can talk in the morning."

With Steve settled, Damien had some time on his hands. He glanced at his watch and saw it was just a little past nine-thirty.

Cool, he thought. I can still get some work done.

Walking over to his drafting table, he began to sketch.

Chapter 2

Julie barged into her house, slamming the door behind her. Abram and Emma looked at her furious face, and then glanced at each other. Knowing discretion is sometimes best, Emma bent over the sink, washing vegetables and minding her own business.

"We have to talk!" Julie said through gritted teeth.

"Yes madam, we certainly do."

Abram followed her from the kitchen and into her bedroom. Carefully closing the door, he leaned against it, arms crossed against his wide chest.

"Just give me a moment. Much happened since I've left this house. Let me collect my thoughts."

Abram shrugged. "Take all the time you need. I'm not going anywhere."

She rubbed her forehead, eyes closed while she tried to calm herself. She needed to work off this frustration, the fear. Tonight, she would not dance. Tonight, she would hunt and she would take Abram with her.

"First, I walked on the beach. It was glorious, Abram. All wind and rain and solitude. Then, I became aware of someone watching me." She described the man in the window and how it appeared he could see her, was studying her.

"He's not like us, Abram. How can this be? I know he watched me just as I watched him, but I don't understand it."

"Forgive me, madam, but how do you know?"

"I just know, Abram! Do not question me on this!"

Abram bowed his head, afraid of what she would tell him next. He didn't have to wait long.

"Tonight Abram, we will hunt. There is more to tell you, but we will hunt. However, before we do, you will go to this building and find out what you can about this man."

Abram's head snapped up, and he stared at her. Before he could say a word, she waved an imperious hand.

"There's more! Feeling unusually apprehensive, I thought I should come home and tell you this. As I approached my car, that... creature... the one who turned me into what I am, was there. He spouted off how I was promised to him. He informed me I would belong to him. In my fury, I wanted to harm him. He grabbed my throat, Abram! He could have killed me with one shake, but the hunter came out of my car."

As she spoke, Abram straightened, fury etched on his rugged features.

"The hunter is here, as well? Quiet for a moment! I must think about all of this."

Abram had to work through his own anger. How dare that loathsome creature put his hands on her? She had been stupid to go off on her own.

Julie waited, but patience was not one of her virtues.

"Abram, we must find out who this man is!"

"Think for a moment. Suppose he's in the employ of the creature? What then?" Abram thought it possible the unknown man could be in thrall. He could be the creature's minion. It would not be the first time the creature had employed a mortal. It was simple. One bite and the victim would do the master's bidding. He or she would be unable to help it.

Julie's eyes narrowed. How dare he question her? Why couldn't he see his duty as she saw it?

"Are you afraid, Abram? Fine! I'll do it myself!"

Knowing her impetuous nature, Abram was sure she'd make a bad situation worse.

"I'm not afraid. I've protected you all these long years. I will continue to do so. I'll do as you have said. I'll see what this man is about, but we will not hunt tonight. If your sire is here and the hunter as well, something is looming. We cannot take any chances." He rubbed his chin with the back of his hand. "To tell the truth, I too have felt disquiet. I've been having dark and disturbing dreams. I believe it is too dangerous to hunt, madam."

Julie opened her mouth to argue, but this time it was Abram who silenced her.

"We will not hunt, madam. You must give me time to find out what is afoot. Understood?"

Abram had kept her safe through more than a few lifetimes. His instincts were almost as acute as her own. She would not doubt him, now.

"Understood." Seeing the grim look on his face, Julie raised her eyebrows. "Something else, Abram?" She asked.

"Emma says she knows about us."

The Club was just beginning to fill up. Billed as the newest hot spot in Milwaukee, it boasted black and silver walls, a dramatic and transparent dance floor, and a sound system designed to thrill.

Its sophistication appealed to all ages, but this night, it filled with students from the nearby colleges.

Right now, AC/DC was rockin' the house. A few patrons were out on the dance floor doing their thing and having a good time.

Kirsten Charleston and her friends flowed through the door, chattering like magpies.

They were young, attractive, and it was Friday night. Everything was new and exciting. Life was like a great big crème puff and they intended to take a nice big bite out of it.

Kirsten and her friend Trish headed for the dance floor. AC/DC sang about the Highway to Hell and the girls got their groove on.

Sitting in the shadows, Lance watched the blonde curls bounce against Kristen's cheek. Her face was flushed with excitement and excellent health, and her large amber eyes glowed with happiness and enthusiasm.

Raising his head, Lance breathed in the scent of her innocence. This one would do, he decided, until the one he came for would be his or destroyed.

Rising from his seat with effortless grace, he crossed the dance floor just as the music switched to Stevie Ray Vaughn. As the tempo slowed, he held out his hand to the pretty blonde.

"Would you care to dance?"

Kirsten looked at the hand, then up into his eyes and took a step back. Then, she took a second step away from him and shook her head. She sensed there was something wrong about him. A small chill danced up her spine, and she took one more step away, putting more distance between them.

"No thank you. I'm with friends." She turned toward her friends and missed the hard look that flashed over his face.

Turning, he reached out a hand to her friend, the pretty black girl standing a little off to the side, watching him.

"Perhaps you'd care to honor me?" he asked.

Trish giggled and laid her hand in his, allowing him to lead her to the dance floor.

Together, they swayed to the music, and Trish let the sweet, sad melody fill her. She felt transported to another time; another place.

Trish moved in a little closer and wished the music would go on forever. She wanted to dance and dance and dance. She felt more alive than she had ever felt, before, and looking up into those strange eyes, she knew, deep in her core, this man could take her places. Strange and terrifying places, she thought, but being with him was all that mattered.

Kirsten watched her friend dance and noted a glazed look wash over Trish's pretty face.

This is wrong, Kirsten thought. He has mesmerized her or

something. Alarmed, she raced out on the dance floor and grasped Trish's arm, yanking her out of the man's arms, almost breaking the spell.

"Come on, Trish. We're going to get pizza and then I'll take you home."

Trish looked as if she was awakening from a deep sleep. She blinked twice as if awakening from a sleep, and she glared at Kirsten and yanked her hand out of Kirsten's grasp. Anger spurted from her eyes as she turned them on her friend.

"I'm not ready to leave. We just got here, and I'm not ready to leave." Even to her own ears, Trish knew she sounded petulantly bitchy. She did not care. She wanted to stay with this man. He made her feel things she had never felt, before, and it enraged her that Kirsten wanted her to leave.

She's jealous, Trish told herself. He chose me over her, and she can't stand it.

Kirsten would not, could not be swayed from her purpose.

This was a dangerous man and he had Trish in his sights.

She knew she had to get Trish away. Kirsten was terrified for her friend. If only she could call her dad, but there wasn't time. She had to get her friend out of this place, *now!* If Trish wanted to be mad at her, fine, but she was getting them both out of here.

"No, Trish, We're leaving. Everyone wants to go and we're going too. We have an agreement, don't forget."

Trish's bottom lip jutted out and Kirsten knew that meant trouble.

"I said I'm not leaving. I want to stay and dance and dance and dance." She smiled up at the tall man standing quietly next to her.

"That's fine, Trish. You want to stay… then stay. But! We do have an agreement. We arrive together and we leave together. You want to stay I can't stop you. Of course, I'll be calling your dad and letting him know you've decided to break our agreement and he'll have to come down and get you."

"I can see you home, if your friend wishes to leave." Lance interjected smoothly. Trish shook her pretty head. Trish knew Kirsten would follow through on her threat.

The rage that poured through her body shocked her.

She and Kirsten had been friends for ages, ever since they were

16

little girls. Why was she being so unreasonable? She didn't understand it and not understanding made her angrier. She slowly turned until her eyes were burning into Kirsten's.

She also was painfully aware that Kirsten would do exactly as she threatened. She would call her parents and then she would have an awful lot of explaining to do. How could she explain what she, herself, didn't understand?

Trish was backed into a corner and she knew it. What brought her anger up one more notch was the fact that Kirsten knew it, too.

"Fine! I'll leave, Kirsten, but you should know this is probably going to be the last time I speak to you for the rest of my life."

Trish turned in a huff and stalked from the dance floor. She gathered up her purse and jacket, and then stood, her arms crossed against her chest, shooting daggers with her eyes. Her sole target was Kirsten.

Unhappily, Kirsten joined Trish, and the two girls left together.

The stranger watched them go. He wasn't worried. He had made the mental connection while on the dance floor. It had been so easy, and that was just sad.

She had been so receptive and there had been no resistance. He would prefer someone with a little more fire, but for now, this one would do until he found a more suitable playmate.

He watched them go, knowing he could and would find her at his leisure. He would simply follow her scent.

For the time being, the pretty blonde was out of his reach, but he was patient. She had sensed something about him, and that surprised him. Unlike her friend, she was able to resist his powers, and later, he would wonder about that. Nevertheless, he had loads of time and when the time was right, he'd finally have her in his grasp.

Moving casually, not wanting to draw attention, he left The Club and stood outside.

Tonight he needed the hunt. He wanted the thrill of the kill and to feel fresh, hot blood jet down his throat. Raising his head, he flared his nostrils and sniffed the air until he caught the scent he wanted.

In one leap, he reached the top of The Club, then unobserved, raced from rooftop to rooftop. If mere mortals witnessed anything, it would not register. They would see nothing more than a blur on the landscape.

They would naturally assume their eyes were playing tricks on them and disregard what they were seeing.

Sensing his prey was almost to her destination, he poured on the speed. He wanted to get there, first.

He needed time to look around the area and make his plan.

In the past, Lance found doing things on the spur of the moment usually didn't end well. So, he would check out the area, make a plan, and wait.

The girls traveled in silence. Kirsten asked if Trish wanted to get something to eat. Trish gave a tight shake of her head and continued to stare forward. So, Kirsten thought, we're going to be mad at each other. She sighed. She and Trish never quarreled, but now, they were at odds with one another. That made Kirsten sad but angered her, as well. How could Trish not realize that man was seriously bad news, she mused?

Trish sat in the passenger seat, seething, lost in her own thoughts. She didn't want to leave him. She loved how she felt in his arms, and Kirsten had spoiled it all. She would never forgive her and tomorrow, she would find him. Trish felt connected to him. Even now, as they traveled away from the city and into the suburbs, she could sense him. She could still feel his arm around her and the touch of his hand on hers. Yes, she would find him and when she did, nothing would come between them. Nothing!

He arrived at his destination. A pretty house in the suburbs with well-tended lawn and garden. He knew this was the correct house. Her scent was strong, here. He stood in the deep shadows and waited.

He decided on a very simple plan. He would wait for her to come home and wait until she was tucked into her dwelling. Using illusion, he could make his way into the house, kill whoever is with her, make her his, and get out before anyone was the wiser.

It was a simple plan, but a good one. Simple was always better. Now, though, his job was to wait for her to come home.

He didn't have to wait long. He saw the car pull up and watched from the shadows as she emerged, slamming the car door… hard.

The blonde also left the vehicle, and he felt his gut clench. He may have his wish after all, he thought. If she stayed with the other girl, he could have them both. The thought pleased him.

"Trish! Wait! Please. Talk to me."

"We don't have anything to say to each other. He chose me, and you were just jealous."

Trish had worked it all out in her head during the ride to her home.

Kirsten was jealous because the stranger wanted to be with her, had connected with her. That was the only reason Kirsten wanted to leave!

Trish had worked it all out in her mind on the way home. Kirsten was jealous and wanted to ruin everything. Trish would never forgive her.

Kirsten reached out a hand. "Trish, please. You're my friend. We've been friends, forever. If you want, if it means that much to you, I'll take you back to The Club. We can see if we can still find him."

Trish laughed in Kirsten's face, tossing away years of friendship.

"Sure, you say that now, Kirsten. You know he's probably gone. You know this is an empty gesture. Go home Kirsten. I don't want to see or hear from you, again. You ruined my life… thanks so much."

Tears filled Kirsten's eyes. She didn't know this Trish. She didn't understand where the sarcasm, which dripped from Trish's lips like acid, had come from.

Kirsten had to try one more time. Trish meant too much to her, and she couldn't let this go.

"Trish, please. I didn't ruin your life. Can't we talk about this? You're my friend, and I was worried about you. There was something wrong about him." Trish had begun to soften but Kirsten's slur toward the man hardened her, again.

"Go home, Kirsten. Just go home." Trish spun away and raced into the house, leaving Kirsten standing next to her car, crying.

He stood in the shadows, watching. He was about to make his move. Here was the object he wanted and just within his grasp. It would be so simple. All he had to do was reach out and grab her. They would be gone in the blink of an eye, and no one would ever find her.

He stirred, about to make his move, but light spilled from the front porch light and a muscular man emerged from the house. Walking swiftly, he strode to where the girl was standing, tears falling down her face, and reached for Kirsten enfolding her in a huge hug.

"Don't worry about it, baby girl. Trish is just being moody. You know how you women can be. Damned if I can figure any of you out."

Kirsten felt comforted by the enormous embrace. Sighing, she laid her head on Mister Rollings' wide shoulders and let him soothe her. She felt as if her world was crashing in around her. Trish would not talk to her, and that was made very clear.

Of course, it wasn't as if Trish was her only friend. She had many friends, but Trish was her soul sister. They shared everything, until tonight, that is.

She was hurt and confused and needed this little bit of comfort.

Wrapped up in her own misery, she was unaware of the man casually walking up the block toward them. Was unaware until he stopped and placed his hand on her shoulder.

"Is there something wrong? Can I help?" His accent made her think of far off lands and historic battles.

She looked up into his serene blue eyes and felt the world pitch. The next thing she knew, she was on the ground with Mister Rollings calling for his wife to come quickly.

In the shadows, Lance felt renewed fury. The Hunter's interference would not to be tolerated, and someone would pay for his interference. Oh yes, someone would pay, dearly.

He watched as two women ran from the house in answer to the man's call. One was older, obviously the mother, followed by the object of his heightened anger. There was his target, stooping over the prone girl on the sidewalk.

He watched as The Hunter brushed up against her, taking away her anger, breaking his thrall over the girl.

He heard her cry of anguish, seeing her friend lying in a heap in front of her. What the hell was the hunter even *doing* here, Lance wondered.

He watched as Trish cried over the prone girl on the sidewalk. He was forgotten. The little bitch had forgotten all about him. This was not to be tolerated.

Oh, the little minx would pay for betraying him. Her will was too weak. She would never make an appropriate bride.

He had plans for her, would find her useful for the time being and then he would destroy her, painfully and slowly.

He waited, hiding in the shadows and saw The Hunter turn and look directly at him, stare into his eyes.

He felt an unholy joy. The Hunter could interfere no longer. With his strange eyes narrowed, he saw The Hunter turn and murmur to the large black man, kneeling next to the prone girl.

"Guard your precious child well this night. There is danger for her." With that, he gave a slight bow in the direction of the deepest shadows and walked away, moving up the block until he disappeared from view.

Feeling a little foolish, Kirsten got to her feet and looked around, a little disorientated. Trish grabbed her friend and the two girls dissolved into tears.

"I'm so sorry, Trish. I wouldn't hurt you for the world." Kirsten began and was hushed by her friend.

"Shut up. I don't know what got into me. It's not important. My God, Kirsten, you fainted. Why did you faint? Are you okay, now? Maybe you should stay here, tonight."

Kirsten shook her head and patted Trish's cheek. "I can't. I have to get home or mom will scalp me. We have a girl thing going on, tomorrow. Shopping and stuff like that. Ever since she and dad got divorced, it's been like that. Almost as if she has to prove to me she's the better parent. I don't get it. I love both of my parents, but now, I feel like I'm in the middle of a tug of war."

Mister Rollings patted her shoulder. He and Missus Rollings were great friends of the Charlestons. The girls' friendship had trickled up to them, as well. So far, the Rollings had managed to stay above the divorce fray using diplomacy for the most part and avoidance when necessary.

"We parents can sure mess up our kids," Nathan Rollings said, softly. He hugged Kirsten tightly, and then let her go. "Are you sure you don't want to come in? Have something to drink before you head on home?" Again, Kirsten shook her head. "No thanks, I'd better get going."

She turned her head to where the odd stranger had walked and then disappeared. "I just wonder who that guy was, and I wonder where he went."

Nathan shrugged his meaty shoulders. "Must be staying with someone on the block. He sure was an odd duck."

Michele Rollings stood quietly, one arm around Trish and the other around Kirsten. She too looked in the direction the strange and beautiful man had gone.

"I don't think he's staying around here, Nathan, and I doubt we're going to see him, again. There was just something about him--" Her voice trailed off. With a wry grin, she shrugged and turned to Kirsten. "You go on home, then, Sweetie. Tell your mom I'll be calling her in the next couple of days. We have a date to take you girls shopping for dresses for Homecoming. I'm so glad you two made up, or it would have been decidedly awkward."

With a grin, she gave her own daughter a pat on the backside, sending her off toward the house, while she and Nate waited until Kirsten drove away.

With deep sighs, they followed their daughter into the house. At least one confrontation had been avoided, although neither of the Rollings knew what had brought about that little bout of temper from their usually sweet daughter.

"I'll ask Trish about it in the morning," Michele whispered. "For now, I think it's best if she just went to bed."

Nate shrugged. It was probably nothing. Just a little spat between friends.

The stranger's words were forgotten as they closed the door on the night.

Chapter 3

A bram made his preparations for the evening's activities. Taking a packet of blood from the small refrigerator in Julie's room, he poured some into a mug and warmed it before drinking it down.

"I'll be leaving shortly; you need to talk to Emma." Abram paused, "I like her," he added, and then entered his own room to dress for his excursion. His mistress wondered if the man was actually warning her. It was something to consider.

She came down the stairway and wandered into the parlors, the den and the family room. She liked to make sure everything was up to her exacting standards. Her housekeeper never let her down.

Slowly, she made her way to the back of the house, through the formal dining room and toward the kitchen.

Julie watched from the doorway as Emma went about cleaning the kitchen.

"We need to talk, Emma."

If Emma was frightened, she did not show it. "Of course Miss Julie. Let me just peel these apples while we talk. Planned on making apple pie. Abram so loves my apple pie."

Sitting together at the kitchen table, Julie stared into Emma's eyes. It would be so easy to destroy her, Julie thought. I could just reach out, grab her throat, and snap her little neck. Instead, she reached for an apple and bit into it.

"So Emma, what do you think you know?" Her deep brown eyes bored into Emma's calm ones.

Emma sighed. "I know a great deal, Miss Julie. I am not a fool. I noticed how you and Abram sleep during most of the day, never going out much, unless it was dark, or the day was overcast. So, I began to wonder. Then, you have little appetite, although you do eat, but the meat must always be blood rare." Emma shrugged. "Just so many little things. But, I never snooped! That's not my style." Julie took another bite and watched Emma closely.

"And then, one day, I brought your laundry up to your sitting room and your little refrigerator seemed to be leaking something. I didn't want it to ruin the rug, so I cleaned it up and opened your refrigerator. I saw all the packets of blood. Then, I knew for sure. Gave me quite a shock, I must admit." Emma paused and reached over to grasp Julie's hand. "Here I am, living in a household of vampires." Emma shook her head. "Couldn't believe it. Not at first. Who would have thought such a thing in this day and age?" She gave Julie's hand a small squeeze before reaching for another apple. "You have nothing to fear from me, Miss Julie. I've known for months. I would never do something to hurt you or Abram." A small chuckle escaped her lips. "Then again, who would believe me?"

Julie didn't know what to make of the woman's calm acceptance. Anyone else would have run from the house, screaming at the top of their lungs.

Honesty was needed here, before she decided what to do about her housekeeper. The bigger problem, though, was the fact that not only did Abram like the woman, Julie herself was terribly fond of her. Something Julie never expected.

"Emma, listen to me very carefully. I must now decide to either send you away or destroy you. You know entirely too much, so sending you away may not be an option, but I like you. I like you very much and sincerely do not wish to kill you, either. It's a quandary." Julie gazed out the window behind Emma.

Emma shrugged. "Why do either?" Julie's eyes snapped back to Emma's face. Emma smiled gently. "I look at you and Abram as family. You know, my husband... he died young. Went off to Vietnam and came home in a box. We never had kids. No man could compete with my Peter, so I stayed alone. I'm the last of my own family. I figured there was a reason for me being here so long. I'm going to be sixty-eight my next birthday." Emma sighed, then took Julie's cool hand in her warm one again. "I believe you and Abram are the reason. I'll be honest here. I wasn't sure I'd like you. I thought I'd stick it out and see what happened." Emma placed her free hand over her heart. "You two touched me. I've never seen people more lost than the two of you. I don't know how you managed to survive until I came along, but I mean to see to it that you continue to survive. That's a solemn vow." Emma gave Julie an impish grin. "And, if I told, who in the hell would believe me? I'm not sure I believe it. Now, you decide what you need to do, let me know and let me get back to my pie."

Julie shook her head and answered Emma's grin. "For the life of me, Emma, I don't know what to make of you. My first instinct is to kill you, but you've touched me, too. I think you would have made a fabulous mother and it's sad you never had that opportunity. I have to tell you, though, since we are being honest with each other. It may be dangerous for you to remain here. I believe I should send you to my house in London for now." Julie tapped an elegant finger against her lips while she considered this.

A look came across Emma's face. It was the one Peter called her bulldog look. Julie had only seen it once before, and seeing it now caused a small giggle to escape her lips.

"I've never been to London and I don't think I'd like it much without you and Abram." Julie sat back and shook her head, again. She was beginning to understand.

"You have a soft spot for Abram, Emma?"

Emma blushed. "Maybe I do and maybe I don't. At my age, there isn't time for such foolishness, but if I were twenty years younger, I'd give him a run for his money... vampire or not."

Now, Julie reached for Emma's hand, rubbing it softly. "We can discuss Abram another time. Just let me say this. He's older than you... much, much older, and you look great for your age." She took in the softly curling auburn hair and Emma's warm gray eyes. Her face was virtually unlined and her figure was one a much younger woman would envy.

"I must tell you this. Things are going to be happening. Today, I ran into the one who sired me, Emma. He's much older than I am. He's more powerful, more dangerous, and very, very sly. He'll come here one day to finish things between us, I think. He'll kill you without a thought. And, there's another. He has watched me through all these very long years. He has such goodness in him that it hurts me to look at him. With these two in the same area at the same time... this tells me something of some importance is about to happen. I don't want you involved in this. You will get hurt."

Emma shrugged a casual shoulder. "If I'm meant to go this way, than you sending me away won't change things. I've never run and don't intend to run, now." Emma grinned, again. "So... just how old *are* you and Abram? What was your name, you know, before this happened to you."

Julie answered the grin. "Abram was about your age when I turned him. As for me, I'm over two thousand years old. I was named for my mother. Her name was Herodius. Mine is Herodius the Younger and I once danced for King Herod. He was my stepfather. At the time I was turned, I was married and had two small sons. I too, am the last of my line."

Emma's jaw dropped, and before she could stop herself, she blurted out the first thing that popped into her head. "Oh my God. You killed John the Baptist!"

Julie's face began to look like a thundercloud and Emma clapped a hand over her mouth.

Abrams shout of laughter broke the tension.

Julie brought one small fist down on the table. "I did not kill John the Baptist! Yes, I danced for Herod and Pilot, but I did not *kill* the man. I never asked for his head. I asked for his *life*!" Julie shook her head. "You must understand this, Emma. Herod was weak. He was afraid of the Baptist. And, as much as Herod trembled with that fear,

26

Pilot trembled more. My mother's great sin was her ambition and her utter lack of morals. That's all I'm going to say about that."

Emma calmly peeled her apples, her head tilted in thought. "To think you really knew these people, lived during that time. It boggles the mind."

Abram fully entered the kitchen and Emma slid a glance in his direction. "Going out this evening, I see. Shall I hold dinner?"

Abram grinned at the woman's impertinence. Her eyes took in the black pants, shoes and hoody. A mask dangled from his back pocket.

"Don't hold dinner. I'm not sure when I'll return." Giving her a grin and a wink, he turned to his mistress.

"It's dark enough, now. I should have no problems. I'll come to you with what I discover and we will proceed from there. Promise you will remain indoors until I return." Only after gaining Julie's assurance that she would, indeed remain at home did he open the back door, looking around before making his move.

Abram slipped out the back door and was lost in the shadows.

"He's not taking a car?" Emma asked, and Julie shook her head. "No, he's not taking a car." Emma didn't need to know everything about their kind.

Abram stretched a little, standing just outside the door. His soldier's mind told him what to do and he would do it. He wasn't happy about it, but he would do it.

He ran, using the odd speed indicative of his race.

Arriving at the correct building, Abram found a shadowy area behind the building. He carefully checked his surroundings, ensuring no one was around before making the incredible leap to the top of the building.

This ability was one Abram enjoyed. He thought he'd be rather sorry to lose it if his circumstances ever changed and he was mortal, once again.

He scaled down the walls, looking much like a giant black spider, and reaching the balcony, scampered over it, and paused.

Abram used the moment to consider. If his mistress' sire was here and the hunter was here that was not unusual. Adding a mortal into the mix was, however.

He trusted his mistress' instincts. Those instincts had kept them alive through all these centuries. The fact of the matter was, he trusted her completely.

Abram didn't have time to analyze all the angles. He was ordered to investigate this mortal, and he would do just that. Still, he thought, if the mortal is embroiled in this thing between his mistress, the sire, Hunter and himself the logical conclusion would be that something big and powerful was about to happen.

The thought did not make him happy.

It was unlikely his circumstances would *ever* change and he had better keep his mind on the matter at hand. Daydreaming could have painful consequences for one such as he.

Following Julie's detailed instructions, Abram carefully and silently lowered himself to the appropriate balcony. Looking in through the glass doors, he could make out the figure of a very large man, sitting at a drawing table. As Abram watched, he saw the man make a few sketches, erase them and finally sit back in his chair reaching for a toy perched on the desk.

The man, to Abram's eye, looked disconcerted and bewildered. Abram grinned. He was willing to bet he knew exactly why the man was unable to concentrate on his work. His mistress was the type of woman who could fill a man's mind with all sorts of thoughts. It had been that way, forever.

Abram decided he'd wait out on the balcony for the man to go to bed. He could then slip into the apartment and do some snooping. At the very least, he could find out the man's name, perhaps learn what type of business the man indulged in. Whatever it was, it was obviously lucrative.

Abram watched from his perch on the balcony, waiting… and then all hell broke loose.

Chapter 4

Damien sat at his worktable and began to sketch. He had this great idea for an assisted living center. He wanted the apartments to be roomy, functional, but fun, too. He thought he might toss in a little elegance as well.

It sure is good to have Steve back, Damien thought. It was amazing. All the time Steve spent in Italy, learning design from the best of the best had not changed him, much.

Steve carried the polish from living abroad, true; but his core, the real Steve, was the same. That made Damien so damn happy. He wondered how his two years in Italy would change him, but deep down inside, Steve was still Steve.

He and Steven grew up together. Steve came to Damien and his parents when he came out, fear oozing from every pore. Steve's own family disowned him, but Damien's parents embraced him, and then paid his way through school. Now, he was on the brink of success. His own collection would be showcased in New York in just a few months.

Damien shook his head and grinned. The kid was definitely on his way. Damien wondered if Steve's family would relent and come see him, see all that Steve had accomplished. He hoped so. It bothered Damien a great deal. Steve always deferred when asked about his family, allowing everyone to think he had none.

Well, Damien thought, that wasn't quite true. He has us.

Pushing thoughts of Steve aside, he tried to concentrate on his sketch, but it was difficult.

While we worked, the woman he saw on the beach kept intruding. Who was she? Why did he feel this connection to her?

Damien tried to push her from his mind as well and just concentrate on his current project, but she kept popping into his mind. Giving up, he sat back in his chair and reached for the Slinky he kept on his desk.

The strange woman pushed everything from his mind. This is ridiculous, he thought. I don't even know who she is, where she came from. Why can't I get her out of my mind? The fact there was a connection between them puzzled him. How can that be?

He couldn't forget her graceful form, walking along the beach and all that glorious hair whipping around her.

He had wanted to race out of the building, find her and talk with her. He was sorry, now, that he hadn't.

Damien put the Slinky back on his desk and began to move away from it. He'd have a little Irish coffee, he decided. Maybe that would perk him up.

The headache which had nagged at him most of the day was still there. He wished it would just go away. He knew what it meant all too well. He had them off and on since he was seven years old.

It was the residue from being struck by a car at that tender age. And then, waking up, he had been cursed with the headaches and a little something extra. He had second sight, a gift he could have done without.

The headaches always happened to get a little more severe before a vision.

Sometimes, it would take a couple of days, and sometimes, it happened immediately. Damien thought he'd be much happier without

30

both.

He took two steps away from his desk and the vision hit him like a ton of bricks, causing him to lurch back to the desk and reach out, trying to break his fall as his knees gave way.

"Steve! Call Wolf Charleston!" he called out, then, was ripped from his comfortable home into hell itself, or so it seemed.

Abram watched as a slender man ran into the room, trying to lift the larger man onto the sofa. Unsure what to do, he waited until he saw blood ooze from the man's nose, eyes and ears. Going with instinct, he waited for the smaller man to turn his back as he reached for a phone. Abram had to act fast.

Thankful for that wonderful speed of his kind, he slid opened the patio door, raced across the room to the foyer and punched the elevator button, all in the blink of an eye.

The bell of the elevator alerted Steve that someone was coming in and he turned, hoping upon hope it was someone who could help him with Damien.

Steve had seen Damien in the throes of a vision before, but nothing like this. Shaken to his core, Steve thought his friend might be dying and he didn't know who the hell Wolf Charleston was, either.

Abram stood in the foyer, looking puzzled. Spying Steve and the disheveled room, he took a step closer taking in the awful sight before him.

"Hello, I seem to have gotten off on the wrong floor," he began, and then stopped. He widened his piercing eyes as he took in the overturned desk with its piles of papers scattered on the floor and the lamp now lying on its side, the shade dented.

He looked at the large man lying in the middle of the mess and pointed his finger. "What happened, here?" he let his tone become slight accusing.

At this point, Steve was so happy to see someone, he didn't stop to think. He knew no one could have made their way up to Damien's home by accident, but he didn't care. Here was someone who could help him.

"It's not what you think, friend." Steve began. "Look, I'll explain it all to you later, but right now I need help getting Damien onto that couch. He's too big for me to lift alone."

As soon as Abram touched Damien, he knew exactly what was happening. This was a true visionary. That would explain the connection between this man and Julie. Abram knew that connection would be a powerful one. More powerful than anything as mundane as love or chemistry.

And now that the connection was made, it could not be ignored and must be explored.

Letting these thoughts run through his mind, he gathered the groaning man into his arms.

"You can't lift him, alone," Steve began and then goggled as Abram did just that.

"Don't worry about it, friend. I'm stronger than I look." Abram told him with a wry grin. "Perhaps you should call for an ambulance. The bleeding from his ears and eyes is not a good sign."

Steve shook his head. "I can't explain this to you, but this has happened, before. He'll be okay." At least Steve hoped Damien would be okay.

"I'm supposed to call someone named Wolf. I don't know who the hell that is." Frustration pumped through Steve as he ran a shaky hand through his hair.

Abram gestured toward the Rolodex now resting on the floor at their feet.

"Perhaps the party you wish to reach is in there?" Abram suggested helpfully. Steve could have kissed this strange man.

He practically leaped for the Rolodex, quickly going through all of the C's. "It's not in here!" He cried out in frustration. Calmly, Abram held out a hand. "May I?" Steve almost threw the thing at Abram. "Perhaps you would be do kind as to tell me exactly who I'm looking for?" Abram suggested.

"Jesus... let me think a minute. Wolf Charles? No, that's not it... what the hell was that last name?" Tears of frustration stood in Steve's eyes. His body shook from head to toe and Abram thought perhaps he'd have two ill men on his hands.

"Calm yourself," Abram told him. "Panic at this time will not help your friend."

Steve took several deep breaths and ran his shaking hand through his hair again, causing his usually carefully coiffed locks to stand on end.

"Charleston! That's it! Wolf Charleston!" Steve almost smiled at this strange man standing in front of him.

Abram quickly moved through the Rolodex until he found the name he was looking for.

"Here! Detective Wolf Charleston!" Abram grinned at the shaking man. "Would you like me to place the call?" Steve shook his head as he reached for the phone and Abram moved toward the elevator. "Well, if I can no longer be of assistance, perhaps I should be on my way."

Steve reached out with his free hand and shook his head. He didn't know who this guy was, but Steve was pretty sure he wanted the man to stay. He felt calmer in the stranger's presence.

Abram didn't want to be here when the police arrived, and arrive they would. The quaking man before him hadn't yet thought that it would have been impossible for Abram to arrive using the elevator, but the police would. He needed to leave and leave quickly.

"There is nothing more I can do for your friend. The police will arrive, soon, and they will be able to assist you. I must be on my way. I have an appointment that won't keep." Steve nodded, and still quaking, he began to dial as Abram made his way to the elevator.

Steve, frantically punching in numbers never saw the black blur run through the living room. He was briefly aware of a draft as if someone had opened the glass doors, but when he glanced in their direction, he saw they were firmly closed.

Strange though, how the soft drapes seemed to sway ever so gently. Then, even that thought was driven from him mind as Damien groaned softly. Focusing his attention on the number, Steve continued to punch in the number with one hand, the other grasping his friend's arm.

Damien was in the throes of his vision.

The Club was alive with young people, reveling in their youth, their good health and their futures, all bright and shiny.

The man, but not a man, singled out two dancing girls. He could feel the beat of the music in his chest. He watched as the pretty blonde gyrated with her friends, her soft curls bouncing against her smooth cheek. Her long amber eyes were alight with fun. The man who was not a man ambled over as the music switched to something slow and sensuous. He held out his hand to the blonde, and when she rejected him, Damien felt his anger pulse through to his soul.

Damien wanted to call out a warning to the striking young black girl. No, no, he groaned but knew she would take the claw-like hand extended to her. Damien watched as the man who was not a man mesmerized the girl in his arms. This was revenge and it would be ugly.

The two girls quarreled, and the blonde made her friend leave with her. Damien hoped this would be the end, but he knew it wouldn't. He would have to watch the whole thing; helpless to stop what he knew was coming. Kirsten... the blonde girl's name is Kirsten. Damien would have to write it down, tell Wolf. This girl is connected to him, somehow, Damien knew.

Now, they are at the black girl's home and they quarreled, again. The black girl is very angry. She wanted to stay with the man who was not a man... but her friend brought her home, safely. Safely, yes, but the danger still looms. Damien knows this. He can feel the evil lurking, near.

Another man walks down the street. This man is different. He, too, is not a man, but he's pure good. His soul shimmers like precious metal. Damien sighs. Perhaps he can stop the evil.

The blonde crumples to the ground, and an attractive black woman emerges from the house, followed by her rebellious daughter. They see Kirsten laying on the sidewalk, the girl's father hovering over her. He's worried. He doesn't understand. The beautiful being whispers to him and Damien doesn't understand *his* words, either. Nothing is making sense. The gentle man wonders if he should make Kirsten stay. She's so pale. She shouldn't drive home.

Kirsten opens her eyes and smiles. She gets to her feet and waits for a moment, but the spell is over and she must get home.

The man who is not a man watches from the shadows. He sees the beautiful being interfere and he is enraged. Someone will pay. Love means nothing to this creature, and humans are for his entertainment and for food. Little more than cattle.

Damien sees the pretty blonde hug her friend. They are all right, again. The spell has been broken. Perhaps now, Damien will be released. But no, that is not the case. He will have to watch it all. He must take care to notice details. Wolf will want to know.

Now the small family makes its way into the house. The man who is not a man waits. The time is not yet right. Just a few minutes and he will have almost all he desires. He will be lacking only one thing. He wants the blonde, Kirsten. She is to take the place of another, for the time being.

Now is the time. Damien doesn't want to see what happens next, but he's unable to stop, just as he is unable to stop the inevitable. Someone is going to die. He's sure of it, and he's going to be forced to watch.

Chapter 5

He waited, tucked in the shadows, until his keen sense of hearing told him the family was settling in for the night. He heard the click, click, click of dog's nails on hardwood floors and grinned. He rather hoped it would be a large dog. He would kill it, first. That would add so much fear into the people residing in their peaceful little house. The kill and the drinking of their blood would be that much sweeter.

He heard two more things which set his teeth on edge. First, and rather minor, but still an irritation, the television clicked on. The second thing was the girl talking to her mother.

"I don't know what happened, mom. We were at The Club. It's uber cool there, and we were all dancing and having a good time. This guy came up and asked Kirsten to dance, and she refused. You know how she is. Then he asked me to dance and I thought, why not. All my friends are here. I won't get into trouble. The next thing I know, Kirsten is pulling on my arm and tells me she wants to leave. I was so mad at her, mom, and I don't know why. I wouldn't even talk to her on the way home. When we got here, I said some really mean things to her and was convinced I'd never talk to her, again. And then, I saw her on the sidewalk and all my anger just went away." Trish shook her head. "I just don't get it."

"Well, never mind. You girls are friends again and tomorrow Kirsten and you both will have forgotten all about this. Friends have a way of getting under each other's skin and then forgiving each other. I wouldn't worry about it."

"I know, but it's just so strange... my getting mad at her like that. Don't you think it's strange?"

"No. I think it's normal for two friends who are with each other almost constantly to become irritated with one another. Get some sleep. I have to call Kirsten's mom in the morning and set up a date to take you girls shopping. You need to give me your schedule so we can get this thing coordinated. Night Trish. I love you more than life."

"Night Mom. I love you more than life."

The loving exchange brought a sneer to his sensuous mouth. These mortals, he thought, they don't really know anything. They would, however, know true horror this night. Their insipid love couldn't protect them from the bloody storm he would unleash upon them.

He heard the closing of the bedroom door and the opening of another. Now was the time to make his move, he decided. Now, while they felt safe and secure.

He emerged from the shadows and silently made his way to the front door. Grinning, anticipation coursing through his shriveled soul, he rang the doorbell and waited.

Nate glanced at his watch as he headed to the door. He wasn't pleased. All he wanted to do was watch a little news, check the weather report and go to bed. The incident with Trish and Kirsten had unsettled him a little, but it was over. He hoped Kirsten made it home okay and made a mental note to ask Trish if she heard from the girl.

Max, their German shepherd tried to get between his 'dad' and the door, barking his head off.

Growling and snapping, Max just wasn't listening.

"Damn it Max! Quiet down! It's just the damn doorbell! What's the matter with you? Settle down!"

Nate opened the door and saw a frail little man standing on his front porch.

"How can I help you?" Nate's voice all but disappeared under Max's barking and he was hard pressed to hold onto the dog. Max lunged at the man on the porch which was very un-Max like.

"My car broke down some blocks over and your light was the only one on. I wonder if I might use your phone to call my grandson. I don't have a cell phone. I never believed in them until now, but perhaps I should re-think that." Lance smiled charmingly.

Nate pulled his dog back and moved away from the door, waving the gentleman in with his free hand.

"Sure, just let me put Max in the other room. Phone's right this way." Nate led the man into the living room and was about to lead Max into Trish's room when Lance made his move.

Breaking the illusion, Lance showed his true form and Nate's hoarse scream thrilled him. "What the hell are you?" Nate yelled.

Hearing Nate's scream, Michele bolted from their bedroom and ran down the hall in time to see a creature with long fangs and talon-like hands reach out and twist Max's head off his shoulders. The dog let out one yip and then was dead. While Michele looked on in stunned horror, the creature turned to Nate and grabbed him by the throat. The unnaturally red lips drew back, and the long coils of hair flew back, revealing red eyes and a nasty snarl. Then, the creature was on top of Nate, pinning him down while ripping out Nate's throat very slowly and very painfully. His strange red eyes never stopped staring at Michele, and her fear went up another notch until she was almost mindless with it.

The creature growled and sucked loudly, enjoying the terror on Michele's face. This was better than he thought it would be.

Nate's gurgling sounds were coming softer and Michele knew he was dying. There was nothing she could do for him.

Turning from the horrifying scene before her, she began to run down the hall.

Her last rational thought was getting to Trish; protecting her child from this horror which had invaded her home. She managed two quick steps before she felt those talons gripping her hair, pulling her back. Michele opened her mouth to scream to Trish. She wanted to tell her baby to run, but the scream that left her throat was mindless. The creature was ripping her hair out of her head, literally scalping her. The other hand reached around and grabbed her throat, cutting off her screams.

Lance decided it would be fun to toy with the woman. She would be punished for daring to think she could protect the girl. She, a mere mortal, thought she could stop him from taking what he wanted. He would show her who was truly master here.

"Please... don't hurt my daughter." Michele managed to gasp as one sharp nail opened a vein in her arm. She watched in horror as the thing holding on to her in a vice like grip sucked sharply on the open wound.

His mouth, smeared with Nate's blood and now her own, smiled at her. He wanted her fear and she couldn't help herself. Terror settled into every bone.

Gently, like a lover, he licked her throat, flicking his tongue over the carotid artery. He could feel her beginning to lose herself. The time was almost right. Just a little longer, and then he would gorge himself on all that wonderful, sweet, fear induced blood.

His claw-like hands began to paw her... inflicting little wounds here and there, and as the blood oozed, he enjoyed sucking on each wound, heightening her fear. Yes... she was almost ready, he thought. Just a little more.

Then, it happened. Michele's eyes rolled into the back of her head and she went limp. She felt the massive squeeze of her heart just before the heart attack took her.

Rage filled Lance. This was not how it was supposed to be! The woman deprived him of his greatest pleasure. The stupid cow died before he had his fill of her.

Her daughter would pay and pay dearly. He would still make her his bride, but it would be painful and difficult. That would be the result of her mother's treachery!

Letting anger take over, he swiped at the body he still held in his arms and with one motion beheaded the dead woman.

Now, he moved down the hall to his prize. He was sure she heard all that had gone on, before, and it pleased him. Her blood would be the sweetest of all.

Opening the bedroom door, he walked in and found the girl on the floor beside her bed, curled up in a fetal position, clutching a stuffed animal in her quaking arms.

"Come here, girl." He ordered but Trish was too frightened to move.

"I said come here! There will be punishment for disobedience." He growled at her.

Slowly, Trish came to her feet, every inch of her a shivering mess.

Trish looked at the intruder and saw the man she danced with at The Club. She couldn't think, couldn't begin to fathom how he found her and didn't want to think about the screams she heard from the front of the house. She knew, in the part of her mind that was still rational, that her parents were dead. Max was probably dead as well. Now, he had come for her. She hoped it would be quick.

Lance took her in his arms and holding her in a lover's embrace, lowered his lips to her throat. Trish closed her eyes, fearing him. Tears oozed from under her closed lids. And then, he bit. She felt as if acid coursed through her veins. Groaning at the unimaginable pain, her head lolled back against his arm while he sucked away at her blood.

Trish's world went from overly bright to gray. The pain was intolerable. Her very bones seemed to be on fire and the marrow dissolving. She was very near death, she knew, and still the agony went on and on. Would he never allow her to die?

Finally, she was aware of his release of her body. Now, she thought, now it would be over. Then, she felt something being forced between her lips and down her throat. She hated the coppery taste and somehow knew that it was his blood. She knew... just knew he was making her as he was. Then, awareness slipped away as did Lance.

He knew where they would take his prize. He would come for her, there. Until then, he must prepare a place for them. Somewhere discreet and safe.

Taking one last look at his handiwork, he prepared to leave the house.

It didn't surprise him to see the hunter standing under the lone street light, watching. He was always watching.

Lance stood on the front porch and faced his adversary. The hunter gave him a slight insolent bow. Lance returned it with a ghastly smile.

"Our time will come," Lance called out softly. Hunter smiled broadly. "Oh yes, it will come. Soon." Hunter promised before strolling away.

Lance left the carnage behind him and made his way to the seedy portion of Milwaukee. There was much to be done and little time to do it.

Chapter 6

L ogan Henry Charleston eased his six foot six inch frame into his chair and let his massive head drop into his hands. He probably shouldn't have had that fourth Captain's and Coke, but boy they sure went down easy, last night. Now, he suffered the consequences. Leaning back with a deep sigh, he reached for his coffee and sipped it slowly. At forty five years old, he just couldn't do the things to his body he did at twenty five.

Man, he thought, it's hell getting old.

Charleston was the scion of an old Tennessee family. His family practiced the law in one form or another, and it had been expected that he would follow suit. It didn't take him long to realize that criminals had more rights than victims. Oh, he loved the law, just hated lawyers.

His mother, Fancy Rayburn-Charleston, wrung her hands when her son told her he didn't think he could stomach practicing law.

"But Wolf, honey, our family has always practiced the law. There's a judge's seat waiting for you after you get some years under your belt."

It had been his mother who gave him the nickname, Wolf. She took one look at those long amber eyes and the shock of black hair, now turned silver, and blurted out, "Why he looks like a baby Wolf!" and the name stuck. Now, bewildered, she wondered where the boy just got some of those crazy ideas.

His father, Henry Charleston was even more perplexed. "Send him north, you said. He's got to be able to spread his wings, you said. Now, look what you've gone and done, Fancy. You've raised a rebel. That boy is an absolute rebel. Comes from consorting with those damn Yankees." For Henry Charleston, the War Between the States never ended. Now, to his way of thinking, they had a viper in their midst and a crazy one to boot.

"Look, mama and daddy. I still want to be involved in the law. I just don't want to be a lawyer. I'd rather be involved in a more hands on version of the law." He looked at his parents and almost laughed out loud at their stunned faces.

"How the hell can you have a more hands on version of the law, boy? Are you just stupid?" His father thundered, and Wolf couldn't stop the grin that flitted across his rugged face.

"I'm going to finish school, then see about becoming a cop. After that, who knows... maybe, the FBI or something." He thought his mother would faint.

True to his word, he finished law school, even managing to make the Law Review. Immediately after graduation a friend of his told him about some openings in the Milwaukee Police Department. Wolf took the exams, passed with flying colors and eventually was accepted into the academy where he aced every course.

Once a street cop, he did exceptionally well, making detective in five short years. During that time, he met and married a fiery red-head named Rachel, and together, they had one daughter.

It wasn't long before Rachel began making noises about his work as a cop. It galled her that they didn't live in a better neighborhood, although their own neighborhood, a new subdivision, was beautiful. She wanted him to give up working as a cop and become a lawyer. Their life-style would be better, Rachel told him. They'd have more money and be able to take nice vacations. Nothing seemed to please her, and once she realized he meant to stand his ground, she filed for divorce, took their beautiful daughter and left the house.

Now, Wolf was foot loose and fancy free. He didn't miss Rachel much, especially after she became such a harridan, but he sure missed the daily contact with his daughter.

Wolf sighed again and sipped a little more coffee, praying for a quiet evening. Usually, he didn't mind working the "B" shift, but tonight, slightly hung over, he didn't think he could stomach anything too extreme.

His phone rang, bringing his headache to a boil, and cursing softly, he reached across his desk to answer it. Briefly, he wondered where his partner was. Alicia Montoya Smith proved to be a great partner and if she were here, she would have answered the phone and left Wolf to nurse his hangover, but Alicia was nowhere to be seen.

"Charleston! How can I help you?" He barked into the phone then winced. Two tiny fiends behind his eyes gave him a good jab in retaliation for speaking too loudly.

"My name is Steven Worthington and I'm a friend of Damien Crist. I'm assuming you know him?" The voice coming over the phone was soft, melodious and just slightly panicked. Oh-oh, Wolf thought, please God, not tonight.

"Yeah, I know Damien. Something happen to him?" Wolf kept his voice briskly professional.

"You could say that. He had a sort of fit tonight. He's just coming out of it and he asked me to call you. He says it's imperative you come over as soon as possible."

Wolf rubbed the fingers from his free hand against his forehead. God wasn't listening, he decided.

"Okay. I'll be over in a few. Keep Damien quiet and if you need to, call an ambulance."

"Why would you say that?" Steve asked.

"Because if you're a friend of his like you said, then you are as aware of his special talent as I am and the last few episodes have been bad. Very bad. So, if you think he needs an ambulance, call one. I'll find you." Wolf hung up the phone and unfolded his powerful body out of his chair. Where the hell was Alicia?

Wolf headed for the door and almost knocked his partner over. She looked as if she had been crying and that stopped him in his tracks. Alicia never cried.

"Hey, what's up?" Wolf brought his booming voice down to a quiet rumble.

"Jake's had a heart attack. I just ran in here to let you know I'm taking family leave. They're not sure he's going to make it." Alicia's breath shuddered through trembling lips, and Wolf folded her in a huge embrace.

Jake and Alicia were the happiest couple Wolf ever knew, and he and Jake were close friends. "Where is he? Columbia? Okay, you go, take care of Jake and yourself. I got a call. Damien Crist needs to see me. I'll bomb over there, then head up to the hospital as soon as I can. If I miss you there, I'll track you down at home. Your parents coming in?"

Alicia nodded. "Yeah, they're driving up from Illinois, and Jake's folks are flying in from Florida. Oh Wolf. What am I gonna do if he doesn't pull through? He's only forty for God's sake!"

Wolf put his arm around her and steered her out the door.

"Listen Alicia, you just go and do what you need to do. You need something, call me. I'm gonna check in with Damien, catch up with you and if need be, I'll go out to the airport and pick up the in-laws. Okay? I'll fill in the captain, too. Give me those papers. Are they for Family Leave?" Alicia nodded and Wolf gave her shoulder a soft pat. "I'll get these to HR. You just go on, now. Tell Jake to take care of himself. I'll see you later."

Shit fire, Wolf thought. First this thing with Damien, and now it looked like he'd be flying solo. Well, better get on over and see what's up with Mister Crist and then head on to the hospital.

Before he left, he placed a terse note on the bulletin board telling other members of the squad about Jake. If nothing else, the rest of the crew would rally around them and Alicia wouldn't feel so alone... he hoped.

Damien let out a small moan. He could taste the blood seeping from his nose, and as he opened his eyes, he looked into Steve's worried face. He was back in his own home, thankfully, but he felt sick to his stomach. The headache that accompanied these visions was fierce, and this one seemed to be the worst, yet.

"Welcome back, buddy." Steve began, but Damien held up a hand. He lurched to his feet and made his way to the bathroom, letting the contents of his stomach find their way into the toilet. He felt as though a jack-hammer was doing a tattoo in his head, and it even hurt to move his eyes.

Slowly, the nausea passed, but the pain in his head still roared, though. God, he felt like a train wreck.

Steve entered the bathroom, carrying two ice packs. He placed one behind Damien's neck and held the other to his forehead.

"Come on, big guy. Let's get you back on the couch. If you hit the floor, again, I doubt anyone is going to come to my rescue, this time." Steve patted Damien's shoulder.

Damien made his way to the couch and was gingerly sitting down when Steve's words penetrated through the fog of pain. "How do you mean, 'again'?"

Steve shrugged "Some guy got off on your floor, accidentally. He helped me get you to the couch. Kind of a strange guy... neat accent, though."

Damien peered up at Steve. "You can't enter my apartment accidentally, Steve. You need the code to get up here."

An icy finger crept up Steve's spine. "Damien! I'm telling you, I looked up and this guy was standing in the foyer. Made me feel creepy, but he got you onto the sofa. As the matter of fact, he helped me find that detective's number and then, he took off." Steve pushed a hand through his hair. "Come to think of it, I didn't see him leave, either. Maybe I'd better check."

Damien waved a shaking hand. "Forget about it, Steve. I doubt he's still here, but I've got a feeling we're going to see him again."

A small chime as the elevator arrived had him glancing over. He gave a hefty sigh and wished with all his being that his head would stop pounding. He needed to talk to Wolf, needed to be clear on the things he saw, and he was afraid he couldn't do that with the demons doing a tap-dance in his skull.

Steve glanced up as the elevator doors opened. His jaw dropped as he caught sight of the man Damien referred to as "Wolf". The name suited the guy.

"Hey Damien. You look like hell, boy. Kinda how I feel." Wolf's grin was contagious. He'd worked with Damien, before on other cases, and their friendship was deep and lasting. Still, Wolf felt a twinge. He'd seen Damien after one of his visions, before, but never did he look like this. This had to have been a bad one.

"Thanks for coming over, Wolf. I have to talk to you. Sit down, and Steve here will get you coffee. You look like you could use a gallon, and after I tell you what I've seen, you may need something a little stronger."

Steve complied, handing the big cop a steaming mug of the hot brew. Wolf took a small sip and sighed. It was just the way he liked it.

"This was a bad one, Wolf. Just give me a few to get my thoughts together."

"Sure, take your time. I can wait." Wolf sincerely hoped he could wait, but was smart enough to realize Damien needed to organize his thoughts, or it would just come out as gibberish and would take more time to get it all straightened out so they both would understand.

Wolf glanced over at Steve and sighed. He would be an unknown quantity in the mix, and Wolf wondered just how he fit into all of this.

"Steve is my oldest friend, Wolf. We've been best friends since we were kids. He's seen me like this, before, and knew pretty much what to do. Seems to be a little confused, though. He tells me some guy managed to get up here 'accidentally'. What we can't figure out is how. No code, no entry." Damien scrubbed at his forehead with his fingers, trying to relieve the headache that still plagued him. His stomach was still rolling, as well, and he wished he could just go to sleep and forget about the things he had 'seen', but that wasn't to be.

"Oh yeah? What'd this guy look like?" Wolf took out a small notebook and jotted down the brief description Steve gave him.

"Seemed like he was pretty calm for a guy walking into the mouth of hell," Steve commented, "But I never thought about how he managed to get up here. I mean, I knew about needing to know Damien's code and all, but jeez... the guy just appeared as if out of thin air."

"He say anything?" Wolf asked and Steve shook his head.

"Okay, we'll get into that, later. Right now, Damien, if you're ready, how about you talk to me. Tell me why I'm here."

Abram lurked outside Damien's condo, listening to the men, inside. At one point, Wolf walked over to peer outside the patio doors, and Abram scurried up the side of the building. If anyone had thought to look up, they would have thought he was a giant spider, sitting on the side of the building. A very large spider.

Abram was grateful Damien lived at the top of the fourteen floor building. It made spying on him so much easier.

Abram could hear, quite clearly, Damien's description of the enemy, the things done to the girl and her family and heard the huge cop cuss blue fire as Damien drove home the fact that Wolf's own daughter was in danger.

"How the hell do you know Kristen is involved and this murdered girl is her friend? How the hell do you know that for sure, Damien?" Wolf ran his hand through his shock of silver hair and glared at the man lying on the sofa. Damien stared back calmly and waited for Wolf to regain some composure.

"Because I know, Wolf." The simple statement said in a calm voice jolted Wolf to his core. He'd check into this, of course. Once he assured himself that Trish and her family were all safe, he'd be able to tell Damien that for once, he was wrong. He had to be wrong! God knew he would move Heaven and Hell to keep his daughter safe.

"All right, tell me about this man who isn't a man, Damien. What the hell is he? Do you know how crazy this sounds? Are we talking demons, here, or what?"

Wanting to hear more, Abram moved slowly down the side of the wall until he was looking inside the room. He could make out the three men quite clearly. That was important. The mistress would need to know all he could tell her about the trio.

Abram's first instinct was to travel home and inform Julie of what he discovered, but realized his information was incomplete. The first two men were easy. He knew exactly where to find the seer and his friend. This big man was another story, and knowing his mistress, she would want to know about him, as well. So, for the time being, Abram stayed put. Out of this whole mess, though, the one thing Abram was sure of was this; his mistress and the seer were connected and he had the feeling, the very distinct feeling, the cop was connected, as well.

While the men talked, trying to figure things out without all the facts, Wolf's phone went off.

"Yeah?" He barked into the phone, and Damien watched as those long amber eyes narrowed, then cut over to where he was laying.

"Yeah, I know the place. I'll be there in ten." Wolf bounded for the door. Stopped once, and glanced back to Damien who watched him with calm gray eyes. "Get this figured out, Crist. If my daughter's involved, I want to know everything. Everything!"

Abram scurried up the building to the rooftop, and then drifted down to the ground. He gathered himself, and with that rare speed, made his way home. He had much to tell his mistress, it would seem.

Chapter 7

W olf bolted from Damien's building, his cell phone jammed against his ear. Even as the dispatcher gave him the address, Wolf knew where he was going. The address was all too familiar.

Climbing into his vehicle, he prayed the call was a mistake or some sort of horrible joke, but in his heart of hearts he knew. Nate, Michele and Trish were dead. Kirsten, somehow involved was in danger, and while he would move heaven and hell to keep his daughter safe, he feared he was in over his head.

If the things Damien told him happened to be true, how could he protect his daughter from this kind of evil? Wolf's mind raced. Damien could be wrong, he thought. The thought that Damien could be wrong wormed his way into Wolf's mind and became a litany. He had to be wrong. Things like this didn't happen. Not in this day and age. No, Damien didn't know what he saw. That had to be the answer. So it followed, if Damien didn't know what he had seen in his vision, then

Kirsten wouldn't be in danger, and he was worrying for nothing.

The practical side of his brain kicked in. Don't be stupid, Wolf, it told him. You are racing to your friend's house. They are all dead. This is really happening, son, and you better get prepared for whatever you are going to find. You better get prepared to protect your kid.

Still fighting with himself, Wolf braked in front of Nate's home. Uniformed cops swarmed the premises, taping everything off so as not to disturb the crime scene, and judging by the pale faces of even the most seasoned cops, Wolf's fear jumped up another notch.

"This is a bad one, Wolf." One of the senior uniformed cops told him. "Never saw one worse. I don't know what the hell went on in that house, but it's a mess."

Wolf glanced at the cop and hurried inside. Nothing could have prepared him for the scene as he came through the front door.

Blood, as thick as paint, covered the floor and walls of the home he knew was usually pristine. Michele took pride in her home, and now, it looked like a slaughter house.

The first thing he saw was Nate's German shepherd, or what was left of him. Then, his eyes tracked to where his friend lay. He wanted to walk over, gather the dead man in his arms and wail like a baby, but he knew he couldn't do that. It would disturb the crime scene and ruin any trace evidence. Giving one last anguished look at his friend's body, he carefully stepped over him and moved into the hall. There, he found Michele, her face still a mask of terror, and Wolf began to shake. He would have to turn this case over to other detectives, but he vowed he would work on this on his own time.

Wolf knew he worked with some of the best, but this hit too close to home, and mixed in with his grief was fear. Seeing all of this, terror for Kirsten raced up his spine, and his heart began to pound. He thought he may have a heart attack, and then gave himself a good mental shake. Keep your mind on the job, Charleston, he thought. You can't help these folks, but you can help Kirsten, so keep it all together.

The talking to helped until he walked into Trish's bedroom and saw his daughter's best friend lying on the floor. Compared to her parents' faces, she looked almost peaceful, but there was something different about her, as well. Something about her face looked a little hard, and he wondered if death had caused the usually soft features to change in such a way. She looked hard and somehow, older.

Wolf was joined in the bedroom by two other detectives. One of them, Harry Harrilson, placed a comforting arm on Wolf's shoulder.

"You knew them, Charleston?" Harry's voice was rough. The scene inside that house shook him, as well.

Wolf nodded. "The male victim is my best friend. His wife is close with my ex-wife and this girl," Wolf gestured toward Trish's body with a shaking hand. He swallowed hard against the lump of grief gathered in his throat, "this girl and my daughter are best friends. She's like a daughter to me."

Harry squeezed Wolf's shoulder. "We'll find him. Whoever did this, Wolf... we'll find him." Harry promised. Wolf nodded. With one last anguished look at Trish, he turned to leave. "If I can help in anyway, you let me know." He told Harry.

Grabbing his cell phone as he left Nate's home, he notified the dispatcher where he was going, then climbing into his car, pointed it in the direction of his ex-wife's house.

§

Abram eased himself into the kitchen and made his way to his room. He kept his own supply of blood in a small refrigerator in his room, and feeling drained, he needed to replenish himself. Once, he would have hunted and taken what he needed, but it wasn't allowed. Julie had been adamant about that, and since he trusted her completely, he usually refrained. But damn, he so missed the hunting.

Opening the packet of the pig's blood he and Julie drank, he poured the contents into a cup and heated it in a small microwave he kept in his room for just this purpose. A noise behind him caused him to turn, and there stood Julie, dressed in a silk nightshirt. She was in the process of shrugging into her robe when he was alerted to her presence.

"I heard you come in and couldn't wait." Seeing the cup in the microwave, she shrugged. "Replenish yourself, and then come to my room. We must talk."

Abram gave her a small bow, and she hurried from his room. Some things they preferred to do in private. Drinking the blood was one of them, even though there had been a time when they hunted, together.

Julie sat on a small settee and waited. She knew he would not keep her waiting long. Abram never kept her waiting long.

True to form, he joined her quickly and began to talk. She listened closely as he told her of Damien, his vision, and Wolf Charleston.

"You think he is a true visionary? A true seer of things?" Julie folded her hands, a sure sign she was paying close attention.

"I am positive of this, Madam. I listened after the policeman came in. It is apparent they have worked together, before. The other man, the small man, he also seemed to believe. He said he and the seer were childhood friends. The news of the murders also upset the policeman a great deal. The seer made it very plain. There is no question. The policeman's daughter is also involved. It is my belief the evil one has designs on the girl. I am, however, unsure as to why the evil one killed the black girl."

Julie tapped a finger against her cheek, another sign she was considering all Abram had to say.

"If what I suspect is true, Abram, he's looking for a bride. More than one, I would dare to say. We must be vigilant." She sighed and, feeling restless, walked over to gaze out the double doors leading to her veranda.

"Watch the newspapers, Abram. I believe this young girl is not truly dead but is turned. He is beginning to build a following." Julie said. "I wonder if the Hunter is aware of all of this," Julie pursed her lips. "But, of course he is. He is aware of everything, and yet does nothing. I do not understand him." She turned to Abram. "Go rest. We will consider this, later. I am going to try to rest, as well."

They both knew rest would be impossible. They both felt they were on the cusp of something huge and terrible. Julie briefly wondered where it would end.

Abram gave a shallow bow and headed for the door. Julie's voice stopped him. "We must think of what we will do with Emma. I do not wish to destroy her, Abram, but she could be a weak link."

Abram grinned. "Somehow, Madam, I do not think so. I am beginning to think she could be a real asset. Time will tell."

Abram left Julie to ponder the situation. She considered everything

Abram told her and weighed her options. They would, of course keep an open eye. She was sure the girl the evil one killed, tonight, would come back as his bride. Julie wasn't too sure how to deal with that. It's not like she could just wander into the county morgue and remove the girl's head for her. Sadly, the girl would be hungry when she woke, and Julie would just bet everything she had, that the evil one would be waiting. If he held true, he would keep the girl from doing anything too outlandish, but deaths would begin. That was inevitable.

Fidgety, Julie made her way to the kitchen. She wasn't too surprised to see Abram sitting at the table, peeling a pear. He glanced up as she entered the room.

"I thought you'd be resting." He murmured, causing her to give a wry smile.

"I could say the same about you." She reached in the fruit bowl and chose a peach for herself. Together, they snacked, speaking in low tones. A noise from the pantry caused both of their heads to snap in that direction. They were shocked to see Emma emerge, rubber gloves on both hands and a pail of soapy water.

"Pantry needed scrubbing. I couldn't sleep, so thought I'd tackle that, now. I see neither of you care sleeping, either." She dumped the dirty water down the sink, chattering as she worked. "No point in pretending I didn't hear you two, either."

Abram grinned. She really was something else.

"So, it seems to me you have a few major problems. I may have some ideas." She cleaned out the sink as she talked. "Obviously, you will have to deal with the dead girl, and I'll leave that to you. I wouldn't know how to begin to tell you what to do on that point. I do have a couple of other ideas, though, if you're interested." Not waiting for either Julie or Abram to comment, she kept on chattering. "You are going to have to contact this Damien Crist, as well as the cop you mentioned. Then, there's the problem of his daughter, as well. Well, that is simple. Arrange a dinner party. Small, intimate. You entertain just enough, Miss, to garner the gossips' interest. This one we'll keep very quiet, of course. I say this because an invitation to dinner, coming from you, will intrigue. It's one way to get the lay of the land, so to speak."

Moving to the coffee maker, Emma began measuring out freshly ground coffee into the basket.

Abram and Julie exchanged grins behind her back, and Julie shook her head. Perhaps Abram was correct. Emma could be an asset.

Wolf pulled up in his ex-wife's driveway just as his cell phone went off. Glancing down, his lips tightened. Alicia. The news couldn't be too good.

"Hey Alicia! What's up?" He could hear his partner sobbing softly.

"Jake died, Wolf. Twenty minutes ago. A couple of uniforms picked up the parents at the airport, and they made it just in time. I'm so glad they made it in time, Wolf. I can't talk. I'll call you, soon. You've been a great partner. I just wanted you to know that, Wolf. You've been a great partner, and one of the guys filled me in on your latest case. Don't be a fool. Let others take care of it. You're too close to it. Keep in touch. I'll call you, soon." She hung up before Wolf could say anything.

Jamming the phone into his pocket, he launched himself out of the car. Damn, first the Rollings are all murdered, and now, this. This is a real red letter day, Charleston, he thought. Yep. A day to go down as the original day from hell.

Walking up to the front door, Wolf looked around. He had that eerie feeling of being watched. Peering into the darkness around his ex-wife's home, he saw no one, but if experience taught him anything, it was this: always go with instinct.

Loosening his gun, he walked slow and quiet around the house. Finding no one lurking in the shadows, he shrugged and then, went back to the front door and pressed the button for the bell.

Movement from behind the door alerted him to his ex-wife's presence. He thought he'd rather face a bear in its cave than face Rachel, but this had to be done.

Rachel opened the door, and Wolf watched her face harden.

"Wolf, we've discussed this. You can't just come here any old time you want to. You're supposed to call, and yet, here you are, in the middle of the damn night. Are you drunk?"

"Shut up Rachel. This isn't a social visit." Grief hardened his voice. "I need to talk to you and Kirsten, and this can't wait, so put your engine in neutral and let me in."

"You know, you really can't come here and tell me what to do anymore, Wolf. What do you want?"

Wolf looked at his ex-wife and wondered why he hadn't caught on to the fact that she was, in fact, a harridan.

"Fine Rachel. We'll do this your way, as always." Wolf ran a shaking hand through his thick mane. "The Rollings family... the *whole* family, Rachel, were murdered, tonight. Still want to talk about it with me standing out here, or are you going to let me in?" Seeing Rachel's face turn chalky filled him with a great deal of satisfaction, just as telling her the rest of his news would be just as satisfactory. The woman thought she could rule everything. She'd find out just how wrong she was.

Rachel raised a shaking hand to her mouth and opened the door with the other. Her eyes were large and burning green in the dim light. She looked as if her red hair had drained all the color from her face, and her lips trembled. He'd give her that. Michele Rollings was her closest friend. She had loved Trish like her own and thought of Nate as a brother. Rachel leaned hard on Nate while going through the divorce, even though Nate had been careful not to take sides. God, Wolf was really going to miss him.

"Come into the kitchen, Wolf. Kirsten is home, and I don't want her to hear us. We have time to tell her. What happened?" She led him into the kitchen and began to set for coffee, her hands shaking.

"I can't go into detail, Rachel. It was a pretty bad scene. The perp even killed the damn dog." He paused, then told her the rest. "Rachel... there's more. There are indications that Kirsten could be involved."

Rachel spun around, her green eyes blazing. "Are you freakin' kidding me? Kirsten wouldn't hurt a fly. Much less her best friend! What the hell is the matter with you, Wolf?"

"As usual, you are jumping to conclusions! I said she *could* be involved, but not in the sense you are taking it. Shut up for a moment and let me explain." Rachel was fuming, and Wolf waited for her to settle down, a little, before continuing.

"You said there were indications Kirsten was involved! How? In what way?" Rachel drummed her fingers on the counter, a sure sign she was trying to keep her considerable temper under control.

"The girls were at The Club tonight," glancing at his watch, Wolf saw it was after midnight, "or rather, last night. It's possible Kirsten is the true target and the killer took out the Rollings as either a substitute or out of revenge. I need to talk to Kirsten. It's my understanding she rebuffed someone at The Club. This could be a lead."

"Dad?" Kirsten's soft voice reached Wolf as his daughter made her way into the kitchen. "What are you doing here, dad? What's happened?" Her seeking eyes took in her mother's pale face and her father's furious one.

"Sit down, Sweetie." Rachel's voice was soft as she guided Kirsten to a chair. "Your dad needs to talk to you." Wolf could see mother and daughter were both confused. He needed to question his daughter without alarming both the women. Yeah, he thought, good luck with that.

"Dad? What's going on? You're really scaring me." Wolf looked into his daughter's eyes, so like his own, and saw her love and concern.

"Kirsten, there's no easy way to tell you this, so I'm just gonna tell you." He took a deep breath, and then continued. "Last night, Trish and her parents were murdered." He saw Kirsten's eyes fill with tears and reached for her hand, clasping her tiny cold one between his large warm ones. "I need you to tell me everything you remember about last night, honey. I can't go into details, but it's very important. I need to know where you were and what happened, last night."

Kirsten took a trembling breath, her sobs hovering, trying to get out. "We went to The Club last night. It's really cool there, and we were there with a bunch of our friends." Kirsten was crying now, trying to keep her composure and failing. "There was this older guy, there. He asked me to dance, but he was... I don't know..." Kirsten shrugged and wiped the tears falling onto her cheeks. "He was creepy, dad. He asked me to dance, but I went with my gut, like you always told me. He asked Trish to dance, and it was weird. She didn't look like herself." Kirsten shrugged again, trying to find the correct words. "It seemed like she was in a trance, or something. Her eyes were so wide and kind of wild, and she looked older and sorta hard." Kirsten wiped at her falling tears, and then took a deep breath. "We fought, dad. I wanted to get her away from that creep. She was s-s-so mad at me, and we argued. She went into the house, and Uncle Nate came out. This really neat guy walked passed and said something to Uncle Nate, and then, I passed out. I don't know why. It wasn't like I was feeling sick or anything, but the neat guy put his hand on my shoulder and down I went. Trish came out with Aunt Michele, and we made up. They were gonna call you, mom, and make plans to go dress shopping for Homecoming." Kirsten laid her head on her arm and let the sobs come.

Wolf and Rachel waited until she cried herself out, both parents hovering, and Rachel worrying her hands. They were all dealing with grief in their own way.

Wolf reached over and rubbed her head, then jerked his own toward the front door, silently telling Rachel to follow him. Lowering his voice to a whisper, he filled his ex-wife in on the rest.

"There is a possibility that Kirsten was the target." He raised his hand for silence before continuing. "I can't tell you any more than that, Rachel, so don't ask. Keep her close. Don't let anyone in. I'd say keep her home from school, but she would suspect something, and we don't want to alarm her, do we?" His golden eyes bored into Rachel's green orbs. He half opened the door, then turned to Rachel, again. "We don't get along, Rachel, but we both want what's best for Kirsten, so for once in your life, listen to me. Keep her safe until we find the maniac who did this." Heading toward his car, he stopped. "One other thing. You may want to call Alicia sometime in the next couple of days. You seemed to like her, and Jake died tonight."

Leaving Rachel standing in the doorway, he headed to his car. Crist had some questions to answer, and there was no time like the present.

Chapter 8

J ulie sat at her writing table, deep in thought. What was her sire's plan, she wondered, and exactly where did this girl fit in? She let out a deep breath of sheer exasperation and began to pace around her room.

So, the sire is making brides. Why? Oh, he had other brides in other lifetimes, but he had been sloppy, taking who ever crossed his path. This is different. He's picking and choosing, if all that Abram said was true.

Something big was about to happen, this she figured out for herself, but how did the other's fit in? What the hell was she supposed to do? She thought back to the afternoon and her encounter with the big man staring down at her from his building. He, too, was involved. If Abram is correct, she mused, and he is a true seer, then obviously he is here to either help her, or visa versa.

More questions than answers. Julie didn't like it. She managed to survive millennium after millennium because she kept herself aware.

Julie knew where every threat came from and managed to get herself and Abram out of harm's way. Now, she felt like she was flying blind, and she didn't like it.

A soft knock on the door interrupted her thoughts.

"What is it?" Her voice sounded harsh. She didn't want to be disturbed while she pondered this new turn of events. She relaxed somewhat when Emma entered the room. The woman had a good head on her shoulders and a kind heart, as well. Still, Julie thought, she could be a liability.

"Didn't mean to interrupt you, Miss Julie, but there's someone at the door and I... well... I didn't know how to turn him away." Emma's cheek turned pink. "There's just something about him, but if you say so, I'll tell him to go."

"That's all right, Emma. I'll come down." Walking toward the door, Julie stopped and spun around to face her housekeeper. "How long would it take you to put together a small dinner party?" Emma shrugged. "Three or four days at the most."

Julie smiled. "I suspect you are a treasure, Emma. Let's plan it for four days from now. Hire a couple of girls to help with the housecleaning. Everything must be spotless. I'll leave the menu in your capable hands." Emma nodded her head as she followed Julie out of the room. "That will be all right, Miss Julie. Ummm... just one thing. Do we announce it to the papers or keep this quiet?" A small smile flitted across Julie's face. "No, this one we keep quiet, I think."

Going down the long stairway, Julie came to an abrupt halt. "Well, well, well. Hunter! What on earth are you doing, here?" Julie didn't know if she should be cross, afraid, or happy to see him. The Hunter in close proximity usually set her teeth on edge, but for once, she was happy to see him… or, maybe not.

Hunter, seeing Julie's conflicted face, smiled.

"You are in a quandary." Hunter's smile broadened into a grin. "Why do you think that is?"

Julie shrugged. As always, it irritated her. He read her so well.

"Makes no difference to me, Hunter. You never explain yourself, anyway." Seeing Emma on the staircase, Julie waved her hand, dismissing the housekeeper. Hunter flashed a charming smile at Emma, and Julie felt her irritation go up another notch as Emma's cheeks turned pink.

"Hunter, really! There's enough going on without you having to charm my housekeeper." Her scowl told him she meant business. "Now, suppose you tell me why you are here."

Hunter shrugged a broad shoulder. "You're going to have a meeting, so to speak. I wish to be included in your little party."

At his words, Julie raised an eyebrow. This was a first. Hunter always stayed in the background, until now, that is. Julie considered his words. His words added to her confusion, and she felt herself losing control of the situation, whatever that situation happened to be. Frankly, she didn't like it.

"Why would I include you? Why would you ask me this? Or, are you going to finally give me some tangible assistance, Hunter? That's something that's been lacking throughout our very long association with each other."

"My dear, I help you more than you can possibly know, but this is different. You are going to meet with some strong resistance when you bring these people together. I want to make sure you don't do something foolish." He almost laughed in her frustrated face. "You do have a temper, my dear. There are times you have to be reminded you are no longer the princess of the house."

"Really! I never do anything foolish, and I'm quite capable of controlling myself, as you very well know." She scrubbed her face with her hands, then peered up at the being standing so confidently in her living room. "Fine! You can come! Now, if there's nothing else, I have things to do."

Hunter did laugh, this time, seeing her anger flare in those exquisite brown eyes. "Actually, there is one more thing. The adversary is moving quickly," he lowered his voice to a whisper, "and I think it best if I stay close. I'll be staying here for the time we have. Surely, that won't be a problem." Julie had the feeling it didn't matter if it was a problem, or not. He waited, expecting her to refuse him. She chose to surprise. "Of course, Hunter. I'll have Emma make up a guest room."

She left him standing in the living room as she made her way to the kitchen. She wasn't quite sure how they came to be in the living room, but there they were. Just another one of Hunter's little tricks, she supposed.

Walking into the kitchen, she found Abram and Emma deep in conversation. Since they both stopped talking, she supposed she had been the topic.

"Emma, Hunter will be a guest. Would you mind?" That was the thing about Emma. One didn't need to draw pictures for her.

Emma wiped her hands and nodded. "Of course. I'll make up a room, right away." She hustled from the room.

Julie turned and watched her leave, then turned back to Abram. "Care to tell me what that little chat was all about?" She tapped one finger on a spotless counter and waited, much to Abram's amusement. He knew his mistress so very well.

"Sure. We were talking about you and your little dilemma. How do you feel having Hunter staying here? He'll be keeping a closer eye on you, you know."

Julie glared. "I know exactly what he'll be doing. It's fine. I don't care. Something is going to happen, and perhaps, it's best to keep him close. If only he would tell me the secret, Abram. All these centuries and I still don't know what he wants from me. I thought, if I stopped hunting, that would make him happy. Nothing! Then, I thought, if I gave to charity, that would make him happy! Still nothing! No matter what I do, it's never good enough! What does he want from me?" She ran a frustrated hand through her heavy curls. "All these years and I still haven't figured it out. I've done good things, Abram, thinking it would all end this nightmare, but still here we are." She stopped her rant and peered at him. "Do you ever resent me, Abram? Do you hate me for turning you?" The question caught him off guard. He took a moment to answer her.

"In the beginning, Princess, yes. I watched from a distance as my wife and sons grew old and died. There was nothing I could do. It was the natural way of things. I watched my grandchildren grow, age, and die and still, I remained. Yes, I resented you, but I also knew my duty. It was to guard you at all costs. I have honored that all this time. Perhaps, someday, you will know how to break this endless cycle, but for now, I am happy to serve you, as always."

Julie stared into his face, amazed. In all their time together, he never spoke so freely, and it touched her. Walking over, she slipped her arms around his slim waist and hugged him, hard. "If ever I find a way to end this, I will free you, Abram. I promise." Both were embarrassed at this show of affection, and Julie quickly moved away.

"Now then, Abram... we need to discuss the situation. If what I believe has happened, the girl will rise in three nights. The Evil One will be there to welcome his little bride. We must stop this, or there will be more deaths. That would cause us to have to leave, once again, and I like it here. I'm comfortable. We will need to find out where her body is and take steps to counter his plans. Are you in agreement?" Abram nodded.

"They will have taken her to the morgue, I believe it is called. We shall find a way in and destroy her, if at all possible. I will, of course, endeavor to find the location and will take care of this matter." He told her.

Julie nodded. Leaving the kitchen, she stopped and turned back to Abram. "I hope it will be that easy, but somehow I doubt it."

Damien emerged from his shower, his golden hair dark from the water. Steve eyed him, suspiciously. Damien didn't look too hot, and that worried Steve. Although Steve had witnessed many of Damien's visions while they were growing up, none had been as bad as the one last night. He wasn't sure how many more like that Damien could survive.

"Go to bed, old pal. You look like shit." Steve took in the pale face and the deep circles under Damien's calm gray eyes. "As the matter of fact, I've never seen you look this bad. Just go to bed before you fall flat on your face."

Damien shook his head. "No. Wolf will be back. He's on his way here, now. I can wait. I feel a little better." Damien forced a grin, and Steve winced. It looked more like a death grimace than Damien's usually easy smile.

"I don't think so, pal. Besides, it's after three in the morning. He'll have gone home, now, or on to more police work, or something. He won't be back here, tonight. You need your rest, Damien. You scared the hell out of me. As the matter of fact, you're still scaring the hell out of me."

Steve began to pace. He had been making plans of his own and knew Damien would fight him tooth and nail. Steve knew he had to be in New York for Fashion Week, but he wasn't leaving, now. Damien needed him, if for nothing more than to keep him grounded. He would make some changes to his collection and be ready to go for the spring shows. Luckily, he saved enough money while in Italy. He didn't have to work, right now, and he'd get his publicist to put a spin on things. It could work out to his advantage, he told himself. At least he hoped it would.

Damien sat on the long, white sofa and rubbed his knuckles against his forehead. If only the pain would just go away, he thought. He couldn't think clearly with the demons doing a tap dance in his skull.

"Damien, listen to me. That cop won't be back here, tonight. Trust me. It's late. He'll have other things to do. Just go to bed. Get some rest. It'll all be here when you wake up."

Again Damien gave a slight shake to his head and instantly regretted it. "No."

The two men settled in and waited. They didn't have to wait long.

Wolf arrived in the parking garage of Damien's building, and using the code the psychic had given him, he rode the elevator up to the top floor. Wolf wasn't in the least bit surprised when he stepped off the elevator and saw Damien sitting on the leather sofa.

"Okay Crist! Start explaining this to me."

Damien sighed while Steve stared at the big cop. He thought Wolf would have gone home, but here he was, big as life and twice as angry, standing in the middle of Damien's living room.

"I think I'm going to make some coffee. This is going to be a long night." He said and wandered off into the kitchen.

"What do you want to know?" Damien's voice was weary and didn't have its usual vibrant timbre to it.

Wolf paused and looked at the big man. Nice going, asshole, Wolf thought to himself. Damien looked like death warmed over, and here he was, barging in like a gangbuster. Wolf shook his head.

"Sorry kid. It's just been a bad night all the way around." He patted Damien's shoulder before taking a chair across from the other man.

"Take your time, but I've got questions that need answering."

Damien nodded, and again regretted it. "I know you do. It would be easier for me if I just tell you what I know."

That sounded reasonable to Wolf and taking out a notebook he reserved just for Damien's visions, he prepared to take notes.

"This being, Wolf. I can't call him a man because that isn't what he is, anymore, but this being is here for a purpose. I don't know what it is. That was hidden from me... but he's up to absolutely no good." Damien sighed. "He killed that girl, Damien, because he couldn't get to your daughter. She's in danger. Very real danger, and I don't know how you can protect her. And, there's more. The woman I saw walking on the beach. It's all connected somehow. Steve filled me in on the man who helped me during the vision. He's connected, too. I just don't know if they are friend or foe... but I have the sense this thing... the one that killed your friends... he has plans, and they include your daughter."

Wolf tried to take notes and remain calm but was failing, miserably.

"How the hell did he get in, Damien? I know... knew... Nate. He never would have let someone into his house. He wouldn't have let anyone in that late at night, for sure."

Damien sighed. How could he explain this? "Here's the thing, Wolf. Your friend thought it was safe. He thought he was letting in a frail old man. He didn't know."

"What the hell are you saying? This guy is a shape sifter or something?"

Damien shook his head. "No. Not a shape shifter. It was illusion. That's how he gets what he wants, Wolf. He uses illusion. He wanted your friend to see an old, harmless man, and that's what your friend saw."

Steve came in with a tray with three steaming mugs and offered one to each of the men before taking one for himself.

Damien sensed, rather than saw, Wolf stiffen, and he smiled slightly. "It's okay, Wolf. Steve and I have been friends since we were kids. He knows about my ability, and don't forget, he was here when the fun began."

Wolf relaxed, slightly, and sipped the brew. Damn, this was really good coffee.

Again, Damien smiled, then taking a deep breath, returned to the subject at hand.

"He went after the girl to punish your daughter. He made his move at The Club shortly after the girls and their friends arrived, but your daughter either has excellent instincts or she was damn lucky. She blew him off. He didn't like it."

A cold finger of fear teased Wolf's spine. "So, you think he's going to make another move toward Kirsten?" Wolf had to ask. He didn't feel any better when Damien nodded.

"Oh yeah. He'll try again. We just need to find out for what purpose. I think that's where the woman from the beach and the guy who made his way into my place comes in. Like I said, it's all connected, somehow."

The three men sat silently, each lost in his own thoughts.

Wolf finished his coffee. There wasn't more to say at this point, and he still wanted to swing past Alicia's house before going home. He needed to see her, make sure she was okay. Glancing at his watch, he was shocked to see it creeping toward four in the morning. Well, he decided, he'd see if there were lights on. If there were, he'd stop; otherwise, he'd just go on home.

Chapter 9

L ance waited outside the morgue. He still had a few hours before the sun would come up. He didn't fear the sun, exactly, but he didn't like it. He told himself to be patient. Sooner or later, the bustle would die down. Once that happened, he'd simply go in, claim what belonged to him and stroll back out again.

He saw no reason to wait until the girl woke up. He would take her, now… take her to the apartment he obtained.

That had been easy, too. He simply waited for the little family to go to bed. He'd gained access through an open window, which was technically an open invitation, and then once inside, slaughtered the little family. He'd disposed of their bodies in the river, which was quite handy, and simply took over the place.

He had to admit, the apartment was rather seedy, but it was good enough, for now.

While he waited, he went over his plan, once again. It was so simple, really.

First, he would get this girl, bring her back to his lair and wait for her to waken. She would do his bidding because, of course, she would now belong to him. This girl, he thought, would give him access to the little blonde. After he secured both, he would teach them the old ways. He smiled as he imagined both young girls, sitting at his feet, learning all he had to teach. Well, he corrected himself, certainly not all. That would give them too much power.

Once the girls were secured, he would begin to build his army. This world was ripe for the picking. Such selfish young people, he thought. Surely, they would stream to him, willing to accept what he had to offer. They wouldn't refuse him.

After he obtained enough followers, and only then, he would make his move. Finally, all the promises made to him by his own sire, would come to be. That proud beauty he turned so long ago would be his and his alone. Together, they would build a race of their own kind, and the world would be theirs for the taking.

Pleased at the thought, he beamed at a pair of young men passing by him. For just a brief moment, he considered taking these two, now. They were presentable enough, and their small smiles told him they would be willing, but he stopped. It would be best to stick with his plan. The few times he had strayed from his plan of action had ended in disaster. He couldn't afford any more costly errors.

Moving on silent feet, he made his way into the building housing the morgue. The first person he met walking down the long, dark corridor was a security guard. The man was tall, with a muscular frame, but this didn't stop Lance. He waited, poised for the time to strike. The guard didn't disappoint.

"Can I help you, sir? You're not supposed to be here, unless escorted by someone on staff or a cop. You're going to have to leave. NOW!" Lance smiled and waited. The guard came closer, and Lance's hand snaked out, grabbing the surprised guard by the throat, and gave him a hard shake. The last thing the surprised guard saw was his own larynx resting in the other man's elegant palm.

Lance dragged the body to what he correctly surmised was a broom closet and stuffed it inside... laying the organ on the man's chest.

Lance's hand was covered in blood, but that didn't faze him in the least. His hands would be a lot dirtier, he supposed, before the end of this night.

At the far end of the corridor, he saw double doors without windows. Guessing that this was where they kept the bodies, he moved carefully into the large room. The smell of death was everywhere, and he almost lapped up the scent, like a cook laps up a sauce. Enjoying the atmosphere, he shot a casual glance at a small woman entering the cavernous room from a small side door. She was dead before she could speak to him.

Moving rapidly, he went through the door the woman had emerged from and found three men eating lunch at a small table. With the odd speed he was blessed with, Lance killed all three. However, he sank his fangs into the last man's carotid artery. All this killing made him a little peckish. He relieved his thirst and went to find his prize, licking the blood from his hand, much as one would lick frosting from one's fingers.

It didn't take him long to find Trish's body. Gathering her up in his arms, he carried her out the back doors to his waiting car. She would wake the next night. Until then, he had much to do.

Wolf drove down the street where Alicia and Jake made their home. He'd do a drive-by, he decided. If lights shown from the windows, he would stop, otherwise, he would catch up with Alicia whenever he could. Damn, he thought, she was the best partner he ever had. If she held true to her word, and Wolf had every inclination that she would, Alicia would be leaving Wisconsin and heading back to Florida with her folks. He couldn't blame her. Jake and their kids meant everything to her, and he had to admit, she and Jake were good, together. He and Rachel never were. With Rachel, life was a tug of war. "Give up police work, Wolf. Make something of yourself." Rachel always began the same way. "You have your law degree, quit wasting yourself." On and on it went, until his ears would ring and his brain would freeze. He didn't know who was more relieved when Rachel finally filed for divorce. He suspected that, just maybe, he was.

Alicia called it on that one, too. "It's a power play, Wolf. She thinks you'll back down and do whatever it is she wants you to do. You need to decide what it is you want. You want to be a lawyer? Be a lawyer. You'd make a damn good one. No one knows law like you do, but Wolf, in the end, you have to do what's right for you... and for Kirsten."

So, Wolf didn't back down, and now, he was happily divorced. Well, if he was going to be honest with himself, not entirely happily divorced. He missed the daily connection with Kirsten. The kid was great about that, though. She'd come to see him three or four times a week at the precinct or his apartment. Not so bad really, but if Rachel knew about their meetings, she'd pitch a fit from here to the Gulf of Mexico and back. So, he and Kirsten kept it their little secret.

As Wolf drove along, he could see lights shining from the neat ranch Alicia and Jake shared. Had shared, he corrected himself. Well, he decided, he'd go to the back door and just knock on the window. If Alicia was up, she would hear him. If she was sleeping, which he hoped for, he'd just leave her a note and go on home.

He killed the engine and his headlights as he pulled into the driveway. No sense waking the household. The kids would need their sleep.

Wolf made his way to the back door and tapped lightly on the window. Almost immediately, Alicia opened the door and fell into his arms, weeping.

"I knew you'd come, Wolf. Been waiting for you." She began sobbing. Her whole body was wracked with sobs. "What am I gonna do without him? He and the kids are my life. Now, he's gone. What am I supposed to do with this life of mine, now?"

Wolf half carried her into the kitchen and gently sat her down. She clasped his hand and pulled him down next to her. "It was so quick, Wolf. We didn't have time to prepare. He had the heart attack at work. They called me, and I raced to the hospital. I'm not sure when it was I called his parents and then mine, but all of a sudden, I knew they were coming. A couple of the guys from the office went out to the airport and picked them all up and brought them to me. His poor parents. They're so bewildered." Alicia composed herself, pushed herself away from the table and poured two cups of coffee. She placed one in front of Wolf and wrapped her hands around the other. "He was in a coma when I got there. I don't know if he knew I was there or not, but I kept talking to him, willing him to come back to me." Alicia shook her head at him. "He never did wake up."

"Honey, I'm so damn sorry. I tried to get there, but I walked into a real mess. Couple of other detectives are handling this case. The victims are... were friends of mine. The daughter was my daughter's best friend. I handed the case over to the other guys. They can handle it. They're good men. I know you don't want to hear about this right now, but I wish you'd reconsider leaving the department. Dammit Alicia! You're the best partner I ever had... and I'm making this about me. Sorry."

Alicia flashed him a wan smile. "I know what you're saying, Wolf, but my kids are going to need a full time mother, now. I don't have any choice. They have to come first with me. That's the way it has to be and the way I want it." She rubbed his hand. "You know, for a southern boy, you ain't so bad. You'll break in a new partner, and you'll be fine." She peered into his rugged face, took a deep breath and gave him one word of advice. "Maybe, you should think about cutting back on your drinking, though. I don't think you have a problem... yet... but you keep going like you are and you soon will be."

She leaned back in her chair and watched him, closely. She waited for him to deny he might have a problem, but he didn't. He just nodded his head.

"Look, Alicia, I'm gonna go on home and let you get some rest. This case... I'm not working it, officially, but Kirsten is involved, somehow. I'm thinking about taking a leave for a while. I have the time coming to me, and I think I'm going to take it. The guys said they'd keep me in the loop, but something else is developing. Crist is involved, as well. I need to be loose, able to move around without calling in all the damn time. What do you think of that?"

Alicia scrubbed her face and ran a shaking hand through her hair. "I think you need to do what you need to do, hon. Just like me."

Wolf finished off his coffee and going over to the sink, rinsed out his mug. "You need help with the arrangements for Jake?" He asked. She shook her head. "No, our folks are here, and we had talked about it, before. The subject came up a time or two when you and I worked some pretty harsh cases. He knew what I wanted, and I know what he wants. It'll be okay. I'll let you know the when and where when I find out." She walked with him to the back door and hugged him, hard. "Wolf, you are a great partner and a wonderful friend. Jake loved you like a brother. I hate to ask you in light of the developments of tonight, but if you could see your way to help carry him, I know it's what he wanted." Wolf hugged her tight. "I'd be honored, honey. Just call me with the details. I'll be there."

Wolf walked to his car and turned around for another look at the house. It was dark and silent, now. Alicia had waited for him, and now, she would take to her lonely bed, probably cry herself to sleep and tomorrow, would deal with this low blow life had tossed in her lap. She would be all right. He was sure of it. He wondered if he would be.

Chapter 10

Lance congratulated himself on just how well everything was going. He managed to secure his newest candidate from that house of death, while obtaining his objective.

He had even taken the time to run around to the house of his main prize. Using his talents, he was able to read the thoughts of the mortals dwelling there. "Hmmm... So they know about me," He thought. This was useful information.

Better get back, he thought, before someone misses this car I've helped myself to. Especially since he had the twit's body tucked securely in the trunk.

Arriving at his newly appropriated living quarters, he checked carefully. It wouldn't be a good thing for someone to see him lifting a body from the boot of the miserable machine. Next time, he would simply have to outfit himself with something more appropriate, he decided. He thought a Cadillac would do nicely.

Seeing no one in the vicinity, he ripped open the trunk and put Trish's body over his shoulder. Taking the stairs two at a time, he didn't stop until he reached his apartment.

Opening the door, he kicked trash out of his way. The previous occupant hadn't cared much for housekeeping. Well, perhaps when the little twit woke up, he'd make her clean. This really wasn't suitable quarters for someone of his station.

He kicked the door shut and crossed the room, carrying the still lifeless body of Trish over his shoulder.

Roughly, and without a care, he took Trish's body and tossed it on a sofa. She would rest until the next evening. This would give him time to put the next part of his plan into action.

She would be hungry when she woke. That would be a bother. He would have to secure something fresh for her to feast on.

He thought, maybe a child, and then rejected the idea. No, a small man or woman would suffice. Securing a child was just too much trouble. However, if the opportunity presented itself, he wouldn't hesitate.

Of course, he thought, if all went well and he secured the one he truly desired, he would destroy this shallow girl now waiting to raise up. If Julie, as she called herself, came willingly to him, all would be well, but if the haughty wench still fought him, he would simply use the mortal woman dwelling there to gain entry into her house, and then, end them all.

He looked down at the body on his sofa. She would do for the time being, he decided.

His thoughts turned to Kirsten. Now, that innocent beauty would soon be his, and he knew just how to get her, too. Perhaps, once he had all within his grasp, he would end this one. His interest in her was purely superficial. He needed her to acquire the beautiful, innocent Kirsten. Although, if this one proved to be entertaining, he could make room for her in his plans. He would just wait and see how events unfolded. For now, it was time to make his move.

He glanced at the sky and judged he still had several hours of nighttime, yet. This shouldn't take long.

Moving quickly, he made his way to Julie's home. Time to put his plan into action.

$\partial \! \! \! \int$

Julie wandered through her house, touching objects here and there, lost in thought. Emma was on to something, she decided. She would invite these people to dinner. Her name, having been in the papers just often enough to generate interest, would make acceptance of her invitation a sure thing. She would leave it to Abram to deliver those invitations. That should perk up even more interest. She thought it would be best not to notify the gossip columns, however. This was one party she didn't want discussed, nor speculated on.

Deep in thought, she was overcome with a feeling of dread. A coppery taste filled her mouth, and she knew. Her sire was killing, again, and he wanted her to feel it, wanted her to taste what he tasted, and wanted her to react in his favor. After all these centuries, he knew she didn't hunt, anymore, and he wanted her to feel that thrill.

A movement behind her caught her attention and she spun around, coming face to face with Abram. He saw her fangs beginning to elongate and saw her eyes burn red, and he knew what these things meant. He just hoped he could talk her down from this sudden urge to kill.

"It's your sire, isn't it?" Abram walked the rest of the way into the room and closed the door. "He's killing, and he wants you to know that. Are you going to give him what he wants, Madam?"

Julie's small tongue darted in and out, tasting the air and smelling her housekeeper, downstairs. It would be such an easy thing. She only had to walk down those stairs, stroll into the kitchen, and reach out to take what she craved. Abram couldn't stop her. No one could stop her.

Abram waited, just as he always waited. If Julie chose to make a meal out of their housekeeper, there wasn't much he could really do about it. His hope was to keep talking to her and bring her around back to sanity.

"It would be so easy, wouldn't it, Madam. Just reach out and take. After all, housekeepers like Emma are a dime a dozen, are they not?" Warily, he watched the craftiness come into her eyes, and watched the coldness settle on her features.

"Don't try to talk me out of this, Abram." Her usually soft voice was harsh, guttural. The hairs went up on the back of his arms. She was deep in thrall, and it would take all of his cunning to talk her out of the madness.

"I wouldn't presume to try, Madam. I am but your humble servant." He placed a hand over the place his non-beating heart was and gave a small bow.

Julie laughed in his face. "My humble servant, Abram? I doubt it." She lowered her voice to a whisper, all the while, edging around Abram and making her way toward the door. Abram's heart sank. He was losing her. He could feel it. Thinking rapidly, he tried to come up with an idea that would save Emma... and Julie.

"We could share her, Abram. She has no family. No one would miss her. Come on! We can feast just as we did so long ago."

Taking his courage in both hands, he stepped closer to Julie. He would physically restrain her if need be. He knew Julie had the power to destroy him, and she could prolong his agony before finally ending him. Abram also knew his own mind. He would happily tolerate the torture if it meant Emma would be safe.

His thoughts jolted him into action. He had not been aware just how much he cared for the housekeeper. He wondered if he would exist long enough to figure out what that meant.

"Come on, Abram. What do you care of a mere mortal? We can join with my sire, and we will have the world at our fingertips. We can begin with the mortal woman in the kitchen. I promise you. She won't be missed, and it will feel so good, so very good to hunt, once again."

A soft knock at the bedroom door caught both of their attention. A tiny shiver of fear raced up Abram's spine. If Emma stood on the other side, Julie would attack her before he could react. The knock was repeated and with a sly smile, Julie flung open the door, prepared to pounce. It was not Emma who stood in the doorway. Hunter casually leaned against the door jam, and hearing Julie's soft curse, smiled.

The room filled with the goodness he radiated, and Julie shrunk away from him, slinking to the far side of her immense bedroom. She wanted to be far from him. She didn't want to look into those gentle eyes, so full of understanding and love. Hunter, in fact, was the only being who could fill her with shame.

"Looking for a little snack, are we?" Hunter flashed a wry smile.

He knew the battle raging within her.

Abram was hopeful that he could talk her out of going on a killing spree.

"Get out of here, Hunter. You have no business, here. Get out of my room, get out of my house, and get out of my life!" Julie growled at him.

"Certainly, Princess. I think I'll take Emma with me, if you don't mind. After all, just because she's been loyal and supportive..." he shrugged one of his massive shoulders, "That's no reason for you to show her the same consideration. And, what of Abram? When will you destroy him, as well? After all, it's what your sire wants... nay, expects of you."

Hunter's gentle tone penetrated the fog that enveloped her mind before his words did.

Abram sighed with relief as he witnessed the change begin to come over her.

Her eyes lost their craftiness and some warmth returned to them as the red faded. Her fangs retreated back, and that incessant flicking of her tongue halted. He was amazed to see she even had the grace to look ashamed of herself.

With a shiver, Julie regained her composure. Maybe it wasn't the words Hunter spoke, as much as the loving amusement in those clear, blue eyes.

Shaken to her core, Julie sank down onto the settee and clasped her shaking hands, together.

"I don't know what came over me, Hunter. Truly I don't. One minute I was pondering the dinner we're going to have, and the next thing I know, I wanted to kill Emma. Sweet gentle Emma who has been nothing but kind to me, and I was going to hunt her. If Abram would have tried to stop me, I would have ended him, as well."

"Yes, well, we know where those feelings came from, my dear. He still has a hold on you, and you will need to be very careful from now on. Now, let's go down to the kitchen and see if there's any of that excellent apple pie left. Besides, I think Emma is about to confront a crisis of her own. It's best if we are with her."

Hunter turned on his heel and led the way down the stairs. Abram didn't feel hungry but did feel a great deal of relief. That had been close... too close. He could only be thankful Hunter appeared when he did.

Julie followed the two men. Apple pie or blood. What a strange choice to make, she thought. She also thought her life was about to get a whole lot more strange.

Emma heard a noise behind her, and to her amazement, watched as Julie, the stranger and Abram invaded her domain. "What on earth are you three doing here? I thought you'd all be in your rooms, resting." She took in Julie's tense face and Abram's solemn one. Hunter was his usual jovial self.

"We've come to raid the larder, Miss Emma. That pie you made was calling to us. We heard it all the way upstairs." Hunter's grin broke into a wide smile as Emma blushed with pleasure. She didn't understand it, but the man made her feel twenty years younger, if not more.

"Well, sit down and I'll just dish it up. You're going to want Ice Cream with that, of course. I'll just warm up slices, and it won't take me but a moment."

Hunter flashed a beautiful smile that lit up his incredible blue eyes as Emma bustled about the kitchen. She set fresh coffee perking and proceeded to get slices for everyone. Topping them off with French Vanilla Bean, she placed the treats in front of her unexpected guests and poured three hearty mugs of fresh coffee to go with it.

Emma had been feeling restless all evening, and now in the wee hours of the morning, it felt good to have something to occupy her. She didn't know what was making her so edgy, but she was as nervous as a blind cat in a room full of rocking chairs. She hoped these small tasks would tire her enough to sleep.

Lost in thought, and seeing to her guests at the kitchen table, she didn't hear the soft knock on the back door. It came a little harder, now, as if the person knocking didn't want to wake the household. You've got to be kidding me, she thought, this household never sleeps.

Emma opened the door and felt the blood drain from her face. She felt the room tip a little, and she reached out a hand to steady herself, gripping the door jamb for support.

Dimly, she was aware of a commotion behind her as Julie, Abram and Hunter all leapt to their feet. Abram was about to rush forward, but Hunter put a calming hand on his arm. The gentle touch burned Abram just a little, but he didn't feel any pain. All of his concentration was centered on Emma and what her next action would be.

Emma gazed up into the face of a man she loved so long ago. Standing there, looking dapper in his uniform was her Peter, looking just as he did forty years ago when he went off to a war and never returned

"Hello Baby. Gonna ask me in?" There was that crooked smile that won her heart. His warm, brown eyes brimmed with happiness, and his voice was still the same soft boom she remembered.

Emma's shaking hand crept to her throat as she stood there, gazing at her long dead husband. A soft sob escaped from between her quivering lips, and she could only stand there and gaze at that face, the face she so loved.

"C'mon, Baby. Aren't you gonna ask me in? It's been a long time. We've both been alone, too long. Let me in," he urged her.

"You haven't aged, Peter. How is that possible? You haven't aged a day." Emma fought for control. Something was terribly wrong. How could Peter be standing here when she had buried him a very long time ago? Nothing made sense to her. She knew Peter was dead, and yet here he was, standing in front of her, urging her to let him in.

With a sudden movement, Emma flung the door wide open. She saw the small triumphant smile he flashed at the people standing behind her, and she remembered Miss Julie's warning. "He's very old and very sly," and then, Emma understood.

Abram tensed, preparing to rush at the vision in the door, but Hunter once again raised a hand to stop him. "It's all about free will, my friend. Let's see what the lady does with it."

Emma gazed at the face she once loved, and her lips parted. Raising one eyebrow, she grasped the door in her hand as she told the being in front of her, "Blow it out your ass!" And then slammed the door in his face with enough force to shake the walls...

The sounds of Lance's fury permeated the entire house.

He banged on the outside door with such force, Emma thought it would shatter. When that didn't happen, he pounded on the walls, screaming in an age-old language that only the three in the kitchen with her, understood.

Emma leaned against the counter, her body shaking from head to foot. Fear mixed with rage, and she thought she'd very much like to claw his face until whatever ran through his veins poured from the wounds inflicted by her. Never had she been so angry, and at the same time, terrified. The threats Lance directed at her in his fury echoed in her brain, until Hunter's roar of laughter penetrated the fog in her mind.

Hunter wrapped her in a huge embrace, his laughter still ringing in her ears. "Well done, Miss Emma! Oh, exceptionally well done!"

Hunter kept her wrapped in his arms until the shivering subsided. Gently and with a beautiful smile, he led her to a kitchen chair and pressed her down. "Rest yourself, dear lady. You have fought a terrific battle and came out the winner."

As the renewed sounds of Lance's anger penetrated the house, Hunter grinned. Stepping to the door, he opened it and confronted his adversary. "Come, come. Time to leave the premises. You've been bested this day and by a mere mortal. Take the stench of your defeat and leave. Our time will come, perhaps sooner than you think."

Unable to stand being in the presence of such goodness, the vampire ran like the coward he is, and Hunter closed the door, securing the lock.

Julie knelt in front of her housekeeper, and taking the woman's hands in her own, gazed up into the now tearful face. "How did you know, Emma? How did you know it was my sire?"

Emma loosened one of her hands and gently stroked the pale face before her. "You warned me, Miss Julie. Remember? When we were discussing what to do about me, since I discovered your secret. You told me he was very old and sneaky. It was a shock to see Peter standing there, I'll admit that, but then your words came back to me, and I just knew. Besides, I had buried Peter. A part of me knew, after the shock of seeing him again… a part of me knew it couldn't possibly be my Peter. The rest fell into place." Emma threw her head back and stared at the ceiling. "It also made me angry that he would use a fine man like Peter to try to get in this house. But, I don't understand something. Why did he try? Surely he knew you and Abram would stop him, so why did he try?"

Julie sighed and stroked the work-worn hand she still held. "Because, my dear. Had he gained access, he would have destroyed me, first. Since I sired Abram, with me ended, Abram wouldn't have been able to save himself, much less you. I suspect that was part of his reasoning."

To everyone's amazement, Emma snorted. "Fat lot he knew." she glanced up at Hunter. "He'll be back?" she asked. Hunter shrugged one massive shoulder. "I don't know. Perhaps he will, but only after he has whatever it is he's looking for. We must remain vigilant, but he won't be back any more, this night. You've given his ego a huge dent. He won't forget that, either."

Emma considered what Hunter was saying and read into what he hadn't said. Sooner or later, that creature would be back for her. Straightening her shoulders and giving Julie one more caress on her pale cheek, she stood.

"If he comes for me, the bastard better bring friends." She gave a short nod and marched off to her room, leaving the three to gape after her.

The son-of-a-bitch, she fumed. He made her feel all the love and all the grief, all over again. And for what!

Emma didn't know how or when, but somehow, she would pay him back for his wretched trick.

Chapter 11

Wolf pulled into his parking spot and killed the motor. It had been one hell of a day, and he still felt wired.

Jake's death, along with the Rollings family, cast a pall over him and he wasn't sure he was ready to handle it. Losing Jake, along with Nate and his family, had Wolf pretty sure this was a completely crappy day.

He would need to take leave. He couldn't work on the Rollings' killings, he was too close. He wasn't even sure if he had the heart left in him to continue working as a cop. He felt tired in his soul, but plotted out his course of action. Later on in the morning, he'd go see the captain and put in his request for leave of absence. He had the time coming to him, and he needed the time off, now. He also planned on seeing Crist, again. He still had questions that needed answering. After that, he'd have another go-round with the ex-wife. Had she always been a shrew, he wondered? He gave a mental shrug. It didn't matter, anymore. All that mattered was keeping his baby safe. To do that, he would fight the devil, himself. He wondered if that was exactly who he'd be fighting.

Wolf let himself into his apartment and headed straight into the kitchen, not bothering to turn on any lights. He snatched a large tumbler from the cabinet and reached into another to find a bottle of Jack.

Grabbing some ice, he tossed the cubes into the glass and, using the light from the refrigerator, poured himself three fingers. Taking the bottle and his glass into the living room, he plopped down on the couch and put his feet on the coffee table. Maybe, he'd kill the bottle. That would stop him from thinking. He didn't want to think about anything, anymore tonight. He just wanted to feel the numbness the whiskey would bring him.

Wolf polished off his first drink and made himself another, tossing that one back, as well. Not bothering with ice or his glass, he proceeded to drink right out of the bottle.

He waited for the whiskey to take effect, but it just wasn't happening. He still felt keyed up, and he wondered if there was enough booze in the whole world to make him stop feeling… stop thinking. He wanted to forget how Nate and Michele looked lying in pools of blood. He wanted to forget how small and defenseless Trish looked. He should have protected her, this child of Nate and Michele. He would have died to protect her, but he wasn't there. He was never there to stop these killings.

Defeated, he lowered his massive head into his hands and waited for the tears to come. He needed the release they would bring, but it never came.

A soft sound caught his attention, and his hand snaked out, turning on the light. He almost had a heart attack, seeing Nate sitting in his favorite chair.

"What the hell?" Wolf managed to ground out before the shakes set in. Nate grinned at him, but it was a terrible grin.

"Hey buddy. How're you doing?" Nate's voice sounded hollow.

"You… you can't be here, Nate! You're dead! I saw you and Michele and Trish! I saw all three of you! You're dead, and you're not here!"

Nate chuckled. "Yeah, Wolf. We're dead. I'm here to tell you to pull your head out of your ass and get yourself together!" Nate pointed at the bottle. "Quit the damn drinking. How much good are you gonna do Kirsten if you're drunk? Get off the sauce! Your kid needs you more than you know. You couldn't save mine, but you can save your own! Can't do it if you're all curled up in a bottle now, can ya?" Nate's brown eyes gave him a shaming glance before he stood and glided toward the door.

"Wait! Nate! Don't go, yet! I've got questions. Who did this to you? Can't you help me nail this bastard?"

Nate shook his head. "I gotta go, Wolf. You'll find the answers. Just do your job, man. You're already on the right track. Just keep going. Keep the faith." Nate stopped at the door. "We'll see each other again, bud."

Wolf watched with his mouth hanging open as Nate glided through the door and disappeared.

Shaking his head, Wolf took the rest of the bottle of Jack Daniels and poured it down the drain.

"Well Charleston, you've either snapped your damn cap, or the impossible just happened." He washed out his glass, having lost the taste for any sort of alcoholic beverage, and wandered back into the living room.

He stared at the chair Nate sat in, seeking answers. A small spot of something blended in with the brown leather, and Wolf ran his fingers over it. They came up red. It was blood! The impossible had happened. Wolf just didn't know what to make of it, but it was something he could and would bring up to Crist later in the day.

First things first, though. He needed to get a little sleep, then go see the captain and get that all squared away. Once that was done, he could head over and have a nice long chat with Damien. He would tell him what happened and see what the psychic would have to say about all of this. Somehow, he didn't think Damien was going to be too surprised.

While Wolf was dealing with the events in his apartment, in another home in a different part of the city, an elderly lady was having her own experience.

Matilda White, known as Mattie to family and friends, was sprawled across her bed, sobbing for her slain daughter, son-in-law and granddaughter. Michele Rollings had been Mattie's pride and joy;

her only child. Now, she was dead. They were all dead, and Mattie prayed for the strength to get through this wall of grief.

"Mama? Mama, don't cry anymore. You'll make yourself sick." The soft voice came from the side of the bed, and Mattie rolled over, looking in the direction the voice had come from. To her utter shock, Michele stood, bathed in a soft glow and looking ever so peaceful. Michele smiled at her mother.

"It's really okay, mom. Nate and I are fine." Michele's doe eyes saddened as she stared at her mother. "Trish isn't. Mama, you are going to have to harden your heart, a little. Trish isn't dead like Nate and me. She's been turned into something wrong, something evil. She'll come to you. Don't let her in. Promise me you won't let her in."

Mattie stared, dumbstruck. All she could manage was a small nod.

"It's important, mama. Don't let her in." Michele smiled, then, and continued. "It's beautiful here, mama, and we'll see each other, again. I love you. Just remember, don't let Trish in. It may look like her, but it's not Trish! I love you, mom. I love you so much, but I have to go, now." And then, with a soft smile, Michele faded away.

Mattie didn't know what to think. Ghosts didn't exist, and yet, Michele stood there, tall and straight and beautiful.

There was only one man she could trust with this. Glancing at her small bedside clock, she saw it was four in the morning. She would wait a few hours, and then call the one man who would give her some straight answers. She would call Wolf Charleston.

Chapter 12

Julie, with her peculiar and adept hearing, listened to Emma's sobs until daybreak. Only after hearing that the older woman was moving around and coffee scenting the air, did Julie go down. She needed to be sure the housekeeper was all right.

Last night had to have been terrifying for the lady. With that thought in mind, Julie decided she would once again give Emma the option to leave. Julie would see to it the woman would be safe.

A smile flitted across her cool features. Damn, she thought, the woman had been magnificent, though.

"Emma," Julie called softly. Emma turned, and Julie studied the woman's wan face. She looked drawn and tired, and her eyes were rimmed red and swollen from crying.

"Emma, come sit down. We need to talk." She smiled again as Emma nodded and sank into a kitchen chair.

"You told me, Miss Julie, you said he was sneaky and sly and evil! What frosted my cookies was him using Peter that way! Peter was a fine, decent and brave man. He died honorably! That creature should never have used him like that!" Emma's head came up, and her eyes snapped fire. Julie reached for one of Emma's hands and rubbed it gently with her thumb.

No one was more shocked than Julie, though, when feelings long-dead began to surface. She began to feel much like a daughter would feel toward a mother. She shook her head, pushing the thought from her mind. She would think about that, later. At present, Emma needed tending.

"You never told me. What happened to him?" Julie asked. Again, she shocked herself.

For centuries she never gave a second thought to her underlings. Now, she was delving into the woman's past and actually wanted to hear.

Emma took a deep breath, then began. "They were out on patrol and were ambushed. They said Peter took the rear and opened fire. The gun he used sat on a tripod sort of thing, and he set it up and began firing at the enemy. It gave his friends time to get away, but Peter kept firing until a sniper took him. One of his guys saw him go down, killed the sniper, and brought Peter's body back to the firebase. That's all they told me, but Peter," Emma raised her head proudly, "Peter was awarded the Silver Star."

Julie squeezed Emma's hand as she took in the proud tilt to the graying head and the tears that stood in the woman's eyes.

"A brave man, indeed. It's a sad thing you never had children." Julie wished she could bite her tongue off. She wanted to offer comfort, not hurt the woman more, but Emma, sensing what Julie was feeling, offered the younger woman a brilliant smile.

"We would have had a dozen, if he had lived. We made plans, but it wasn't to be. Everything happens for a reason, Miss Julie. Maybe, what happened in the past is what led me, here." Emma shrugged. "Who knows?" She whispered.

"I was married, Emma. Did you know that? I was married to a King. Phillip. He, too, was a warrior. All kings were warriors in those days. I didn't love him, at least not like you loved your man, but we were pleasant together. We had two sons." Julie got up and poured two mugs of coffee and offered one to Emma. "I watched from a distance as they grew up and had children. I watched them all grow old and wither and die. I never felt a connection to any of them, though. Not like you had with your man. I'd say you are a very lucky woman."

"You were never tempted to make them like you?" Emma asked. Julie shook her head. "I could have, but no, I did not. As my sons grew, I wanted them to have a full normal life. Oh, I was tempted. I was very tempted, but even then, Hunter was always lurking about. Finally, when the temptation became great, Abram and I left Palestine and traveled. We ended up in Gaul for a while and feasted on peasants and high born. It didn't matter. Then, it became too dangerous to remain, so we left and ended up in Spain, then Egypt and Africa."

Julie shrugged. "The time came, I think it was in the early nineteen twenties, that Europe became dangerous for us. We were living in Germany, and I sensed the new Chancellor was not right in his head, so Abram and I packed up everything we owned. Abram, by this time, mastered the art of making false passports and identification papers. We left Europe and came here. Oh, we've been back, since then. I have a villa in Italy, a home in Paris, another in London, and several here in this country, along with estates in South America. I leave each for two generations or so, and then go back, but I pay to keep them all up. I never know where I want to settle."

"Why Wisconsin? Why Milwaukee?" Emma just had to ask. Julie laughed. "I like Wisconsin. The country reminds me of Germany. I like Milwaukee, as well. It's a large city, but it feels like a small town. People are friendly, here, and they respect privacy. It's a good place, but now with my sire here, I feel I may lose everything."

"Ahh... this may be the final showdown, then." Emma murmured, and Julie nodded.

Abram sauntered into the kitchen and made a bee-line for the coffee. He waved Emma back into her chair as she began to stand. "Sit! I can get this!" He poured the brew and inhaled deeply. "Emma, no one makes coffee like you do." He grinned at her.

Emma smiled back. "Don't try to flatter me, Abram. What is it you want?"

Abram chuckled. "Is there any of that pie left? I never got to finish mine, last night."

Emma pointed toward the covered cake plate, and Abram snapped up one of the two pieces left.

Julie studied Emma, her eyes cool and solemn. "Emma, what are we going to do about you?" Julie asked and received a shrug.

"Well Miss. I would think that's up to you, isn't it? If you believe I'm a threat, then that leaves you two choices, to my way of thinking. You either have to kill me, or send me away."

"Actually, there is a third option." Hunter entered the kitchen and snagged the last piece of pie, causing Abram to grumble.

"She can stay, continue to take care of you and Abram, and you can hope she would be strong enough to stand up to the adversary once again." He cocked his head toward Julie, watching her with his beautiful, clear blue eyes. "What will you, my dear?" He asked.

Julie tapped an impatient finger on the kitchen table. Emma leaned over and gently patted her hand. "It's all right, Miss Julie. All that matters is that you and Abram are safe, while we find a way to stop this creature from hurting others. I don't matter all that much."

Julie was taken aback. Never, in her long years of existence, had she ever met anyone quite like Emma.

Julie sat back, weighing her options. Hunter cut into her thoughts. "Let's take the options one at a time, shall we?" He grinned at Julie's petulant face.

He is supposed to be here as a spectator, she thought, why is he butting in, now? Still, she nodded. She needed all the help she could get.

"First, if you send Emma away, he can always find her. Travel, as we all know, is not a problem for him. Therefore, it's easy to figure he will just track her down and either turn her or destroy her. Killing her would be an option, but highly selfish. She's done nothing more than defend, protect and serve you. Killing her would be a highly selfish move on your part, Madam. She proved last night she has a strong will and is not easily fooled. He's angry, yes, but with some small precautions, she will be safe enough." He flashed a charming smile at the three scowling at him. "As a plus, I am here, too. I would be honored to defend such a lovely woman as you." He took one of Emma's hands and put it to his lips, kissing her knuckle softly.

Julie felt a subtle shift in the dynamics of the quad sitting in the kitchen. She didn't know quite what it meant, and she didn't have time to ponder it, now. They were waiting for her decision, and looking into Emma's sweet face, Julie felt another shift. In a deep dark secret place in her non-beating heart, Julie wished Emma had been her mother. She would have been a loving one.

These feeling surprised Julie, but again, she pushed the thoughts away. Time to get down to business.

"Emma lives, and she stays." Julie raised an imperious hand, demanding silence just as Abram opened his mouth to speak. "Not now, Abram, we have plans to make." Julie looked around the room before continuing. "Events of last night and the night before show my sire is working on something big. Hunter, you're here, so you must sense the same as I do. Emma, we're going to have to arrange a small dinner and get these people together. Together, perhaps we will figure out what it all means, and knowledge is power. Emma, you have until tomorrow night to arrange something. Can you do this?"

Emma nodded. "Of course. I'll bring in a couple of the girls we use for larger parties to help me with the cleaning. Dinner won't be fancy, but it won't be plain, either. I won't let you down, Miss."

Julie patted Emma's shoulder before moving on. "Abram, stay close. I will write out invitations by hand. Can you find those I will be inviting?" Abram nodded. He was pretty sure he knew who would be invited. It would take a little bit of doing to find the daughter, but not impossible.

"Good! Let's get on it, then."

Julie marched from the room and took the stairs two at a time, leaving the other three of her household to grin at each other.

Emma stood. "Time to get to work, gentlemen. I suggest you get the hell out of my way."

Wolf woke, fully dressed on his sofa, where he more or less passed out in the early morning hours. Checking his watch, he noticed that it was just after seven. He would have time to catch a fast shower, and then, go have a chat with his captain. After that, he would have another little talk with Crist. Still too many unanswered questions. The only things he knew, for sure, was his best friends and their daughter were slaughtered, and his own daughter was in danger.

Add in the little visit from Nate in the wee hours, and Wolf was pretty sure he was losing his mind. There just was no such thing as ghosts. He didn't care what he thought he saw. He discounted the blood on his recliner. He convinced himself he must have transferred some home with him. That's the only reasonable explanation there could be.

He needed a shower. That would clear his head and help him get rid of the after effects of his drinking. He decided he would just grab a coffee on the fly before he headed to the precinct. It would have to do.

Emerging from the bathroom, the ringing phone startled him. Wolf was probably the last person in the city to have a land line, and the ringing jarred his pounding head. The shower didn't help much.

"Yeah? Charleston, here." He growled into the phone. The soft voice that responded was the last voice he expected to hear.

"Detective, this is Mattie White. Michele's mama? Do you remember me?" Wolf was taken aback. "Yes ma'am, I sure do. What can I do for you?" She hesitated a fraction of a second before answering. "If you have time, would you be so kind as to stop by and see me sometime today?"

Now it was Wolf's turn to hesitate. "I'm not sure that would be a good idea, ma'am. I'm not working the case, you know. Department rules, you know, and there's nothing I can tell you."

"It's not like that, Detective. Something happened here early this morning. I don't know who else to talk to. Please come." The desperation in her voice reached through Wolf's hang-over.

"Okay," He agreed, "I have a couple of things I need to take care of, then I'll be over late this morning. That okay?"

"Yes, that will be fine. Thank you, Detective. Thank you very much."

In a hurry, now, he slammed out of his apartment, raced down the stairs, and more or less bounced into his car. He drove to the precinct, after snagging a cup of coffee from a convenience store, sipping as he drove.

Wolf kept his mind on his driving, not ready to think about the events of the previous day. He just wasn't ready to deal, yet. He wished he could just make his mind a blank. Then he'd never have to think about anything, ever again.

Wolf knew he was wallowing, but he just didn't care. Only the thought of his beloved Kirsten kept him moving forward.

He parked in his usual spot and raced into the precinct. The captain's door was closed, which was never a good sign, and he couldn't help but notice the hush that fell over the office as he entered. Now, he thought, what in tarnation is that all about? He would find out, soon enough.

Harry Harrilson, the lead detective on the Rollings' killings, sauntered over to him. Harrilson's usual florid face was pasty, and the shadows under his eyes, unusually deep.

"Hey Wolf. How're you doin'?" Even Harrilson's usual greeting sounded forced to Wolf's ears. "I'm doin', Harry. How 'bout you?"

Harry shrugged. "Some new developments, Wolf. Captain's gonna wanna talk to you when he gets off the phone with the Chief."

Wolf's interest picked up. Whatever those developments were, they must be important if the Chief of Police is involved. Wolf wondered if he'd be able to take a leave of absence, after all.

A few minutes later, Captain Tobias emerged from his office, pale and shaken. Spying Wolf, Tobias gestured with his head for the big cop to join him in his very small office.

Wolf entered, and Tobias closed the door and drew the blinds across his window. Oh, oh, Wolf thought. This can't be good. He wondered if he was about to be fired.

"Okay Wolf. There's no easy way to say this, so I'm just gonna say it to you. We had five killings at the morgue last night. Five good people, including the little girl who was one dynamite assistant coroner. They were slaughtered, and one was drained of all his blood. You are not going to handle that case, either, Wolf. I assigned it to a couple of other detectives. You won't be handling the Rollings' murders, either. I know they were friends of yours and all, but you're too close to it. So, my question is, what do I do with you?"

Wolf stared at Tobias. He could have handled the murders at the morgue, and then, changed his mind. He was still reeling from the night before. Sighing, Wolf placed his shaking hands on his knees. "Let me make this easy on you, Cap. I have leave time coming. I'd like to take it. I know you're going to be short, what with Alicia leaving, but you're right. I'm not feeling particularly professional at the moment, and the last thing you need is a loose cannon on board. So, if you'll approve the paperwork, I'll take a leave for a while and get the hell out of your hair."

Tobias sighed, relieved that Wolf was making this easy for him. Dammit, Tobias thought, the man is one of his best detectives, but he could see Wolf was pretty shaky.

Wolf was taken aback to see Tobias pull out a leave request. All he had to do was sign the damn thing, and he would be relieved of his official duties.

Unofficially, of course, he would do what he could to bring in the killer or killers, but Tobias didn't have to know that.

"What are you going to do, now?" Tobias asked after Wolf finished.

Wolf shrugged. "I'm gonna take a few days and get my head wrapped around this mess. I want to spend time with my kid, too. She and the Rollings' daughter were best friends. I need to make sure she's okay."

Tobias' pallor increased. "Damn Wolf. I knew you were tight with the family, but I didn't realize Kirsten and the Rollings' girl were tight, too. Wolf, I gotta tell you. Her body disappeared, last night. We figure that's why those five were slaughtered. Someone wanted the girl's body pretty damn bad."

Wolf gaped at Tobias as his mind went into a deep freeze. Nothing was making sense. Trish's body stolen? Why? Wolf couldn't think.

Tobias heaved his bulk out of his chair and held out his hand to the grieving man. "Get out of here, Wolf. Go spend time with your kid. We've got this."

Wolf nodded and left the office. He made a mental note. He would run over and see Mattie White, then swing by Damien's place. They had a lot to talk about.

Wolf took a moment to look up Mattie White's address, bounded out to his car, cranked it over and then, eased it into traffic. He wished he hadn't promised Mattie he would come to see her, but the promise was made, and she was expecting him. He'd take care of this visit quickly, and then head over and have a chat with Damien.

Too many things didn't add up, Wolf thought. Damn! Give him a nice straight-forward shooting or robbery and he'd solve it in less than a month. This was beyond him. He told himself he was dealing with something out of the ordinary. Briefly, he wondered if he'd survive. Hell, he wondered if *any* of them would survive.

Wolf pulled up in front of a neat and well-tended bungalow. He threw the car into park and emerged from the vehicle, heading up the sidewalk. Mattie must have been watching for him, because he was half way to the door when she opened it and stepped out onto the spacious porch.

Fall flowers in assorted pots adorned the space, and the flowerbeds were well cared for. It was a cozy house and reflected the woman waiting to greet him.

Wolf extended his large hand, and Mattie took it in her small frail one, pulling him into the clean and tidy home.

"Thank you for coming, Detective." Mattie looked worn and sad, but her eyes were direct and calm as she stared up at the big cop.

Lord, she thought, he just fills her living room. Still, gracious as always, Mattie indicated to Wolf to take a seat on the sofa. "You look like you could use a cup of coffee, Detective. I'll just be a moment."

Wolf wasn't stupid. He knew she needed time to tell him whatever she had to tell him. It wouldn't do to rush her.

She returned with two white mugs on a tray, along with a plate of cookies arranged on a charming plate, adorned with violets.

"Detective," she began and Wolf stopped her.

"Please ma'am. You can call me Wolf." He told her.

She cocked her head to the side and studied him. "The name suits you," she grinned, and then, immediately sobered. "Detective Harrilson and his partner came by this morning. They're going to be working on this?" her lips trembled. She just couldn't bring herself to say the word, 'murders'.

Wolf nodded. "They're good men, ma'am. They'll find out who did this. You don't fret about that."

Mattie gave him a small smile. "Please call me Mattie. Everyone does." She told him, and then, sobered again. "Detective Harrilson told me about Trish's body. Why would someone steal that girl's body, Wolf? Lord, I don't even want to think about what they could want it

94

for." She shook her head. "It's an evil world we live in, Wolf. You know that better than anyone, but why would someone do this?"

Wolf studied her. There was more, here, although rightfully upset over the disappearance of her granddaughter's body, there was something more; something she was hesitant to bring up. Best to let her do this in her own time, he decided, and just not rush her.

"I don't want you to worry about that, Mattie. Harrilson will get to the bottom of this whole thing. Like I said, he's a good man. He'll do a good job." Even to his own ears his words sounded hollow and trite. It was the best he had to offer.

Mattie nodded, again, and leaning back in the over-stuffed chair, sipped her coffee.

"There's more, Wolf. I'm going to tell you what happened, last night, and then you're going to think I lost my mind. I can promise you, what I'm about to tell you really did happen. It was not a dream. I have proof." She opened a small chest on a table next to the chair and plucked out a perfect yellow rose.

"Last night, Michele came to me. She tried to comfort me, Wolf. At first, I thought I was going insane. I cried myself to sleep. This morning, while making my bed, I found this. The odd thing is, I didn't put it in water. I placed it right here in this box. It should be dying now, but it's not. I think Michele left this for me." She peered at him, her eyes sharp and focused. "Am I losing my mind?"

Wolf shook his head. "No ma'am, you are not." A huge sigh exploded from between his lips. "Up until this minute, I didn't plan on telling anyone this, but I'm gonna tell you."

Mattie noticed his Tennessee drawl became more pronounced as he became a little more agitated. "Last night, I was having a couple of drinks in my apartment. Nate came to see me, too. At first I thought I got ahold of some bad liquor, or something, but after he left, there was a spot on my recliner. It was blood." Wolf hung his head before going on. "I didn't have the guts to have it tested, Mattie. I didn't have the guts to tell anyone like you just did. I'm not sure what it all means, either. Maybe if we share what they had to say, I'll be able to start putting the pieces together."

Mattie told him of Michele's warning and Wolf, swallowing his pride, shared the message from Nate. Mattie was silent, digesting everything Wolf told her.

She nodded her graying head and gave him a small smile. "I'd say Nate was telling you to get your act together, Wolf, and I'd say Michele came to warn me. Now, I don't believe in this supernatural stuff but when my own daughter comes back from the dead, warns me and leaves me that," She pointed at the rose, "I believe I better listen." She turned to point at Wolf, "And you better listen, too."

She leaned back into her chair and propped her head against a fist. All the fight flowed out of her, and tears stood in her eyes. "So much to deal with. So much to contend with. Will this ever end? This pain? Will it ever go away?" Wolf had no answers for her, but stood and held out his arms to her. She went into them, gratefully, letting her head rest on his broad shoulder.

"I have to go, Mattie. You need something, ma'am, you call me." He produced a card and handed it to her. "All of my numbers are on it, but I'm not going to be in the office much. My private home number and personal cell number are on that card, too." Taking it back, he circled his personal numbers and handed it back to her.

"You be careful, Wolf. You be careful and keep yourself together. Nate and Michele are counting on you."

Wolf could only nod as he left the house. His next stop would be Damien's place. He had even more to ask the psychic, and Damien better not try to fend him off with cryptic crap, either.

Chapter 13

L ance Ebon was in a rage. He had been so sure his little ruse would work and access would have been gained to Julie's house. It had been his intention to destroy her household and force her to come with him. Together, they could, and would, build a mighty race. Humans would be much like cattle, kept alive for their betters to feed on. He would build a mighty army, and they would spread everywhere. It was his destiny. He had been promised all of this by his own sire, whom he destroyed after learning all there had been to learn.

Now, everything he wanted was just out of his grasp, and he let his fierce anger be known to the occupants of Julie's house.

Lance pounded on the doors and the side of the house. In his rage, he threw back his head and howled before assaulting the portals, once again. If it had been within his power, he would have torn down that brick structure with his own two hands. Hearing Hunter's laugh drove Lance's ire up another notch.

He dared to laugh at him! At Lance Ebon! By all the demons, this could not be tolerated! That creature would pay, Lance vowed. He promised Hunter a slow and very painful death. Hunter would beg for release, and still, Lance would keep him alive, just for the unholy joy of tormenting him.

By the time Lance left Julie's place, his rage knew no bounds, and on his way back to his lair in the apartment Lance currently called home, he made a detour under a bridge where the homeless liked to hang out. He swooped down and snatched up a frail elderly woman, asleep in her cardboard box.

Lance snatched up the painfully thin body and watched her eyes widen with terror as she took in his fiery eyes and elongated canines. He enjoyed her fear as he pushed her head back, exposing her carotid artery. As the first gush of blood blasted down his throat, he reveled in the fear he could taste. The woman's terror sweetened the blood, and he drank every drop.

The poor old dear felt the razor-like teeth bite into her flesh. The pain he was inflicting on her was white hot. She felt as if her organs and bones were melting in the awful heat, and her heart began to flutter in a meager attempt to keep beating. She was dying, and she knew she was dying. The old woman prayed for her death to come quickly, and when it finally came for her, she felt no regret, only release.

Lance found some cinder blocks and secured them to the old lady's body. He didn't want it found, just yet. He suspected he may have made a rather large mistake, killing those five at that morgue. It would draw the attention of the police and could draw attention to him. It was too soon. He would have to be more careful, he thought.

Once the cinder blocks were secured, he lifted the old lady's lifeless body and tossed it into the Milwaukee River. She wouldn't be missed, but Lance knew he would need to find another victim. His rage still pounded through him, and he needed to assuage it.

"Hey, what the hell you doin' with Gert?" A rough voice called out. Lance spun around, taking in the dirty and very skinny form staggering toward him. "I said what did you do to Gert?" The voice became more belligerent, actually threatening. Lance stepped closer to this threat.

"I merely sent her where she and her like belong. I sent her to the bottom of the river, and you, my friend, will soon join her."

Not giving the wino a moment to think, Lance was on him, using his teeth in a sawing motion until he pulled back with the man's esophagus in his mouth. Lance's eyes glowed with glee as the wino took one look to register what it was and dropped dead at Lance's feet.

That was enjoyable, Lance thought. It almost put him in a good mood.

Again, securing more blocks to this corpse, he effortlessly carried the dead body and pitched him in, letting him join his friend.

About to leave, he realized he would need a little something for Trish to feast on when she woke the next night. Luck was with him and seeing a car housing a woman and her two small children; he made himself presentable and ambled over to the dead vehicle.

"Good evening, my dear. This is not a safe place for you and your children. Have you nowhere else to go?" His tone was careful and solicitous.

The woman shook her head. "This is all we've got. The shelters were full before we could get there." Sheer desperation sounded in her voice.

The children whimpered from cold and hunger in the back seat where they were huddled. The crying irritated him. The satisfaction of killing the old lady and the wino were gone. Taking these three would satisfy some of his lust with the added feature of giving his new treasure some much needed nourishment. He would feast on the mother and have the satisfaction of watching Trish feast on the two small bodies.

"I have a small apartment building, madam. If you would allow me the privilege of helping you, I would be more than happy to put you up in one of the apartments for tonight. We shall see what tomorrow brings."

Not believing her luck, she roused her children from the back seat of the vehicle and ushered them toward this elegant man standing patiently, a beautiful smile on his elegant features. A boy and a girl, Lance thought, how absolutely perfect.

He tousled the hair of the boy and beamed at them. "I bet you're hungry. We'll stop at George Webb's and get some burgers to take to your new home."

The woman and her children smiled back. To them, George Webb's, a diner that stayed open all night, could have been manna from Heaven.

"God bless you, sir. It's getting so cold out; I didn't know what I was going to do. God bless you." She took one of his cold hands and held it to her lips. Lance sneered down at her bowed head. God bless, indeed.

§

Lance made good on his promise. They stopped off at George Webb's, and he purchased three large bags of burgers. That should tide them over, he thought, at least for tonight and tomorrow. After that, there would be no need to feed them, again. Grinning, he reminded himself that they would be lunch.

Lance ushered them into a small apartment that was partially furnished. It was dusty and musty, but the woman decided it was better than nothing. At least it had running water, sort of. She and the kids could wash up, eat, and the kids would be asleep in no time. Tomorrow, she would turn herself in and see what the county could do for her. Sighing, she looked at herself in the small, dingy mirror in the bathroom. She certainly had made a mess of her life, she knew. Tomorrow, she would try to correct it. Maybe kick the drugs that led to her downfall. Once she did that, she would be a good mother.

Her kids quietly ate, and the kind man left them alone. After munching down a couple of burgers each, the kids yawned wide and couldn't keep their eyes open. She quickly ushered them into the bathroom and washed them up as best she could. No soap or wash cloths at hand, she used her own clothes. Water was better than nothing.

Cupping her hands under the faucet, she gave them each a drink of water and led them to the bed. They were asleep almost before their heads hit the pillow.

Tears filled her eyes. "Mommy's so sorry, guys. I'll do better, I promise. Someday, we'll have a real home, again, and lots to eat. I sure did mess up, but I'll make it all up to you, I promise." Her own eyes

100

sagged shut, and before she knew it, she was sound asleep.

She never heard the sounds of fury coming from the apartment below her. Lance's rage returned four-fold, and it was the sight of Trish, lying so still, that caused him to almost lose control.

Trish was the reminder of his failures of the night, before. If the sun wouldn't be rising in the next hour, he would venture out and get to the pretty, innocent blond he wanted.

They laughed at him; he thought, and it brought fresh anger to a fever pitch. That creature, he thought, had dared laugh at him!

Lance pounded the walls in anger, whirling around the room like a crazy dervish. He picked up a bed and smashed it into pieces, and punched holes in the walls, almost causing two or three windows to fall out of their casings. He eyed Trish's still body still lying on the sofa and yanked it up, shaking her like a rag doll. This isn't who he wanted! A cheap substitute is all she is, he stormed.

Grasping her head in his powerful hands, he wanted to yank that head off her shoulders. He wanted to desecrate the still body in ways that would shock and stun and bring terror to everyone who heard of it.

Then, just as he was about to act on his impulse, a cooling thought came into his feverish brain. "No," he whispered, "Through you, I will have all I desire. Only after I have succeeded... only then will I destroy you."

He let Trish's lifeless body fall to the floor. He didn't bother to pick her up, again, leaving her to rest on the dirty floor. He would rest, he decided. Tomorrow, while Trish feasted on those two young cows, he would hunt their mother. That should perk him up.

Julie sat at her writing desk. She'd drawn the shades against the sunlight while she concentrated on the invitations. She would see to it that Abram applied the lotion she had developed, laughingly referred to as Super Sun block, and hand deliver each of these. She too had become convinced that time was of the essence. They could not delay. Even losing one day could mean defeat for herself and her friends.

Hunter came in holding a slip of paper. "You are going to need this. It's the address of the girl and her mother. Abram knows how to reach everyone else."

To Julie, Hunter appeared agitated, something she had never seen before. Small beads of perspiration stood on his upper lip, and his eyes darted around the room.

Julie got to her feet and placed a hand on his arm. "What's the matter with you?" She demanded and was further surprised when Hunter shook her hand off.

"I have to go. I need to take care of something, and I can't delay. This is the address you needed. I'll..." He took a deep breath and gave himself a mental shake. "I'll explain it to you later, if at all possible."

His long legs ate up the distance between her desk and the door. Before she could blink, he was gone from sight and she could hear him pounding down the stairs, followed by the slamming of the front door.

"What on earth?" she muttered and then turning back to her desk, she concentrated on the chore at hand, forcing Hunter's odd behavior from her mind.

Once clear of the house, Hunter moved on silent feet, gaining speed until he was a mere blur. He raced toward a certain run-down and abandoned apartment house and made his way to the second floor.

It had surprised him when his brother sauntered into his room in Julie's house, just moments before.

"Hello Brother. It's been a very long time. We miss you." Hunter stood, hearing the familiar voice. It was one he had not heard in too long.

"Gabriel! What are you doing, here?" Pure joy sang in Hunter's voice. Gabriel's characteristic shrug made Hunter laugh in absolute pleasure.

"Delivering a message... as usual. This one comes from the top, Brother." Gabriel's handsome face turned solemn. Sadness crept into his golden eyes and his generous lips trembled. "There are some innocents you are to rescue and see to it they arrive home, safely. You must move quickly, Brother. There isn't much time to spare."

Hunter strode to the small writing table in his room and scribbled something on a piece of paper. "I must deliver this to the mistress of this house, and then, I will do as I am bid."

Gabriel embraced Hunter. "Do you think she has figured out what it is that's desired of her?" Gabriel wondered and his beautiful face hardened a little as Hunter shook his head. "I know we are not to question, but it has been too long since you've been home. You are missed by all."

Hunter patted Gabriel's shoulder, which was as massive as his own. "I know, Gabriel. But, I am charged with a task, and I must see it through."

The two hugged, again, and Gabriel sauntered to the door. He turned and flashed a radiant smile in Hunter's direction. "Maybe, this time, she'll get it right. Hope springs eternal," He quipped, and then, was gone.

Hunter stood in the middle of his room and closed his eyes for a moment. In a flash, understanding came. He knew where he needed to go and what had to be done. Sighing, he hurried from his room and delivered the address he had written down.

Now, arriving at the tenement, he quietly entered the building. Carefully skirting the doorway where the evil one rested, Hunter made his way up the stairs, taking them two at a time.

He found the woman and her two children, quietly asleep. Hunter felt a great sadness for the small family as he watched them sleep. Life had not been kind to them, he knew. The children in particular touched his generous heart.

Moving quietly, so as not to instill fear, he wrapped the two children in a loving embrace and held them quietly. When he was finished, he reached for the mother. Her time was at an end, anyway, he knew. Judging by the smell of her, she would have been dead in a matter of days. Better for this to happen, he thought. He carefully lay down along side of her and held her close. Again, once finished, he rose and stared down at the small family. He knew when they awoke; they would be warm and happy. It was the most any mortal could ask for.

Hunter quietly left the building and headed in the direction of the beach. He would stare out across the majestic Lake Michigan and gather himself.

Lord, he thought, I am so tired. Let this all end, soon.

Still, he had a job to do, and he would do it for however long it would take.

Homesick, he made his way back to Julie's home. He would rest for the day and see what else developed. As he walked along, a small smile broke across his face. He would give anything to see the evil one's reaction once he realized another plan had been thwarted. The thought made Hunter laugh as he quickly headed back.

Lance roused himself late in the afternoon. He strolled over to Trish's body where it lay on the floor, just where he dropped it. He nudged it with his foot and watched. There! She moved a little. Now was the time to get her new playmates. Perhaps, he would allow the mother to run free. It would be more of a hunt, that way, and the terror coursing through her thin body would make the kill all the sweeter.

Happy with his decision and looking forward to an evening of sport, he took the stairs two at a time. He thought, perhaps, he would simply grab the two brats and bring them down to his apartment, and then, torment the mother. Now that's a great plan, he decided. What could possibly go wrong?

Entering the apartment, the first thing he noticed was the stench. It was not the odor of unwashed bodies. No, it was something far more awful. It was the stench of everything good. He could detect a faint hint of roses and lavender in the air, along with violets and baking bread. He even detected a hint of sea spray, clean and wild.

He looked at the small bed the three had slept on, and he was shaken all the way deep into his shriveled soulless heart. Their faces looked peaceful, even beautiful, and they were lifeless.

With a growl, he covered the slight distance to the bed and snatched them up, shaking them as a cat shakes a rat, and then, tossing them to the side.

"What the hell is this?" He screamed. Losing control, he grabbed the mother and shook her again. "Who did this?" Her head lolled to the side, and in his frustration, Lance swiped at it, removing it from her shoulders. And still, that beautiful smile remained.

He knew who was responsible!

"Hunter!" He growled out. "You will not stop me, Hunter! This is just a delay, but I will win!"

He stalked down the stairs and checked on Trish. Yes, she was wakening, and she would be hungry. He'd have to move fast. He'd have to find a substitute, bring it back here, see to it that she fed and do all of that before he could satisfy his own hunger. This was really becoming a bother, and if he wasn't positive he needed this one, he would simply destroy her, here and now.

He began to wonder if the blonde girl was worth all this. Calming himself, he sat for a moment and thought things through. Yes, the blonde was worth it, even if it was just the entertainment value of destroying such loathsome innocence. And, she would be an excellent substitute for the proud beauty, should it become necessary to destroy Julie as well.

A small growl from Trish's blue lips drew his attention. This one would be necessary to lure the blonde princess to him. That one, he thought, had been canny and sensed he was dangerous, but this one had been her friend. He would need Trish's assistance to secure her friend.

He would simply have to find her a little dinner before sending her on her way. Perhaps tonight, he would have the pretty blonde in his grasp. The thought made him feel much better.

He left the apartment, taking care to secure the door. It wouldn't do to have his playmate roaming around the city. Satisfied Trish was locked up; he strolled from his apartment building and made his way to the downtown area. There were always thrill seekers around, if one simply knew where to look.

It didn't take Lance long to find what he was looking for. A young man, with a slight build and dead eyes was nestled behind a parking garage. His head nodded, and Lance could tell the kid had just taken a hit of some sort of powerful opiate. Lance didn't care. He would be easier to convince.

Lance crouched down next to the young man and tapped him on the shoulder. "Hey kid! What's your name?" The boy's head came up, and Lance figured he was at least in his early twenties. So much the better. He may even have a little fight left in him, Lance thought.

Once again, he tapped the young man's shoulder. "I said, what is your name?" It took some doing, but the young man finally focused on Lance's face. "What's it to you? You a cop?" The words came out slurred and snarky. "Leave me alone!" His eyes focused on Lance's face with some difficulty. He saw exactly what Lance wanted him to see. He saw another young man, a junky like himself, and he relaxed a little.

"C'mon, man. You don't have to stay out here. It's cold and I gotta place. Got some good shit, too, and a pretty little thing that will make you feel like a real man. We can share her. She won't mind."

The junky smiled, showing teeth that were rotten and broken. "We're gonna have a party?" He asked, and Lance nodded.

"One you won't ever forget. Come on. Let's get in where it's warm." The junky stumbled to his feet. "You got food, man? I'm hungry." Lance nodded. "Yeah, I got food like you wouldn't believe."

Together, they made their way back to the apartment. The sun was set, and judging by the growls and hissing coming from the room he had left Trish, it was apparent his young apprentice was awake and hungry.

Lance opened the door and led the young man inside. He turned on a small lamp and spun around, grabbing his guest by the throat.

"What the hell? I thought you said this was a party! Let go! You're hurting me!" The kid began to sob. He didn't know what was wrong, but he was pretty sure he wasn't going to make it out of this room alive.

"Come here, little girl." Lance called out in a deceptively soft voice. "Come see what I have for you."

Trish emerged from the shadows, her eyes red and her tongue flickering in and out between her long canines. She watched Lance with a feral caution. She didn't understand what was happening. She didn't understand the changes happening to her body and mind. All she knew is, she could hear the young man's heart beating frantically, and she could almost taste the blood coursing through his veins.

"Come here. I will show you what must be done." The junky tried to fight; tried to get away, but Lance's grip on his throat was too strong.

He watched the thing coming toward him and felt his bowels and bladder let go. By the time Trish reached him, he had lost his slight grip on reality and was babbling, unable to form a coherent sentence.

Trish looked up at her master and waited. Instinct told her it was the smart thing to do, so she stopped and waited for his command.

In short order, she understood what she was to do and fell on their guest, sinking her teeth into his dirty neck and relishing the spurt of hot blood coursing down her throat. A small part of her that still housed a tinge of humanity felt sorry for her victim, but not sorry enough to stop. She was hungry. This was her meal. She hoped there would be others.

Dimly, she became aware that her victim stopped moving, but she continued to drink until there was nothing left. Disgusted, she tossed his lifeless body from her and turned to Lance. Blood dripped from her lips, but she was getting stronger.

Perhaps later, if she did everything her master asked of her, he would let her drink again, only maybe next time, he would allow her to hunt her next meal by herself.

"Well done, child. Now, I have a task for you. Not tonight, you are still too weak, and I have things I must teach you, first. In two nights, we will set out on this task. In the meantime, your lessons will begin. If you're a good girl and please me, I will allow you to hunt before the sun comes up. We shall see."

Trish settled herself at his feet and began to learn the old ways.

Chapter 14

olf drove into the underground parking and pulled into a
visitor's slot. Whipping out his notebook, he found the
code to punch into the elevator. His large fingers were
awkward as he tried to key in the numbers. Mission accomplished, and
he waited as the elevator took him up to Damien's place.

Arriving in the main lobby, the doors opened to allow a couple of
tenants to enter. As the doors closed, Wolf noticed a powerfully built
man with exotic features and the bearing of a soldier hand a large
cream envelope to the concierge. Wolf and the man made eye contact,
and before the doors closed, the stranger gave Wolf a wide grin,
flashing impossibly white teeth at him. Then, the doors closed and
Wolf continued his ascent.

Damien sat at his large worktable and worked on the sketch he had
begun two days ago. His head still hurt, but the work would do him
some good, he decided.

Steve decided to get some work of his own finished. He had

purchased a dress dummy, shopped around for fabric and was in the throes of creating something sensational. He didn't have a sewing machine handy, but he figured he could put it all together, make some changes as he saw fit, and if the need arose, he could always purchase one. It was a good plan, and he felt good working, although he would move on silent feet and check on Damien, now and then. Steve didn't want to admit it, but that vision two nights ago scared the bejesus out of him.

Pushing the thought from his mind, he worked on his own sketch and then began draping the fabric, his sheers flying as he cut the cloth and draped and pinned.

The opening elevator doors caught Damien's attention, and he wasn't shocked to see Wolf get off the elevator.

"I rather thought you'd be showing up sooner or later, Wolf." Damien smiled. He got to his feet and walked over, his hand extended. The two men shook, and Damien led the big cop into the living room and pointed at the sofa. "Sit down; I'll get us something cold to drink. Coke all right with you?" Wolf nodded and Damien went over to the refrigerator and liberated two cans.

"What can I do for you, Wolf? You look like a man with a lot on his mind." Both men glanced toward the hallway as Steve emerged into the living room. "I thought I heard voices. Is this a private conversation? I can return to my lair if you like."

Wolf shook his head. "You know what's going on, so you don't have to leave." Wolf gave the smaller one a questioning look, and Steve smiled.

"Steve Worthington." The two men shook hands and then walking over to the refrigerator, Steve snagged himself a Coke and settled into an overstuffed chair that seemed to swallow his slight frame.

Wolf wondered where to begin. This was sure as hell out of his realm, and he wasn't entirely comfortable with the topic they must discuss. He gave a huge sigh. Give him a good old fashioned murder and he was on top of things. This situation is entirely different, and he wasn't sure just where to begin. He gave Damien an imploring look, but before Damien could say anything, the bell rang, alerting him that someone else was seeking entry to his home.

Steve waved Damien back into his chair. "Sit down. I'll get it. You still look like hell." Steve pressed a button and the doors slid open, revealing the concierge. In his hand, he held two large cream-colored envelopes. One was made out to Damien and himself, the other to Wolf.

He handed Damien his and sat back and waited. Damien grinned at Wolf. "Looks like things are going to get pretty interesting." He pulled out a hand-written invitation, done with an elegant hand on heavy cream paper. A gold crown served as the logo.

The invitation was signed with a flourish and read Julie King. Steve couldn't contain his excitement. "Holy cow! Julie King is inviting us to dinner? God! I can't get over this." He peered over at Damien and scowled. "How the hell do you know Julie King? You been holdin' out on me, pal?"

Damien shook his head. "I've never had the pleasure, but unless I miss my guess, I'm willing to bet she's the mystery woman I saw walking on the beach two days ago."

Wolf cleared his throat. "Who the hell is Julie King?" He was examining his own invitation and looked up, hearing Steve's faint groan.

"My dear detective," Steve grinned, "She is only the most fabulous hostess on the planet. She's active in some charity work, as well, but she's also a true fashionista! Every major fashion house throughout the entire world is panting for her business. We were lucky! She bought from my mentor!" He was so excited he could hardly contain himself.

Wolf grinned in spite of himself. His phone vibrated, and he scowled when he saw who was calling him. "What is it, Rachel? I'm in the middle of a conversation." Rachel's voice came over the phone, loud, clear and highly excited.

"I just received an invitation to Julie King's for a dinner party, Wolf!" He cut her off before she could go off on her usual tirade of how they could hob nob with a better quality of people if he would just practice law and give up the police business.

"Yeah? I got one, too." It satisfied him a great deal when she sputtered into silence. Damien was making motions toward Wolf, and Wolf held the phone a little away from his ear.

"Ask her if Kirsten was included." Damien thought he could see where this could be going.

Wolf nodded then turned back to his phone. "Was Kirsten asked as well?" He nodded toward Damien as he quickly wrapped up the conversation with his ex-wife.

Damien sat back in his chair, deep in thought. Steve and Wolf waited.

"I think this little dinner party is all about Kirsten, Wolf. I have the sense that Ms. King is aware of what is going on, why it's going on and who is responsible. This should be a very interesting dinner, all in all."

"Why invite me?" Steve wanted to know, and Damien shrugged.

"You were here when I had that episode." Damien always referred to his visions as 'episodes'.

Damien got to his feet and walked over to his table. "We should get a few answers at that dinner, tomorrow night." He told the room in general.

"Maybe you can give me a couple of answers, right now, Damien." Damien glanced over to Wolf and shrugged. "Sorry Wolf, I'm in the dark, too."

Steve tapped an elegant finger to his temple, then shrugged. He was in the dark, as well.

"I don't think so, Dame." Wolf gave the two men a chilling smile. "Maybe you two can tell me how I was able to see Nate, last night, in my apartment and why Mattie White, Michele's mother, had a visit from her dead daughter. Either one of you geniuses want to explain that little gem to me?"

Wolf sat back and watched the expressions on the two men's faces turn to surprise, shock and then utter confusion.

Julie paced through her home, touching small treasures every now and then.

She felt on edge, but didn't know why. Emma followed her into the main parlor, checking for dust bunnies or anything else that may have escaped her sharp eyes.

"Sorry Miss. I thought you were upstairs, resting." Emma looked around and found everything in order. She caught Julie's small frown and turned to leave the room. If Julie wanted to be left alone, Emma would leave her alone.

"Wait, Emma! I feel uneasy, and I'm not sure just why." Julie flung herself on a gold settee and pointed to a matching chair across from her. "Sit down for a moment. We'll talk about our plans for tomorrow night. Everything is in order?" Emma nodded. "I called the girls I use for other parties to come and help me. The house is clean; the menu is finished and waiting for your approval. That will just leave the shopping, and I have time for that."

Julie sighed. "Very good. You know, I am not sure if this party is a good idea, or not, but perhaps it is the most effective way to get all parties to come together. Abram delivered all the invitations, this afternoon." Julie scowled again. "He thinks we may have problems with the woman. He told me when he delivered the invitations to her and her daughter, her reaction was quite strange. She almost burst at the seams, according to Abram and then peppered him with questions. He tells me she is quite bold and very headstrong. She would not allow him to leave gracefully, demanding answers to her questions. He finally told her he was a mere messenger and her questions would be answered tomorrow evening." Julie gave a small laugh. "A 'mere messenger'. As if Abram could be a mere anything." Emma grinned but kept silent.

The two women sat, both looking off into space. Julie finally broke the silence. "Emma, let's go into the kitchen. I will review the menu. Maybe that will ease my mind." Together they headed for the kitchen.

In the hallway, Julie was overcome by nausea and dizziness. She stood very still and waited for the feeling to pass, clutching Emma's arm. Alarmed, Emma placed her free arm around Julie's slim waist and held on, tightly. Julie, her head down, shivered. Her head snapped up and she knew. Her grasp on Emma's arm tightened, and Emma could feel the blood pool under Julie's grip.

"He's made another!" Julie gasped. Shaking off Emma's hand, she raced in search of Abram, calling over her shoulder. "Abram is back?" She headed for the garage before Emma could answer her. Abram was just entering the kitchen from the garage as Julie raced in from the front parlor.

112

"Abram! He's made another!" She grasped his arm and gave it a small shake. "We have to move fast! It will be hungry!"

Hunter sauntered into the kitchen and nosed around the covered cake plate. He had developed a fondness for sweets, and Emma always had a generous supply of donuts, cakes or pies. He gave Abram and Julie a casual glance and resumed his nosing about.

"How can you think of your stomach at a time like this?" Julie demanded, and Hunter gave her an easy shrug. "There is one grandparent left. It will go there. Family always lets you in, you know. I have the address. You'll go and stop this newest creature. Be on guard. I doubt the enemy will be so foolish to allow her to go, alone, but one can always hope."

With a triumphant shout, he found the three-layer chocolate cake Emma baked, that morning. He cocked an eyebrow at her, and she gave him a small swat on the arm.

"Go sit down, I'll bring you a nice, large slice." She cut a generous piece, putting it on a plate and poured him a large mug of coffee. She had not been sure she would like this stranger, but if he was helping her, Julie and Abram, then he was all right with her.

Abram looked out the window over the sink and turned to his mistress. "Madam. I best be on my way. The sun is almost all the way down." Turning to Hunter, he saw a small piece of paper in the other man's powerful hand. Snatching it out of Hunter's hand, he made a beeline to his room and changed into what he referred to as his uniform. Black pants and boots, topped off by a black hoody and ski mask.

A sense of urgency filled him as he hustled to the back door. "I'll find it," he reassured Julie, "I'll find it, and I'll destroy it. I won't let you down."

He raced out the door, and using his peculiar speed, was quickly on his way. Hunter grinned. "He never has let you down, has he Princess?"

Julie shook her head. "No Hunter. He never has." Turning to Emma she gestured to the kitchen table. "Let's hope for the best. In the meantime, we will go over the menu. If he fails, we'll have to think of something else."

Trish sat at his feet, learning all Lance could teach her. "You will go to your grandmother. Family will always let you in. You, my young protégé, are not capable of illusion. That will come in time. As you grow stronger, become accustomed to your new form, many things will become easier for you. You will have strength beyond your wildest dreams. You will learn to appear in other forms. This is a great gift I have given to you. You must show me you are worthy of such a gift."

Trish was hungry. The junkie she had for breakfast was not enough. His blood was thin and tainted. She still felt the after effects of drinking blood laced with narcotics. She wanted more. She knew her grandmother's blood would nourish her. She couldn't wait to sink her teeth into such a nourishing meal. After drinking granny's blood, she thought, she'd find a nice toddler to feast on. Children's blood, she thought, will be pure and nourishing and wonderful.

These thoughts bouncing around in her awakening brain caused her to lose her focus. She listened to her sire with half an ear and that earned a sharp cuff to the side of her head. The pain was sharp and immediate, and she snarled at Lance in response. Trish was aware of just how cruel her sire could be, but that didn't mean she would take his slaps without retribution. Not now, she considered, she was too weak. The day would come when he would pay for this slap and any future ones he dished out.

"You better listen to me, child. This is new to you. Mistakes can cost us a great deal. Now, pay attention."

Lance saw the red eyes and the elongated canines. He knew she was angry, and he knew that, in time, she could destroy him. He would have to be careful with her, at least, until her usefulness was at an end. Then, he would destroy her before she became too strong.

"It is full dark, child. Time for you to visit your grandmother. Drink your fill, but do so carefully. Be certain she is dead, and do not think of making her like us. That is not your place." Lance tapped a long, elegant finger against his red lips. "Only I will decide who is to be given this gift which you now enjoy. Now go, I did some shopping

114

and bought you fitting clothes. Put them on, and then we will send you on your way."

Excited, Trish entered the small and dingy bedroom. She found the clothes Lance purchased for her and slid them on, hands shaking with anticipation. She did not fully understand everything happening to her, but she liked the changes in her body. Even now, with the tainted blood in her system, Trish felt incredibly strong. She was invincible. Better still, the man of her dreams chose her! How wonderful this all was; how very wonderful.

Her ringing ear reminded her of how quickly and cruelly Lance disciplined her. He may be the man of her dreams, she mused, but that didn't mean he wouldn't pay for hitting her. She decided she would enjoy him, learn all he could teach her, and then, make her move. Perhaps, if he pleaded prettily, she would allow him to survive, but if and when he hit her again, his fate would be in her hands. Smiling at the thought, she dressed quickly.

Emerging from the bedroom, Lance looked her over, carefully. Dressed all in black, he thought the color suited her. The narrow pants worn over sharp-heeled boots were becoming, as was the black cable knit sweater. A short black leather coat completed her ensemble. She was ready.

"Go child. I know you hunger, still. Enjoy your dinner. I shall be out and about, seeing to my own appetite."

Lance's incredible ego would not allow him to consider failure. The twit would feast and come back to him. Her next test would be securing the pretty blonde. Once he had her in his grasp, this one would cease to exist. A simple plan. It couldn't fail.

Trish eased herself out of the rundown building. She walked briskly toward the downtown area, aware that Lance was following her. A cold sneer crossed her lips, and her eyes blazed with a sort of madness. Two young punks, who started walking toward her, saw the look and decided it may be healthier to avoid this stunning creature. Something about her hit them as wrong, and they didn't want to mess with her.

She turned down a street which was mostly deserted, and picking up speed, she found this particular perk amazing. There was some initial clumsiness, but she quickly overcame that. Moving with a sudden burst of speed, she raced up the block and around the corner. Let him try to keep up with me, she thought. He was old, and she was not. It could be a lesson to him, something for him to think about in the future.

Trish loved this speed, along with the other changes in her body. Her eyesight, so much more acute, took in sights she knew she would have missed before her change.

Her hearing, so much sharper now, could pick out conversations inside buildings that looked deserted. As she sped past a tenement building, a small cry caught her attention. Ah, she thought, a baby. She filed the information away for future reference. Yes, she loved these changes. If only she wasn't so damn hungry, she could have really enjoyed herself.

Knowing that granny would help relieve that hunger, she moved faster still.

A few blocks from Mattie's house, she slowed down. Anticipation of her coming meal caused Trish to tremble in anticipation. She ran a shaking hand over her hair in an attempt to smooth it into place. She couldn't very well go to the old woman looking half-mad and a mess.

Trish arrived at Mattie's house and was pleased to see the block dark. She had no idea what time it was, but she figured it must be pretty late. Most of her grandmother's neighbors worked, so as was their habit, they would have watched the news and retired for the night. How perfect.

She walked around her grandmother's home and was pleased to see all the lights were off. Granny must have retired, as well, she decided. So much the better. The old bat would be confused and disoriented enough and would let Trish in. Lance had stressed that. She *must* be invited in. Oh, this was all going to work out great.

Confident, Trish walked around the bungalow until she found her grandmother's bedroom window. She tapped lightly on the glass. Getting no response, she tapped again, a little harder this time. Still no response. Impatient now, she grated her nails down the glass and listened. She heard Mattie move around and then saw the curtains part.

"Who is it?" Trish could hear the confusion in the old woman's voice. She had been correct. The old woman was befuddled after being woken from a deep sleep.

116

Mattie peered into the darkness, and Trish pushed her face against the glass. The elderly woman put her hand to her mouth, seeing the granddaughter she thought dead, standing in front of her window. "Trish?" Mattie managed to croak out? "Trish, baby, is that you?"

"Grandma! Let me in! I'm scared, and I'm hungry! Please let me in."

Mattie flew to the door. Her Trish was just outside. She wasn't dead, after all! The police had made a mistake! Trish was here, and she was frightened and hungry.

Mattie put her hand on the doorknob and yanked the door wide open. There stood her much loved granddaughter. It was a miracle.

"Grandma! Can I come in?" Trish put on a vulnerable front, but couldn't stop herself from licking her lips in anticipation of that nice, warm gush of blood about to shoot down her throat. Oh yeah, she decided, granny was gonna make a fine meal.

Forgetting Michele's warning, Mattie stepped back and opened her lips to reply.

Chapter 15

K irsten cried herself to sleep. The tears stained her face and soaked through to her pillows. At the heart of the terrible grief she felt horror.

That Trish should die so young was one thing, but to be *murdered*, that was just too hard for Kirsten to wrap her mind around. Kirsten knew Trish had to have been so terrified, and she died feeling that terror, knowing she was on her own and wondering why no one was coming to save her.

Something inside the young girl knew... she just knew the man at The Club must have had something to do with this. Had he followed them home? Was this her fault? Kirsten began to berate herself. She should have been more careful going home. She just never thought to check and see if someone was following them. Now, because she didn't think, her best friend was dead. Not just her best friend, but her friend's parents, who she loved as much as her own parents.

She just couldn't accept this. It had to be a bad dream, and she would wake up and everything would go back to normal. Only, Kirsten's practical side told her, this was real and there was no waking up from this nightmare, and she would have to face life without Trish. That thought brought on fresh sobs and she cried until she didn't have any tears left.

Exhausted, she fell into a light sleep. She was vaguely aware of her mother coming in and pulling a blanket up around her shoulders, before tiptoeing back out again.

The next morning, Kirsten didn't bother getting dressed. She stumbled to the kitchen table and plopped into a chair, staring at her mother. Rachel glanced at her daughter and saw the warning signs. Kirsten would be a handful, today.

"So, I was thinking, Kirsten. We could go shopping. You have homecoming approaching, soon. We could go out, today, check out some dresses, and maybe have lunch? What do you say?"

"I don't want to go shopping, mother. I'm not going to homecoming. Don't you get it? My best friend is dead! Murdered! Her whole family wiped out! Doesn't that bother you? Michele was your best friend, and you stand here like nothing happened!"

Rachel turned and faced her daughter.

"It bothers me a great deal, Kirsten, but life doesn't stop. We have to make the best of things and just push on." Rachel took a sip of coffee, watching Kirsten, carefully. Ever since her divorce from Wolf, Kirsten had been difficult. She blamed Rachel for the break-up, not understanding that Wolf was capable of so much more. They could have had a great life, if only he had used his law degree for what it was meant for. They could have had a bigger house, and Kirsten could have had every advantage.

Wolf loved being a cop and refused to leave the force, and Rachel couldn't tolerate that.

Strong-willed Rachel always found a way to get what she wanted, except when it came to Wolf. She almost hated him for his stubbornness.

In her frustration, Rachel said the wrong thing. "Well, Kirsten, the great detective is on the case. I'm sure he'll have it solved by lunch time."

Kirsten didn't miss the venom in her mother's tone. Exasperated, she pushed away from the table.

"You don't know anything, mother. Dad can't work the case! They won't let him because he's too close! And, here's a thought. I'm involved, somehow! Did you even think of that? I could be next."

Kirsten huffed into the bedroom and Rachel slammed her cup down, prepared to follow her daughter and have it out with her, yet again. The doorbell brought a halt to that.

Rachel peered outside through one of the small windows next to the door. She saw an exotic-looking man standing on her porch. In his hand, he held two large, cream colored envelopes.

She opened the door and gazed into two of the most piercing brown eyes she had ever seen. "Can I help you?" She asked. Abram raised an eyebrow as she kept the screen door as a barrier between the two.

"My employer asked me to deliver these to you and your lovely daughter." His voice, although a deep rumble, was as exotic as he is, and Rachel reddened a little.

"May I ask who your employer is?" Rachel was aware of Kirsten entering the living room, alerted by the voices.

Abram's smile encompassed them both. "Miss Julie King." He replied, and watched as Rachel's jaw dropped. Obviously, she knows who Julie is, he thought. Glancing at the daughter, he grinned. This one was a real beauty, he thought and a few hundred years ago, he would have sought permission to make her his bride. Times change, though, and maybe not for the better, he thought.

Rachel opened the screen door and accepted the two envelopes. Abram gave a small and courtly bow and moved away, while Rachel closed the door. Anticipation made her hands shake.

Why would Julie King send her an invitation, she wondered. Unable to wait, she tossed Kirsten's envelope to her and hastily opened her own. Seeing the request to the small dinner party had Rachel babbling with excitement. She just couldn't wait to tell Wolf about this! This would show him, she thought. What she thought it would show him was unclear, but her mind was racing rapidly. Her next move was to grab her phone and call her ex-husband.

Kirsten read her invitation and put it aside. She knew, of course, who Julie was. For a brief moment, she wondered why they were receiving invitations to a dinner party hosted by the woman. What did she and Ms. King have in common?

Too exhausted and upset to care, Kirsten placed her invitation on the coffee table and turned to go back to her room. She knew she had been unfair to her mother, but her mother had been just as unfair and as usual, not willing to see Kirsten's point of view. And why, she thought, did her mother have to keep attacking her dad? It wasn't fair.

She heard her mother crowing to her father about the invitations and headed back to her room. She didn't want to listen to the never ending saga and accusations between her parents. Her mother's next words stopped her in her tracks. "What do you mean you received one, as well?"

Kirsten turned, slowly, and watched her mother's face. It was slightly amusing to see the self-satisfaction seep from her mother's face as Wolf told her he, too, had indeed received an invitation and at the urging of a friend, would be attending.

Having her small sense of victory snatched from her, Rachel abruptly ended the phone call, telling Wolf she would see him there. "Don't forget to wear a clean shirt." She said in parting.

Satisfied with having the last word, she raced into her room and dove into her closet. She couldn't afford a new outfit, but she just knew she had something suitable.

Rachel scanned her considerable wardrobe until she found a cocktail suit. She had worn it only once, so she guessed it could be considered new. Wolf had never seen it, so that was something. She carefully brought out the burnt orange outfit and examined it, carefully.

The satin lapels and trim skirt along with the abbreviated jacket suited her and showed off a decent figure as well as showcasing her red hair, perfectly. Searching again, she found the razor sharp heels that matched. All she needed was to find the small purse that went with it, and she'd be all set.

Turning from her closet, she saw Kirsten leaning against the door jam, watching her with an amused expression on her young face. "What are you doing, Kirsten? You need to see what you have to wear to this. If you don't have something suitable, we can run out and get you something."

Kirsten shook her head, her soft blond curls gently bobbing against her cheek. Those long amber eyes, so like Wolf's, gazed at her mother in amusement. "Don't worry about it, mother. I have something that will work."

Rachel stopped and stared at her daughter. "No argument? None of this 'I'm not going' nonsense?" Rachel didn't quite trust this sudden acceptance from Kirsten. She narrowed her eyes at her daughter and waited. When Kirsten didn't go off in a huff, Rachel raised an eyebrow, bringing a grin to her daughter's face. "If daddy is going, then there's a reason for me to be there. So, I'm going." Kirsten turned and walked back to her room. She had the distinct feeling that tomorrow night would be very interesting, indeed.

Trish waited impatiently for her grandmother to say the magic words. Granny *had* to invite her in, or there would be no entrance, and Trish knew that would be bad, very bad. Lance would not take her failure well. She simply had to do this and besides, she was so thirsty, so hungry. Grandma would make a fine meal.

Mattie stood in the doorway, staring at her only grandchild. They told her Trish was dead, but here she was! All Mattie had to do was reach out and bring her granddaughter into her house where she would be safe. Still, she wanted to gaze on those beloved features and revel in the fact that Trish was alive and wanting to come in.

First things first, though. Mattie needed to settle down, a little. It wouldn't do for Trish to see her so agitated. They had much to talk about, but that could wait. She would wrap Trish in a loving embrace and never let her go.

Abram stood in the shadows, downwind. Surprise was all he had on his side. Tense, he watched the elderly lady open the door and gaze at the form standing in front of her. He had a pretty good idea of what was going to happen, next, and as much as he hated to do it, he would rush the young vampire before she could do any damage and get her the hell away from here. He only hoped it wouldn't be too much for the old lady. She had been through much. This could be the last straw for her.

Mattie couldn't stop staring at Trish. She took in the face so like Michele's.

Mattie extended her hand toward the girl, now waiting. In her anxious state, wanting to please her master, Trish made a mistake. "Come on Granny! What are you waiting for? Ask me in! I'm cold and hungry and you're just standing there looking at me.!"

Mattie stopped and took a hard look. Trish never spoke to her like that. Then, the warning Michele had brought to her, penetrated through the shock.

Mattie gave a deep sigh, and just as Trish was ready to walk in the door, Mattie shook her head. "I don't know who you are, and I don't care. You're not my granddaughter, though, and of that I am certain. You leave now, girl, before I call the cops on you."

She watched as Trish's face contorted with rage. She saw the girl's eyes turn red and Trish flashed fangs at her. "Let me in, old woman, and I'll make it easy on you." Even Trish's usually soft voice was changed. Now, it was guttural and coarse. Mattie shivered. Slowly, Mattie closed the door in Trish's face, leaned back against it and let the sobs come.

Abram relaxed, slightly. The young vampire had made a grievous mistake, and it cost her that first meal. He wondered what she would do, next. Curious, he decided to follow her and see what she would do, next.

Frustrated and terrified, Trish turned from the door. What was she going to do, now? She couldn't go back to Lance and tell him she failed. She walked down the street, pondering her options. She didn't have to go back to him, she thought. She could just strike out on her own. As quickly as the thought came into her head, Trish pushed it aside. She really couldn't be on her own. Not yet. She had a lot to learn, and only he could teach her. No, she would have to go back and take her punishment. Surely, he wouldn't destroy her. He had chosen her over Kirsten, hadn't he? He would just have to give her another chance to prove herself.

Heading back to the miserable apartment she shared with him, she stumbled across a young runaway. The young girl gave Trish a small smile and hope shined in the girl's eyes. Maybe this pretty black girl could help her get home.

Two days away from home had taught the girl some hard lessons. Her parents hadn't really been that bad, and she had been selfish and irresponsible. Now, she had been beaten, robbed and only luck kept worse from happening to her. Maybe, this pretty lady would help her get home.

Trish sensed the fear in the girl and swooped over her. "Come with me. You can't stay out here," Trish said, reaching for the girl's hand. Willingly, the girl got to her feet and followed Trish.

Abram, following Trish, knew how this would end. He took a moment to debate with himself and decided to act. The recent killings had drawn too much attention, and Julie wouldn't like more attention brought down. They could get caught up in the back-lash. Abram caught up to the two girls, trying to decide how best to proceed. He didn't want to create a scene. It was still fairly early in the evening, and people were milling around. It would never do to draw attention to either this young vampire nor or himself.

Still uncertain, he followed the girls until they came to a stoplight. Waiting for the light to change, Abram took a shot. He struck up a casual conversation with them. The young mortal, who couldn't have been more than fifteen, answered willingly. She liked the looks of this man, and Abram could be quite charming.

The young vampire, on the other hand, showed her annoyance. Her eyes shot daggers in Abram's general direction, and he grinned his most charming smile. This was dangerous territory. If the young vampire created a commotion, the police would be called. There would be a lot of explaining to do.

The young run-away's stomach rumbled loudly, and Abram seized the opportunity.

"You're hungry. Come with me. There's a hamburger place on the next block. We'll get you something to eat. You'll feel better and after you have eaten, we'll decide what to do." He heard Trish's soft growl. He understood the terrible thirst that consumed her at the moment, but this young girl would not become her first meal. She would have to look elsewhere.

Not sure why he felt so protective of the young mortal, Abram walked between the two girls. Trish would have to go through him to get to the young one. In the meantime, he would be on guard. The young vampire's sire could be lurking around, although Abram did not sense nor smell him. Still, he could be in the area, so Abram knew he would have to be careful.

Arriving at the small hamburger shack, Abram opened the door, gesturing with his head for the two girls to go on ahead of him. The young run-away darted through the door, but Trish held back. "This isn't the end, old man." She growled low. "I may not make a meal out of this one, but there are others." Abram shrugged. "Of course there are." His eyes held just enough amusement to irritate her. Turning on her heel, she strode away. Abram knew she was on the hunt. He could not do much about that, but he had saved one young and very frightened girl. He would feed her, and then, see what it was she wanted to do.

Abram settled the young run-away in a booth in the back of the restaurant. He ordered her a cup of hot soup, salad and a burger with the works. For himself, he chose a mug of coffee. While he sipped, he watched her attack the soup with a vengeance. He took in her tousled brown curls, her doe eyes and pale face.

She reminded him of a younger Julie, before the change, and he felt a warm feeling where his heart beat at one time. He knew he could easily over power her, make a meal out of her and be done with it. Even now, the thirst was on him and he promised himself an extra bag of the blood in his refrigerator. He had enough willpower to hold off, until then.

Checking out the bruises on her face and arms, his eyes tightened in anger. She had been worked over pretty well. He hoped worse had not happened to her.

"So, want to tell me your name?" He asked, watching and waiting. If he was going to help her, she would have to trust him. He didn't want to blow this.

"Jenna Hanson."

Abram nodded. "My name is Abram." It was a start. "Care to tell me what happened?" The ball was firmly in her court. He'd wait and see what she did with it before going any further. Jenna sighed as the hot soup penetrated through the cold.

This was the first thing she had eaten in two days, and it felt so good. Abram waited for her to finish off the soup. Then, he would see. If she confided in him, he had a half of plan formed in his mind. He would see to it she was safe until he could get her back to her family. If she decided not to confide in him, he would pay for her meal and leave her to her own devices. He was, after all, no saint.

"I stayed out late. My mom and dad were going to ground me, so I ran away with my supposedly-called boyfriend." A faint blush came into her wan cheeks and she tossed her head. "I refused to sleep with him. I'm only fifteen, for God's sake. He brought me here into the city and ditched me. I live three hours from here, and he took my cell phone so I couldn't even call my folks. They said he wasn't much good. I hate that they were right." Hunger and fatigue made her narrative a little disjointed, but Abram followed.

He nodded at her. "Parents have a way of knowing who is good and who is bad. What do you want to do, now?" He waited.

"I'd like to call my folks and see if they'll come and get me. I just want to go home." Tears stood in those deep brown eyes. Abram excused himself. He needed to call Julie and put his plan into motion.

"Madam, I'm in the Burger Shack with a young run-away. She almost became victim to your sire's latest creation. She wants to go home. I'd like to bring her to your home and have her parents pick her up, there." Julie sighed heavily over the phone.

Why, she wondered, was Abram bringing this problem to her doorstep? "Why?" she asked, her tone snarky.

Abram laughed into the phone. "Because she reminds me of a younger you."

Julie's patience was worn thin, as always. Things seemed to be spiraling out of her control and she didn't like it. "Fine! Bring her here, but get her out of here as soon as possible." She hung up and Abram returned to the restaurant.

"We're going to call your parents to come and fetch you. But! You must promise me you will not do this sort of thing, again! Next time, you may not be so lucky!"

Jenna quickly promised, and Abram handed her his cell phone. "Call them, and after you speak to them, I will tell them where they may find you. I am taking you to the home of my employer, where you will be safe.

Jenna called her parents, and then, after tearfully begging them to come and get her, she handed the phone to Abram. He gave them Julie's address and promised them their daughter would be waiting for them. He assured them she was fine, a little bruised and a little shaken, but he thought she had learned her lesson.

Abram paid the bill after hanging up and seeing Jenna eyeing the pies on the counter, grinned down at her.

"Emma has much better pies. We'll go bug her until she gives us a piece, then you will clean up, put on some fresh clothes, and look presentable when your parents arrive." He took a deep breath, thought about it for a minute, and then decided, what the hell. "You don't know how lucky you are, Jenna. When I say things could have been far worse for you, you don't realize how much worse. Let's just say that you could very easily have ended up very, very dead. You take my warning seriously. You were hovering very close to the river. Someone could have come along, harmed you, killed you and tossed your body into the river... and you would not have been found if they chose. Now promise me you will be a good girl from now on. Choose your friends a little more carefully and do not put yourself, nor your parents, through something like this ever again."

Jenna's eyes had widened. This was the most he had spoken to her since he found her, and there was something in his voice that told her he was not kidding. "I guess I just didn't think things through, Abram." She gave him a shy side glance. "You have a different sort of accent. I guess you aren't from around here, either." She ventured.

He nodded his face solemn. "I am from Israel." Not entirely the truth, but close enough.

"Wow! That is completely cool! Did you serve in the Army, there? My dad says everyone has to serve."

Abram nodded. "But, that was a long time ago."

Now that they were out of the restaurant, Abram was faced with a dilemma. He had been on foot when he started out this evening. It would take him forever to get this girl to Julie's house, and at this time of night, he was pretty sure it would be damn near impossible to get a cab. What the hell was he supposed to do, now, he wondered.

He was still feeling uneasy. He had snatched this innocent right out from under the young vampire's nose. If this was part of her "lesson" for the night, then his thwarting those plans had placed not just the girl but himself in danger, as well. He put himself on high alert.

As they walked, Abram kept his face calm while his mind raced. Ideas came into his head, and were rejected, quickly. He just didn't see how he was going to solve this problem.

They walked about six blocks, Jenna quietly walking with him. She was exhausted but didn't want to complain. The man might change his mind and leave her behind. So, she kept quiet as they continued their journey.

Abram, sensing the girl's fatigue, was about to cave in and call Julie to come pick them up when one of her cars whipped around a corner and came to a stop next to them. Bending down, he made out his mistress behind the wheel. A massive sigh of relief escaped his lips. Opening the door, he motioned Jenna into the back seat, climbed into the passenger seat after she was settled, and whispered a thank you in Aramaic.

Julie answered him in the same language. "Did not think things through, did you Abram." Seeing the guilty look on his face, she sighed. "I rather thought not."

The three made their way to Julie's home in silence. Jenna fell asleep during the ride, finally feeling warm and safe. Abram kept a sharp eye out for their nemesis or his spawn, but the ride home was uneventful.

Once arriving home, they found Emma waiting for them. She hustled Jenna to a shower, searched the girl's backpack and finding nothing clean, and hustled out to find Julie.

"That girl has absolutely nothing clean! Her parents can't see her like that. The bruises alone will be enough to send them into a tizzy." Julie turned from her dressing table. "You're about the same size." Emma added.

"What do you expect me to do?" Julie was definitely in a snarky mood.

"I expect you to give me some clean garments so the girl can look presentable." Because Emma's tone was so motherly, Julie couldn't stop the grin from flitting across her lips. She went to her dresser and pulled out undergarments, then checked her closet. She found a pair of jeans and a light sweater.

"Tell her she may keep these things. I don't wear them, anyway." Satisfied, Emma hustled back into the guest bathroom just as Jenna was stepping from the shower.

"Now you get dressed, and then, Abram will show you to the kitchen. He said you have a fondness for pie, and I think there's one slice left."

Emma went down to the kitchen, found the last piece of an apple pie that Hunter had not gotten into, yet, and placed it on a plate. She poured a glass of milk, and then, sat down and waited until Abram brought the girl into the kitchen.

Julie's clothes were a little big on Jenna's small frame, but all in all, the girl looked clean and presentable.

Julie wandered in and poured a glass of wine, then sipped as she studied the girl sitting at her kitchen table. Abram lounged in another chair, close by. Soon, Hunter sauntered in, took in the little group, studied the young girl now devouring pie and accurately guessed what was going on.

Julie gave him a sultry glance and then zeroed in on Jenna, just wolfing down her desert. For herself, she didn't see a resemblance between herself and this little waif sitting at her kitchen table, but she supposed she could understand Abram's inaccurate assessment.

"So, young lady. You have had quite the adventure, hmmm?" Julie was still feeling a little put out at the intrusion, and Hunter's grin irritated her even further.

"Yes ma'am, I sure did. Learned my lesson, too. I never should have listened to Travis. My parents said he was bad news. I really hate that part... you know... having to admit they were right."

Julie grinned, and her sour mood lifted, a little. The girl may look like a waif, but she had some fire left in her. "You do realize this could have ended badly if Abram had not found you." Julie drove the point home, giving the girl a stern look.

"I know. Some guys came along and roughed me up, some." Jenna pointed to the bruises. "My mother is gonna go nutso when she sees these bruises." She sighed, "I guess I have them coming to me." She added softly.

"What did you learn from this?" Hunter asked her, softly. Jenna turned to him. She felt so good in his presence. Not that she didn't appreciate everything Abram had done for her, but this man just made her feel just plain good!

"I learned to listen to my parents. I learned I don't know everything, and I learned that Travis was a liar and a thief and a loser, just like my mom said."

Hunter nodded. "Young girls often get themselves into trouble by not listening. I think, perhaps, you have learned your lesson, after all. As for this Travis. I have a feeling he is going to learn a very hard lesson, before too long."

He ignored Julie's questioning look and walked around the table. Taking Jenna's face in his hands, he gently stroked it, and then let his hands travel down her arms as well. In an instant, the bruises were gone and Jenna didn't know when she felt this healthy.

The doorbell stopped any questions Jenna may have had and, she rose from the table as Abram ushered her parents in. She was enveloped in a warm hug by both parents, while the occupants of Julie's household watched. Jenna's dad extended his hand to Abram and then Hunter and flashed a beautiful smile at the women.

"We can't thank you enough! We've been so worried. We sort of thought Travis may have brought her here, but we didn't know where to look. Thank you all, so very much. How can we possibly repay you?"

Julie shook her head. "We were happy to be of assistance. Jenna has promised to be a good girl, haven't you?" She gave the young runaway a piercing look, and Jenna's face flushed.

"Yes ma'am. I sure have." Jenna began gathering up her things, preparing to leave. "Jeez dad, you must have broken some laws getting down here so fast." She said. Her dad gave a warm laugh. "Getting you home safe and sound would be worth a few speeding tickets."

Abram ushered them to the door. Jenna stopped, abruptly, and dropped her things before enfolding Abram in a huge hug.

"Thank you!" she whispered, then gathered up her things and followed her parents out the door.

Hunter stood close by, a wide smile on his handsome face.

"Well, all's well that ends well." He slapped Abram's shoulder and wandered back into the house. He knew there was no pie left, but perhaps Emma had chocolate cake. He wandered into the kitchen in search of some.

Chapter 16

Travis Jarvis lurked in the mouth of the alley. Sooner or later, something worthwhile would come along, and he was so ready to strike. He laughed to himself, thinking about Jenna. The silly twit thought he actually cared about her. He shook his head. She didn't know anything.

Travis' father schooled him well in the way of women. The only thing women were good for was breeding. Women were stupid and are only here to serve men.

Girl children were a waste of time, but boys could be raised up to be just like their fathers. Travis learned the lessons very well. Survival of the fittest, he told himself. When it came to that, men had it all over women.

Travis had one slight twinge of regret. He watched his father drink himself into a stupor, night after night, and watched the old man take a belt to his mother, time and again. Travis watched and waited, and two nights ago, his father passed out from his usual bout of Old Crow.

Travis decided that night was the night. He was more fit than his father and his mother was useless. So, while his parents slept, he took a baseball bat to the two of them, and then, calmly went out on a date with Jenna. He deliberately kept her out past her curfew, and talking her into running away was easy. His plan was simple.

He'd turn Jenna out, and she could support the two of them, but he wanted at her, first. She fought him tooth and nail until he smacked her around pretty good. Her screams had brought some busybodies running, and he took off, taking her cell phone with him.

Now, though, here was a sweet young thing coming up the block. He took in the sharp clothes and the exotic look to the black chick and decided he'd have a little fun with her, and then, keep her to himself until he could teach her the tricks of the trade. He was about to become the one thing he admired. He was about to become a pimp.

Trish walked slowly up the street. She was fully aware of the young man waiting for her and had a pretty good idea what he had planned. She gave a dry chuckle. He was about to get the shock of his life. Too bad he wouldn't be around to tell.

She waited until she was almost to the opening to the alley, where Travis waited. She glanced furtively around and gave another laugh. The area was deserted. Good! They would not be disturbed.

Trish's thirst was raging, and she couldn't wait for that most pleasant gush of blood shooting down her throat. Stay calm, she told herself. If she overplayed her hand, he'd run, and Trish didn't think she could wait for another meal to present itself.

Travis waited until the girl was just past him and then sprang into action. He put his hand over her mouth and wrapped a strong arm around her waist, lifting her off her feet.

"Just keep quiet. We're gonna have a good time. Just you and me." He smelled rank, and at one time, Trish would have gagged, but not now. She was too hungry, and she would have no problem getting past the stench of his unwashed body and foul breath.

He made the mistake of taking her silence for fear. He didn't see the feral look in her eyes, nor the satisfied, smug smile.

Trish was new at this, but she wasn't afraid. She would simply follow her instincts and enjoy her meal. She was grateful he had chosen such a private place. She could feed on him in complete privacy, and when she was done, she'd simply use some of the cinderblocks that littered the alley, weigh his body down using his clothes, and toss him into the Milwaukee River. It was, she thought, very considerate of him to choose such a wonderful place. Pity he would never know just how considerate he had been.

Travis thought it strange that the girl in his arms wasn't struggling. What was the fun in that? He liked it when they struggled. It gave him the opportunity to show these twits who was boss. Trish, sensing his thoughts, began to squirm against him, laughing. He took the shaking shoulders as a sign she was crying and he settled down, some. It was good when they cried. He could use the tears as an excuse to rough her up, a little. The other girls he had roughed up had cried. He hadn't killed them, though. He wondered if that had been a mistake.

Travis dragged Trish to the back of the alley, threw her down on a pile of trash and launched himself on top of her. He backhanded her a few times, showing her who was boss. He was so intent on his own plans, he didn't bother to look in her face. Perhaps he should have.

After a few well-placed punches, he grabbed the front of her sweater, planning on ripping it from her body. Trish had other plans. It was the only decent outfit she had, and she wasn't about to let this animal ruin it. She decided now was the time. Her thirst wouldn't wait. She grabbed his hands before he could do any damage and squeezed... hard. It was quite satisfying to hear the bones crunch under the pressure. Trish got a kick at her own strength. She saw him open his mouth to howl and easily flipped him over on his back.

Too late, he saw the red eyes boring into his. He saw the girl's canine's elongate and figured he was in deep trouble.

"What the hell are you? Let me go! I won't tell, just let me go!" Snot flowed from his nose, and to his chagrin, he realized he was sobbing.

"Oh no. I can't do that. I can't let you go. We're going to have a good time. Isn't that what you said?" Trish was toying with him. She flicked her tongue against his throat while easily holding him down. At the touch of her tongue on his skin, Travis flinched, and Trish's hunger went up another level.

"Nothing to say, now?" She taunted. Travis whimpered loudly and she slapped him. "Shut up!"

Trish's voice was guttural, and her eyes took on a sly look. She'd let him go. She rather thought she'd enjoy the hunt. She would let him run, and then catch him. That would be such fun, she thought, and then decided against it. They were not in a secluded enough place for games. Perhaps another time with another victim.

The hunger reminded her that she needed to feed. No point in delaying the inevitable. She couldn't wait any longer.

Throwing back her head, she allowed her fangs to elongate, completely, and then grabbed Travis' hair and bent his head back, exposing the carotid. It was pounding beautifully, and Trish could hear all that lovely blood pulsing through his veins. She bit into his throat and reveled in that wonderful gush of sweet, sweet blood.

Her meal began to fight, in earnest. Two broken hands were nothing compared to the thought he was going to die. His frantic movements enhanced her feeding frenzy, and she got a little carried away. The last thing Travis saw was his esophagus hanging from the girl's mouth.

"Oh shit", He mouthed before giving up the ghost.

Trish disposed of the body, using his belt, his clothes, an old chain she found in a dumpster, and some of those cinderblocks that liberally littered the downtown area. Effortlessly, she picked up the laden body and pitched it into the murky water, and watched with satisfaction as it gracefully sank to the bottom. If he ever surfaced, she didn't really care. She was part of something so much bigger, now. She realized, somewhere along the line, that Lance had plans and she would be part of those plans. The thought elated her as she walked home.

Now that her thirst was satisfied, she felt vibrant and more alive, now, than when she had been alive. Living was for losers, like Kirsten. It would be just her and Lance against the world, and they would win. That thought made her deliriously happy. Just her and Lance. It was just meant to be.

She let herself into the apartment and knew he was waiting for her.

"How did it go?" His voice was silky smooth, and the hair went up on the back of her neck. Trish knew she was in trouble.

Trying to keep up a sense of bravado, she shrugged and turned to face him. "She wouldn't let me in. I don't know why, but she refused to let me in, and I couldn't get her to come out of the house."

No sooner were the words out of her mouth, then she found herself sailing across the room. She landed hard on the floor, hitting her head sharply on the wall behind her. Before she could move, Lance crossed the room and picked her up, his grip tight on her throat.

"You failed!" Gone were the smooth tones. In his rage, he tossed her carelessly across the room, and came at her again. Trish tried to make for the door, but he was too fast. "Failure! I gave you a great gift and you fail me!" He ground out as he grabbed her by the hair.

Spinning her around to face him, he opened his jaw wide and prepared to rip her throat out.

"You should have come with me," she ground out, giving him pause. His grasp on her throat eased a little. "You sent me there, all alone. You knew I didn't know what I was doing, but you sent me there on my own."

Lance roared at her impertinence. "I could kill you right now and not break a sweat. Who do you think you're talking to?" He growled. He gave her a shake and tossed her onto the ratty sofa. Her words had penetrated his fog of fury and he needed to think.

"Perhaps you are correct. Perhaps I should have gone with you, but it was a small task. Surely you could have handled one old lady." He sneered. Trish shook her head. "It was almost as if she had been warned. She opened the door, and I thought I was home free, but then she said I wasn't her granddaughter and slammed the door on me. Who could have warned her, Master?"

Trish thought it wouldn't hurt to toss in the title. His vanity might like it. She was correct. He turned from her and put himself to rights, again. Trish found his preening rather amusing but was careful not to let him see her amusement.

"Was she alone? Did you sense anyone else with her?" He asked. She shook her head, and he frowned. He didn't like this, at all. Something was amiss, but he couldn't put his finger on what that was. Now that his anger had cooled, he had other fish to fry.

"Have you eaten?" He asked and raised a slick eyebrow when she nodded.

"There was a fool who thought he was going to rape me. Dragged me into an alley and hit me a few times. I let him have his fun for a little while, but when he was going to ruin my sweater, I put a stop to it. He was a good meal. I would have preferred someone a little cleaner, but he was rather tasty, after all."

Lance stared at her. He should punish her, but he would wait for the end of her tale. "What did you do with the body when you were finished?" He asked.

Trish noticed the silk was back in his voice. "I weighed him down with some blocks and tossed him into the river. I made sure no one was around, first." She really hoped he was okay with that. She didn't think she could handle another round of punishment from him. A sigh of relief passed her lips when he nodded.

"That was wise. Perhaps you aren't a total failure, after all. Now, get some rest. Tomorrow night we hunt, and the night after that, I will have another chore for you to do." He looked at her sharply. "Do not fail me again."

Chapter 17

The day of the dinner party dawned crisp and clear. It's a nice change after all that rain, Emma thought. She wasn't too pleased with Julie, however.

"I want you to hire those local girls you use for the big parties, Emma. You'll have enough to do, today." Julie told her. "I don't want you fussing with the cleaning, as well as the cooking."

Emma opened her mouth to argue, but Julie raised an imperious hand.

"Don't argue with me. I'm not in the mood. We're having strangers in this house tonight, Emma. Abram tells me the ex-wife of the cop will be difficult, at best. So please, don't argue with me. Simply do as I ask."

Emma did as Julie wished, but she supervised those girls, seeing to it they were careful with Julie's antiques. Wouldn't they be surprised if they knew the lady of the house had purchased them new, she thought.

Seeing the girls were doing their usual good job, she headed into the kitchen. Their house guest, Hunter, was making himself at home with coffee and freshly baked coffee cake.

"Emma, you are a jewel. No one this side of Heaven can bake like you can." He told her, smiling his engaging grin.

"Thank you, Hunter. Now, scoot out of my kitchen. I have a lot to do, today." She flashed him a saucy grin as he gulped down the rest of his breakfast and headed out the door.

The menu for the evening was simple. Emma could have cooked this meal with her eyes closed, but was wise enough to know that prime rib, new potatoes, grilled asparagus and a fruit salad along with French onion soup could all go badly, very quickly.

Moving around the kitchen, she didn't waste a motion. In short order, she had the meat seasoned with her own special rub, the potatoes and asparagus ready to be cooked and her fruit salad cooling in the refrigerator. She was about to get started on her Black Forest Torte when Abram sauntered into the kitchen in search of a hot cup of coffee.

"Busy day today, Emma. The mistress is in a mood, again." Abram said.

"Don't I know it? She insisted I hire on those extra girls, but for the life of me, I don't know why. The house is always clean, it's a small party, and the menu isn't that ambitious. Just a bad case of nerves, I suppose."

Emma poured Abram a cup of coffee, then, took the chair across from him.

"Abram. How bad are things going to get with this enemy lurking about?" She asked. Abram shrugged.

"I believe it's going to be very bad, Emma. Very bad, indeed. Consider this, the mistress must keep her wits about her, at all times. He'll come at her, again, so she can never let her guard down. Then, she must deal with these mortals. Strangers. This makes her very uncomfortable. She's going to be very vulnerable at this time. To make matters worse, if she fails, he'll end her," Abram paused, sipping from his cup, his eyes never leaving Emma's. "He'll end me, too. Still think it's a good idea to remain here?" He asked.

Emma considered. Yes, she was worried. A fool wouldn't be worried. Still, she never ran, before. She always faced problems, head on. She was too old to change, now, and she told Abram that.

"No point in running, now. He'll probably come after me, too. We both know, Abram, that where ever I am, he could find me, so I'll take my chances with you and Julie."

Emma got up from the table, grabbed the coffee pot, and topped off Abram's cup before re-taking her seat.

"This other man, Abram. What's his story?" Abram shrugged.

"Hunter? I'm not sure. He's always been around for as long as I can remember. He never interferes and never tells the mistress what she's doing wrong. The fact, however, that he's here and the adversary is here makes me wonder."

"Wonder what?" Emma bit her lip. She wasn't sure she wanted to hear the answer.

"I wonder if we are coming to the final showdown. I wonder if this is the mistress' last chance at redemption. It makes me..." He looked at Emma.

"Twitchy?" She finished for him, and he nodded. "Yes, twitchy. Very much so."

Emma reached across the table and took his cold hand in her warm one.

"I have faith in Julie, and I have faith in you. I believe with my whole heart we will come out on top. Wait and see." She gave him an impudent wink, then rose and began mixing the ingredients for her torte.

In spite of her brave words to Abram, she was very much worried. She had one request of Abram, but decided to wait. First things first. Right now, her job was to get ready for the evening. With a silent prayer, she hoped it would all go smoothly, but somehow, she rather doubted it.

§

In another part of town, Rachel Charleston dove into her closets, searching for just the right outfit for this evening's dinner party. So intent on finding just the right thing to wear, she didn't realize Kirsten was standing in her doorway, watching her.

"What are you doing? Why is this such a big deal?" Rachel jumped a little at her daughter's words.

"Do you have any idea who Julie King is? She's just the premiere hostess in the whole state," Rachel went back to searching her closet. She really couldn't afford anything new at the moment and she so wanted to make a good impression.

"Are you aware that Trish and her parents are going to be buried tomorrow? Do you have any recollection of that, at all?" Kirsten was definitely in a snarky mood.

"Yes, of course I'm aware. Michelle was my best friend, after all. So, naturally, I'm aware. It's just this is such an opportunity to meet someone worthwhile. I want to look my best." Rachel looked over at her daughter and saw the thunderclouds rolling across her young face. "Speaking of which, what are you planning to wear?"

Kirsten shook her head. Had her mother always been this shallow, she wondered. Is that the reason the marriage broke up? It was, she decided, something to think about.

She headed back to her own room, leaving her mother to shake her head in frustration. Kirsten didn't understand… she never understood. What, after all, was so wrong in wanting the finest things in life? Wolf didn't get it, either.

Not her problem, she thought. She still needed to put together something amazing, and with her lack of imagination, that would not be easy.

Finally, she tossed aside the outfit she had planned to wear and choosing a cocktail suit of teal, she dug out the matching strappy sandals and evening purse.

This would have to do, she decided, and it would make a good impression, she hoped.

Chapter 18

L ance sat and brooded. His little protégé was not working out quite the way he thought she would. A simple task and she failed.

He contemplated ending her, but he still had one more task for her to fulfill. If she failed, again, he would have no choice but to end her.

A few things bothered him a great deal. His first change, Julie King, as she was now known, was an enigma to him. He couldn't read her thoughts, and this was more than just annoying. It was downright scary. If he couldn't read her thoughts, know what was going on in that head of hers, then how could he know what she was plotting.

She was plotting something, of that he was certain. And then, there was the little matter of the Hunter. He appeared to be taking a more active role. That was frightening, in itself. The fact that he aligned himself with Julie made Lance even more wary.

Glancing over at Trish, he kicked her awake.

"I have a chore for you. Do not fail me again."

Trish stumbled from her pallet and wondered about the legend of sleeping in a coffin. A nice coffin would suit her, about now, rather than taking her rest on this hard floor. Her sire could at least let her rest on the sofa, she thought, but no, he took the sofa and made her take the floor.

Trish was not happy. What she was, however, was smart enough to keep her unhappy thoughts to herself. And, that was another thing that gave her pause. Why couldn't he sense what she was thinking? All the stories she read had said there was a connection between sire and victim. It was something to think about when she was alone, she thought.

"I need you to go to this address. It's a nicer neighborhood, so you will need to dress appropriately. There is a new outfit hanging in the bathroom. Cleanse yourself and get dressed. When you're finished, I'll tell you what I want you to do." Lance reached out and grasped Trish around the throat. "Do not fail me, again."

He looked into her eyes and saw the hunger there. "I'll get you a little something to eat. Just enough to ease that peckish impulse." He smiled a ghastly grin. No need for illusion, here. Trish knew exactly what he is.

She couldn't help herself. She tried to draw back, revulsion filling her sordid soul. He grasped her all the tighter. Her small rejection of his person irritated him. Here, he had given her a gift, and she showed her gratefulness by rejecting him.

To make himself feel better, he backhanded her, sending her sprawling onto the worn sofa.

"Go make yourself presentable while I do a little shopping. Do not leave until I return."

While Trish made herself presentable, Lance cruised the parks until he found just what he was looking for. Just a little snack to tide his protégé over, until later. If she accomplished her task, they would hunt, together. If she failed, again, he would be dining alone.

Lance scanned the playground until he found exactly what he was looking for.

She looked like a sunbeam, playing in the sandbox and chanting, "No more monkeys jumping on the bed."

He took offense at her blonde curls and bright blue eyes. He took offense at just about everything about her. He loathed her innocence, purity and her happy little life.

The only use he had for mortals and their spawn was for food and, one of the reasons he managed to stay under the radar for millennium after millennium was simple.

Lance preferred to nest in poor countries. Brazil was a particular favorite of his. He could hunt, and no one was the wiser.

Now, though, in this time and place, he knew he had to be careful. Still, children, those loathsome little creatures, came up missing every day, and this one would satisfy Trish's hunger for the time being.

Lance never considered turning a child. He had just one child on his mind, and that was his own. He had been promised, and Julie King was part of that promise.

He and the elusive Ms. King would have a child, together. He doubted she would live during the ordeal of giving his son life. It didn't matter. All that mattered was his son and all they would accomplish. Together, they would rule all of the earth. Just as it should be.

His own sire taught him well. He learned the signs to watch for. The time was now, and finally, after centuries of waiting and hiding, he would be free to roam at will, do as he wanted. Finally, the time of waiting was over, and that haughty wench he turned so long ago, would not stop him.

He had a plan. He would begin to build his army. He only needed a few men. He rather thought it would be a good idea to keep Trish. She would be entertainment for his troops, while he considered the two that would be his prizes. One would be his mate, and the pretty blonde would be his toy.

Mortals would be kept alive for amusement and for food. It was, he thought, all they were good for.

Making his move, utilizing his incredible speed, he snatched the child out of the sandbox and was back at the quarters he shared before the child could utter a single squeal.

He dumped the little one onto the dusty sofa and gave it a smack across the face as the toddler's face puckered and she began to wail.

The sounds brought Trish from the spare bedroom and the sight of the wailing little girl moved something in her, where her soul had resided.

Perhaps it was the values instilled in her by loving parents. Trish didn't know, and maybe, she would never know. The one thing she was sure of, though, she would see to it this little one returned to her parents unharmed.

"Take it into the other room. I don't want to see it, again. Be quick about it, too. Oh, and when you are finished, dispose of it on your way out. You have the address, and I would advise you to hurry." Lance ordered.

Ever so gently, Trish picked up the sobbing little girl and moved to the spare room, closing the door behind her.

It never occurred to Lance that Trish would defy him. It's what she was counting on.

She walked with the little one in her arms, until the child quieted.

Trish was sorely tempted to sample but even as she bared her fangs, she knew she wouldn't do it.

Unsure, Trish raised the window and looked down. She has as yet, to try out all of her new powers.

"No time like the present," She whispered. Holding the little one close, she jumped. Her landing was a little rough, but at least the two of them were out of the apartment, out in the street and miracle of miracles, in one piece.

She breathed in the child's scent, then raised her head and followed the scent trail back to the park.

A great many people were searching bushes and paths. It didn't take a rocket scientist to figure out who they were looking for.

"I found her!" Trish called out, and a woman raced over to Trish and gathered her daughter into her arms.

"Where did you find her? Oh! I can't thank you enough!" She gushed, and Trish plastered a pleasant smile on her face as she faced the distraught mother. If you only knew what this has cost me, Trish thought.

"I found her a couple of blocks over, following a dog. I thought she may have been playing here, so brought her back as quickly as I could, hoping I'd find someone who knew her. Poor little thing is so sleepy, though."

The relieved mom tried to push money into Trish's hands, but the girl backed away. Guilt overrode any other emotion. I thought, she mused to herself, that vampires didn't have a conscience. Looks like another legend shot to hell.

A young cop walked over, pointing toward the tree line. "Someone you know?" He asked Trish.

Michele stood quietly, watching her daughter, infinite sadness marred her handsome features.

"My mom," Trish told him. She left out the part about her mom being dead. He wouldn't believe her, anyway, and probably would think she had snapped her cap. She doubted he'd believe that she, herself, was a vamp. Such things just didn't happen in the modern world.

Trish began to walk over to Michele, but watched with swimming eyes as her mother smiled at her then walked into the trees. A moment later, she was gone and Trish felt the pain of loss. Another reason to detest her sire.

If it took forever, she would find a way to make him pay. One way or another.

In the meantime, she had a job to do, and she had better get at it.

Chapter 19

Damien emerged from the shower and wrapped one large towel around his waist. He reached for another, quickly toweling his hair as he walked to his room. He didn't feel too great. Headaches had plagued him for the past week, but they were manageable, at least for now.

"Worried about you, old buddy." Steven Worthington's voice came from behind him. "You've been looking a tad peaked. Anything going on I should know about?" Damien knew where Steve was going with that and shook his head.

"Nah. At least I don't think so. Just seems to be a nagging headache I can't seem to shake." Damien peered down at his diminutive friend. "Got any ideas about this little dinner party we're going to be attending, tonight?"

Steve shook his head. "If anyone would have an idea, it would be you, pal of mine. I must admit, though. I'm curious as hell. Everyone knows who our illustrious hostess is. An invite from her is like one to

Buckingham Palace, or something. I'm figuring I'm just a tag-along, but hey, anything to get to see the enigmatic Julie King up close and personal."

Damien walked into his room, his fingers digging into his forehead. He turned toward his closet and found himself on a playground.

The little girl, playing in the sandbox looked like pure sunlight. Her blonde curls beamed in the light, and her little face was alight with happiness.

He could see her lips move, but couldn't make out quite what she was chanting. Something about monkeys and a bed.

In horror, he watched the creature swoop down and snatch her up. Damien's heart fell to his knees. No, he thought, not this innocent. Please God, not this innocent. He groaned, feeling helpless, and his soul cringed.

He flashed to a shabby apartment and watched as the creature tossed her so carelessly onto a dusty and broken down sofa. He watched as the male vampire slapped that little face. Tears streaked her cheeks as a female vampire emerged from a side room. He watched helplessly as the female took the child and re-entered the room she had just vacated.

Before he knew it, he was witnessing a miracle. The young vampire shushed and comforted the child, then against all odds, took her from the apartment through a window.

The two floated to the ground, and the young female lifted her nose, caught a scent and broke into a run.

Moving with the obscene speed of her race, she took the child back to the playground and re-united her with the mother.

Standing in the line of trees, Damien dimly made out a female figure, quietly watching to see what the female vampire would do.

The girl, for that was what she was, did see the figure and Damien watched her shoulders slump in grief, huge tears swimming in those cold brown eyes.

The young cop, walking up to talk to the girl, also noticed the figure in the trees and pointed. The young vamp replied briefly to the officer before turning away and walking toward the trees.

Damien took a deep breath and was back in his room, facing his closet.

Steve came in with a cold cloth and placed it on Damien's neck, holding another to his nose.

"Welcome back, pal. You okay?" Steve's handsome face was creased with concern.

"Yeah, I'm okay. Just a mother of a headache." Damien's knees folded, and he slid to sit on the side of his bed.

"Look. I'll call Ms. King and cancel. You look like hell." Steve offered, but Damien shook his head.

"I think this is too important to miss, Steve. Be a bud, though, and grab me some aspirin, would ya? I feel like my spine is coming through my brain."

Steve hustled off to do Damien's bidding and quickly returned with a bottle of Aleve and a large glass of water.

Damien shook four of the tablets into his palm and shot them straight into his mouth, quickly washing them down. All he could do, now, was wait until the pain eased some.

"I'm just gonna head back into my room and finish dressing. Call me if you need anything. We have a little time, Damien. Why don't you just lay back and let those pills take effect. If you don't feel better, we'll cancel."

"Give me twenty, Steve. I'll be okay." Steve turned to leave the room, and Damien's voice stopped him.

"Steve. I don't know for sure what is going on, but I *do* know whatever it is, it's huge. We can't not go. It's all related, somehow. And those deaths at the morgue? They're related, too. I think, tonight, we'll be getting some answers."

Steve shrugged. "Okay pal. You're the boss, but I'm driving. That will give you a little extra time to recover."

Damien laid back and stared at the ceiling. Was there ever a time that Steve hadn't been a pal? Damien couldn't remember a single episode where Steve let him down.

Maybe it was good that Steve was back, but he had overheard a phone call Steve made. He was pushing his show back until late winter for the spring collection. This bothered Damien a great deal. His friend was putting everything he worked toward on hold with no questions asked.

Damien would talk to Wolf. If Steve was in any kind of danger, perhaps between the two of them, they could talk the young designer into leaving. He could go to New York and wait there until whatever was brewing was over. He'd see what Wolf thought, tonight.

In the meantime, it was his job to get up, get dressed, and get moving.

Carefully, he sat up and swung his feet to the side of the bed. His head no longer pounded, and the smell of dried blood was gone.

Taking his time, he dressed carefully. Damien thought about swallowing a couple more pills, but decided against it. They would just make him sick to his stomach and fuzzy. He needed his wits about him, tonight.

Emerging from his room, he walked into the living room and found Steve perched on the arm of the sofa. It was a habit Steve had from childhood and only did it when he was worried.

Steve was worried now. He didn't like these headaches Damien was plagued with. Oh, he knew his friend suffered from headaches, before, but he couldn't remember them being this severe and this constant.

The visions worried him, as well. They came faster, now, and with little warning, they brought Damien to his knees.

This can't be good, he thought. Briefly, he wondered if he should call Damien's parents and then decided against it. After all, what could he tell them? They knew all about Damien's gift. It scared the hell out of them more than once, but they knew.

Better to let sleeping dogs lie, Steve decided, but he also knew if Damien had one more vision like the one he had the other night, he'd be calling the folks, after all.

Steve knew, deep in his heart, that the visions were killing his friend, and he didn't know how to stop it.

Hearing a soft sound behind him, Steve turned and watched Damien walk toward him.

"I still think we should cancel, Damien. I can whip up something, here, and you need to rest. You're looking mighty peaked, old friend."

Damien waved his advice away. "No. I'm okay, really, and I think tonight is important. I'm going with my gut, here and it's telling me to get my ass over there and see what develops."

150

Steve let out a heavy sigh. "You're one ornery cuss, you know that, son? Okay, we'll go and see if we can find some answers for you. Maybe I'll find a few for myself, who the hell knows."

Damien glanced at his watch. "Time to go." He tossed the keys to his Lexus at Steve.

"You're right about one thing. You're driving."

The two men walked out of the condo, each wondering what the coming evening would bring.

They had no way of knowing they would be walking into a realm of unbelievable proportions.

For once, Damien's sixth sense was leaving him alone.

Chapter 20

Julie threw herself on her bed and placed her forearm across her eyes. In just a few hours, her house would be filled with people. People she didn't know and people she would probably have to deal with. This did not set well with her. Too many variables and too many things that could go wrong.

Fitful, she moved from the bed to her dressing table and studied her reflection. Yeah, she thought, vampires *can* be seen in a mirror. Another legend disproved, although why any self-respecting vamp would want to be able to look at themselves was beyond her.

She looked coarse and tired. Well, she decided, who wouldn't look tired after living among mortals for over two thousand years.

Carefully, she applied her cosmetics, all the while fretting over the coming party. She shouldn't have agreed to this. She should have taken the imitative and found Lance on her own, ended him and be done with all of this.

In the hall, Hunter's laugh drifted through the door and set her teeth on edge. This was another part of the puzzle. Never, in their long history together, had he ever stayed with her. Why now? What was so different about *now*?

Then there was the matter of her dreams. They were more vivid, now. In her long past, she could control them, but not any longer. Why?

Too many questions and no answers. Julie didn't like it.

A soft knock interrupted her thoughts. "Come in!" she called out in a surly tone. She was not pleased when Hunter strolled into her room.

"What do you want?" She snarled and was rewarded with one of his beautiful smiles.

"Feeling a little edgy, are we?" He sat down on the side of her bed and studied her. "You're looking a little out of sorts. Anything I can do?"

She spun toward him. It hurt her eyes to look at him, but her wrath was rising. He would do well, she thought, to remember who and what she was.

"Anything you can do?" Sarcasm dripped from her lips. "Seriously? You ask me this?" She shook her head and braved the discomfort of making eye contact with him. "You could start with telling me exactly how to end this. I'm tired, Hunter. I'm about to have a group of people invade my space. People I don't know and have never even met. This ridiculous party was your idea… you and Emma, and I'm stuck with it. My sire is lurking around, planning only God knows what, and you ask me if there is anything you can do." She gave a very unlady-like snort. "You could have stopped this ions ago and have done nothing. Why are you here, Hunter? What does all of this mean?"

Hunter sat quietly, his eyes closed. She marveled at the serene look on his face, even as all that magnificence hurt her eyes and stirred something where her soul had been.

He opened his unbelievable eyes. To Julie, they seemed to change colors, rapidly and if asked, she would have said she saw eternity in those amazing orbs.

"I can tell you this much, madam. We are coming to the end. These people you are welcoming, tonight, will be your army. If you are victorious over the adversary for the correct reasons, you will have all your heart desires. Your actions in the coming days will determine much."

Julie shook her head. "That isn't much to work with, Hunter. Not much, at all."

Hunter shrugged a refined shoulder. "It's all I can tell you."

He rose and walked to the door and opened it. "I'll leave you to get ready. Remember this, though. Over all these centuries I have watched you evolve. You have gone from slaughtering men, women and children for your own perverse pleasure as well as needing to feed. You have come far but have further yet to go. I hope you succeed."

More ambiguous words, she thought, and still no real answers.

She turned back to her mirror and began to apply her cosmetics. No reason not to look her best.

Down in the kitchen, Emma paid her helpers and sent them on their way. She and Abram would be serving the meal. A task they could easily handle.

"It smells wonderful in here, Emma. You've outdone yourself." Abram grabbed a cup of coffee and leaned against the counter, watching Emma as she put the finishing touches on the desert.

"Not a big deal, Abram. We've handled bigger events."

To Abram, she looked worried and preoccupied. "Something bothering you, Emma?" He asked.

"No, not really. I think I'm just picking up on Miss Julie's case of nerves. Usually, she looks forward to entertaining, but always on her own terms. It's different, this time."

Abram nodded. "That it is. Let's just get through this evening and see what the morrow brings."

Wolf picked up his constantly ringing phone. Of course it was

Rachel, again, all in a dither about something or other.

"What?" He barked and then listened as his ex-wife went off on a tangent.

"You need to wear a suit, Wolf. I think it would be a fine idea if you picked Kirsten and me up and we go to this thing as a family. Did you press your shirt?" The woman flipped from subject to subject, not letting him get a word in, edgewise. Better to wait until she ran out of steam, then try talking.

Rachel finally paused to catch her breath, and Wolf quickly answered her. "I am wearing a suit, my shirt is pressed and if you think it would be better if we arrive together, get off the damn phone, stop calling me, and let me get out of here so we aren't late. You know how you hate being late, Rachel."

She sputtered into the phone, and he heard a definite *click* as she hung up on him.

Kirsten sat on the sofa, waiting for her mother. She didn't want to go to this party. It didn't seem right. Trish and her family would be buried in just two days. She wanted to mourn her friends, but Rachel was dragging her to this party. Kirsten was not happy, and she glared at Rachel as she swept into the room.

"For heaven's sake, Kirsten! This is the opportunity of a lifetime. You'll have to lose the long face, at least for the evening. Try to pretend you're having a good time, will you please?"

"Mom! Trish and her parents will be buried on Monday. Doesn't that mean anything to you? It seems obscene to be going to this party so soon. It doesn't feel right."

Rachel glared at her daughter. Kirsten's so much like her father, she thought.

"I lost my best friends, too. Don't forget that, but Nate and Michele would want us to go. They wouldn't expect us to sit home and mope. Time enough for that on Monday."

Kirsten shook her head and wondered if her mother was truly that shallow, or if she was hiding from her own grief. Kirsten was betting on the shallow.

Michele and Trish had spent a great deal of time with Kirsten and Rachel. Kirsten knew it frustrated her mother, though, that Michele would not join in on bashing Wolf. It irritated Rachel when Michele would change the subject. She wondered if her mother resented Michele for that. It was something to think about.

"Your father will be here shortly, Kirsten. We're going, together, as a family. It should be a pleasant evening, if only you will cooperate just a little."

Rachel checked herself in the full length mirror located on the back of the guest closet door.

The deep blue cocktail suit was stunning. She'd paid too much for it, of course, but it showed off her toned figure and fair skin perfectly.

Her red hair fell in waves down to her shoulders, and Rachel fussed with it. She should have had it trimmed, she thought. Too late, now.

She snatched up the matching blue clutch purse and tossed in keys, a lipstick, and her small wallet. A small vial of her favorite perfume joined the selection, and she was set.

Rachel turned and looked at Kirsten. The girl wore a dull copper pants suit with a cream blouse. Not quite what Rachel would have picked for the girl, but it was a fair choice. She was pleased to see Kirsten had applied a small amount of make-up. Just enough to highlight those long amber eyes, so like Wolf's.

Kirsten had pulled her hair back from her face with clips, and the result was casual but fetching.

They heard Wolf's car pull into the driveway and went out to meet him. Rachel beamed, and Kirsten was still fighting tears.

Chapter 21

Julie emerged from her room, took her time coming down the stairs, and entered the formal parlor. The sight in that room pleased her. Old mahogany gleamed in the late afternoon light. The antique Indian rug showed off its colors of red, blue and yellow and almost sparkled.

Mirrors in gilt frames twinkled like diamonds, and the fresh flowers in beautiful low vases gave the room a peaceful scent.

Julie was just as pleased in the dining room. More flowers graced the long table, and the brocade chair seats looked fresh and clean.

She was pleased with Emma's choice of white on white china and ornate silver flatware. It gave the room just the right balance between formality and casual.

Smiling, she entered the kitchen where Emma was putting the last touches on desert.

"Your girls outdid themselves for this little soiree," Julie said. "I'm more than pleased. I'm sure the evening will be a lovely one."

Emma snorted. "We both know you are dreading the upcoming festivities, so I'm not too sure how lovely the evening will be, but it sure as hell will send a signal to your guests."

Julie walked to the kitchen sink to stare out the window. She turned and raised an eyebrow.

"Emma, you sound positively pissy. Something wrong? Something I should know about?"

Emma shook her head. "No. Nothing's wrong. I just know how you feel about this little get-together. But! The meal will be fine. The desert will bring tears to their eyes, and anything else that comes up... well, you'll handle it just fine."

The peel of the front doorbell had them both turning in the direction of the front door. Abram stopped and looked at the two women, shaking his head, his hands full of champagne flutes. Thrusting them at Emma, he gave a slight bow from his waist.

"Don't worry. I'll get it. I'm not doing anything important." He brushed past them and headed to the front door.

"You're not the only one feeling out-of-sorts about tonight." Emma whispered in Julie's ear. A small giggle escaped her lips as she began to polish the glassware.

"Well Emma... how do I look?" She did a small turn for her housekeeper.

Emma took in the long black tunic, the neat slim pants and black slippers. Silver embroidery broke the monotony of the black tunic. Small swirls and tiny crystals sparkled in the kitchen light.

The pattern on the tunic was carried through to the hem of the pants and the soft black slippers. Around her neck, Julie wore a fine necklace of platinum with a diamond the size of a robin's egg resting in the hollow of her throat. A matching bracelet encrusted with diamonds circled her wrist, and diamonds winked in her ears and fingers.

"Stunning, as ever, Julie. Absolutely stunning. You're going to wow your guests."

On another woman, the clothes and jewelry would have been ostentatious. On Julie, it was exactly right. She looked amazing.

Hearing voices in her foyer, she grimaced at Emma. "Time for the monkey to be on display." Emma chuckled as Julie left to greet her guests.

"Welcome! I'm so pleased you could accept my invitation!" She sang out, a charming smile on her face as she faced the man and two women standing in her foyer.

"Allow me to make the introductions, miss. Detective and Rachel Charleston and their lovely daughter, Kirsten. Your hostess, Julie King."

Ah, Julie thought, the cop, the ex-wife and the daughter.

She paid attention to Wolf in particular. Was this the "one other" Hunter had mentioned? She rather thought so.

Her gaze took in the slight paunch, the tired face, and sad amber eyes. Hmmm, he's a tall one, Julie thought as she shook his hand.

He has a firm handshake and a direct stare. Nothing much gets past this one, she thought, although, it appears he drinks a little more than he should. Still, quiet competence oozed from the man, and Julie found that a favorable trait. He's much like Abram. Perhaps he will be of assistance after all.

She turned to Rachel and recognized the avarice look in those cold green eyes. The sweet expression on Rachel's face didn't fool her for a second.

This woman was all about greed and control. She wouldn't hesitate to throw her own family under the bus if it served her ends. This one would have to be watched.

Finally, she turned to Kirsten. It was almost painful to see all that honesty shining from eyes so like her father's. Julie liked the poise the girl possessed. She would go far, Julie considered, but only if she's allowed to.

Julie greeted each in turn and then gestured toward the parlor.

"Come, we'll be comfortable in the parlor while we await our other guests."

She led them into the room and heard Rachel's soft gasp. Everything is so beautiful, Rachel thought, and she could have something like this if only Wolf would give up the whole cop thing and settle down and practice law. It was what his family wanted and what she, herself, wanted.

Renewed anger surged through her veins, and she shot a nasty look in his direction. Wolf didn't notice. He was too busy studying their hostess.

"You have an unusual accent, Miss King." He stated, watching her closely. Julie was rather glad she had home field advantage. She guessed Wolf Charleston could be quite intimidating in another venue, such as an interrogation room.

"Yes, I was born in the Middle East. Jerusalem to be exact. I've also traveled extensively throughout Europe, South America and now here. This is a beautiful country. I'm so glad I've made it my home."

They chatted while Abram circled the room, offering glasses of champagne. Kirsten shook her head, her blonde curls dancing.

"Something else, perhaps?" Abram whispered and she gave him a sweet smile. "Could I just have a Coke, please?" Abram nodded. "Certainly."

"Kirsten!" Rachel hissed, "Where are your manners?" Rachel's eyes sparkled with anger as she confronted her daughter.

"I don't like to drink, mom. What's the big deal?" The girl's face clouded over, and she lowered her head. Lately, if felt like she couldn't do anything right.

"Please, it's fine." Julie hastened to interject. She reached over and gave Kirsten's hands a small squeeze. She could relate to this girl. Her own mother had been just like Rachel.

Rachel, still simmering, gave a tight nod. "Thank you. Sometimes children can be such a nuisance."

Julie thought back to her own sons, now long dead. A nuisance? Julie didn't think so.

She was saved from having to make a polite reply when Abram ushered in her last two guests.

She rose to greet them, extending her slim hand and gliding over to greet them.

Introductions were made, and Julie made no secret of the fact she was studying Damien closely.

After a time, she turned to welcome Steve and found him staring at her ensemble. Briefly she wondered if there was something wrong with it.

"Excuse me, but the garments you are wearing. It's from the house of Armani, isn't it?" Steve asked.

"Yes, yes it is." Julie raised an eyebrow at him and Steve rewarded her with a radiant smile. He held up the tunic and pointed.

"See here? The initials *SW?* Steven Worthington." Steven gave her a deep bow from the waist. "No one could wear this unless she is an exceptional woman. I'm pleased to see you wearing it with such aplomb."

Julie understood. "You are the young protégé' Giorgio spoke of. I understand you are having a showing this fall of your own collection. Giorgio is very proud of you. I have several of your pieces."

Steve inclined his head. "Under the circumstances, I've postponed showing my collection until spring. However, it would be a delight and a privilege to design for you, anytime."

Julie patted his cheek before gesturing for them to follow her into the parlor.

"Come in and meet my other guests. We're having drinks in the parlor. Come and join us."

She gracefully led the way into the parlor and gestured for the two men to sit.

She needed time to collect herself. The meeting with Damien had shaken her, and she needed a moment to gather her wits about her.

Such a gentle man, she thought. Too gentle for what may be coming for them.

A true visionary, as well. That particular gift would be a true asset, but she wondered at what cost.

Her thoughts were interrupted as Hunter glided into the room, beaming his wonderful smile.

The men, as well as the women, stood as he came into the parlor, bringing his own brand of light with him.

"Well, good evening. I'm glad to see I'm not late." He stared at Julie until she sighed and made the proper introductions.

No one in the room could tear their eyes away from this wonderful creature. Sunbeams seemed to burst from him, and even Rachel felt amazing in his presence.

Wolf looked into those marvelous eyes and had the feeling this man knew all about him and loved him, anyway.

Rachel, making eye contact with Hunter, felt ashamed for all of her pettiness and selfish whims. She rather thought she would like to be friends with this man, but didn't think he would give her the time of day.

Hunter patted her hand, silently telling her everything was okay, but maybe she could change, a little bit. All of this told without a word being uttered. Simply done with eye contact and a gentle pat on her hand.

Turning to Damien, Hunter extended his hand, his face tight with concern. "You aren't feeling well this evening." It was not a question. Hunter stated a fact.

Damien shrugged. "It's nothing. Just a small headache." He said, while accepting Hunter's offered hand. The moment the two hands clasped, Damien's headache vanished. One moment it was plaguing him and the next, it was absolutely gone. Hunter smiled and turned to Steve.

"Such a loyal friend Mr. Crist has in you," Hunter murmured. "It's a very good thing." Steve could only nod and stare at this tall man, still shaking his hand.

Abram came in with three more lutes filled with champagne, and the small party made small talk until Emma announced dinner.

They began with a crisp seafood salad, and as Abram served, Steve recognized him, giving poor Steve quite a shock.

"That's him!" He gently elbowed Damien, drawing his friend's attention away from his salad.

"Who?" Damien looked at Steve, confusion clear on his face.

"That's the guy in your house that night. He picked you up and put you on the couch! That's him!" Steve whispered excitedly.

Damien turned to face Abram as he placed a plate in front of Damien. Abram heard the whispered conversation and grinned.

"Really? Are you sure?" Damien whispered back.

"Yes I'm sure! I'd never forget that man! It's him." Steve was insistent.

Julie heard the whispered conversation, as well, and smiled charmingly.

"Perhaps we should concentrate on this excellent dinner," she said, "and we'll talk later. All, if not most, of your questions will be answered at that time. For now, let's just enjoy."

While they dined on perfectly prepared prime rib, new potatoes and grilled asparagus, Julie felt a heightened sense of awareness. She could tell that something was not quite right, she could tell.

Glancing at Abram who stood in the doorway leading to the kitchen, waiting to bring out the next course, she could tell he felt it, as well.

They both could sense another vampire, and Julie knew this one was very, very close.

Giving him a small nod, he quickly left the house, leaving Emma to finish serving.

None of her guests were aware of anything amiss until Abram returned with an unexpected visitor, and then pandemonium broke out.

Chapter 22

F rom her vantage point in a tree across the road, Trish watched the guests arrive.

She was hungry and would need to feed, soon. Maybe she shouldn't have been so weak and kept the child Lance provided for her. Too late to worry about it, now.

She noted with interest when Wolf's car pulled into the drive. As much as she loved him in life, he would make a fine meal, but she had better wait.

The back door of the sedan opened, and Trish was surprised to feel her eyes well with bloody tears as her friend emerged from the back seat.

Seeing Kirsten leave her dad's car gave the young vampire a pang. She had been with her friend when Kirsten bought that outfit. How weird was it? The first time Kirsten was wearing it and she, Trish, was dead, cut off from her best friend.

She watched Rachel climb out of the car and smiled nastily. Now there would be an even better meal, and since Kirsten didn't get along with her mother, she wouldn't mourn her like she would her father, and if she could convince her sire to join her in the meal, perhaps it would make up for her earlier failures.

It was something to think about.

She watched as the family entered the beautiful Tudor home with its fine lawns and perfect gardens. Obviously, who ever lived here had money. Trish felt another pang. Maybe, just maybe, if she had lived, she would have had a home like this, too.

What was the matter with her, she wondered. First, she made sure she returned that baby to its mother, and now crying over a stupid outfit and wishing she could have had a house like this; a life like this.

Her sire, after all, told her what a great gift he had given her and now, she was sitting here, wallowing in self-pity. To make matters worse, the hunger was growing. She would have to abandon her hiding place, soon, and look for a meal. Just a small one to tide her over until she and her sire hunted, together.

The practical side of her argued back. And what kind of guarantee do you have that he'll let you hunt, she asked herself. He's lied to you, before. He's broken promises to you, before. What makes you think he won't do it again?

What had once been Trish sat in her tree and argued with herself. She was so engrossed in her own thoughts; she almost missed the Lexus with two men pull in behind Wolf's car.

The larger of the two looked pale and sick, but he spun around and looked directly in her direction.

He stood that way until his friend said something to him, and even then, he continued to stare right at her. Trish was sure of it. She was sure he could see her, even though she had taken care to hide herself in the shadows of a very large branch.

Stop it, she ordered herself. It was just coincidence. He hadn't been able to see her. She was in shadow, and it was dark.

Still, she felt a little bit of disquiet. She made a mental note to tell Lance about this odd man. He was the boss, after all. Let *him* figure it out.

She began to slither down the tree, not wanting to bring attention to herself.

A soft sound behind her made her stop and look around. A tall shadow stood just at the base of the tree, so clinging to her perch, she tried to make out who it was.

She couldn't tell if it was a man or a woman. Deciding she could handle anyone, she continued her descent until she was almost to the ground and then jumped the rest of the way, positioning herself to come down right next to whoever was creating the shadow.

She should have, she thought, the element of surprise on her side.

If it was a mortal, she could feast without the hunt. Her thirst was gnawing at her, and this could be a win-win situation.

If it was her sire, he would see for himself that she wasn't as stupid as he liked to think.

And that was another thing that bothered her a great deal. While she was alive, he had taken great pains to be with her, but now that he had turned her, all he did was criticize. What the hell was up with that?

No matter. Right now, her job was to surprise whoever was lurking below her perch, get herself down on the ground, and then get closer to the house so she could hear what was being said.

The more information she brought back, the more pleased her sire would be with her.

Landing softly on her feet, she turned and was rewarded with quite a nasty shock.

Standing at the base of the tree was her mother... but not her mother.

Michele gazed lovingly at the thing that had once been her daughter, tears of sadness welling up in her eyes.

"You can't be here. You aren't here! I know my sire killed you. He killed you and dad. What kind of trick is this?"

Her thirst gave her voice a harsh, guttural quality.

Michele stood with her hands folded at her waist keeping her eyes on Trish.

"Trish. You know what you must do. This existence isn't for you. It isn't right, and it isn't natural. This isn't how we raised you."

Trish cringed. Here she had been thinking about killing, and her mother knew it. Still, there was no censure in her mother.

Her *dead* mother, she reminded herself. Things sure were strange. First she was dead... then she was not dead. She was cursed with a terrible thirst for blood, but was moved seeing Kirsten.

Next she's standing here listening to her *dead* mother lecture her.

What next, she wondered.

She didn't have to wait long. Michele looked over Trish's shoulder and faded away. The next thing Trish knew, she was flat on her back and a very angry man was standing over her.

Trish leaped toward her attacker, intent on ripping his throat out, but he was faster than she, and a lot stronger.

Once again, she found herself on the ground, looking up. He was like her, she knew. She could smell it on him, but she doubted her sire and turned this man.

Again, she made the leap, intent on getting the upper hand, but the man was too fast and too strong for her.

Eyes glowing red, fangs bared, they went after each other, again. Abram was having a hard time controlling his rage, but he knew if he killed this girl without the mistress' permission, there would be hell to pay.

Trish snaked out a hand and caught him on the cheek just below the eye. He retaliated by backhanding her and sending her spinning into the tree.

Trish was too new and too inexperienced to stop the momentum, so she hit the sturdy trunk, head on.

Whirling around, she launched at him, again. The two combatants were snarling at each other, each trying to best the other.

Abram wanted to subdue this creature, and Trish wanted to kill. Neither was getting what they wanted.

Finally, the sounds of the fight penetrated houses in the area, including Julie's home. She knew she would have to intercede before someone noticed the racket, outside, and became curious. The last thing they needed, now, was more complications.

Honestly, she wondered, when did her life become so crowded? She wasn't comfortable with all of this. She was accustomed to a solitary existence, and now, there were more people involved in her life than ever before. She didn't think she liked it.

Still, she had a job to do and obviously, it wouldn't wait.

She excused herself with a charming smile. "There must be dogs fighting. Please, enjoy your dessert while I tend to this. Emma?" Julie left the table and rushed outside, leaving Emma to pour coffee and offer more Torte if they so desired.

Rushing across the road, she raced to where Abram and the strange girl fought.

"Enough!" The command in her voice penetrated the blood lust in Trish's brain.

She stopped and looked at this new threat. There was just something about the elegant woman, standing in total control of herself. Trish felt a kinship to this woman.

"I said enough!" Julie repeated and glared at Trish.

Abram leaned against a tree and fought to re-gain control of himself.

Trish continued to stare and felt some of her own bloodlust begin to fade.

Julie grasped the girl in a fierce grip and gave her a good shake.

"You're the little girl my sire has turned. Foolish child. Do you think you are the first he has turned? Have you bothered to ask yourself where the others might be? No? I'll tell you, anyway. Once they served their purpose, he ended them. He is not to be trusted, girl. And yet, here you are… doing his bidding. The question, now, is what to do with you and find out exactly why he sent you here."

Trish stood, wanting to be defiant, but the woman's words penetrated the fog in her brain. What this woman was saying rang with truth.

She reminded herself of the fact that her sire had sent her to her own grandmother's house to drink the woman's blood.

Confusion swirled around in Trish's brain. Who could she trust? Should she trust this woman? She didn't know what to do. She was too new at this, and then, there was the fact she had seen her dead mother… not just once, but twice.

What was she to make of that?

A soft whisper came to her ear. "Trust her. You know what you must do. Do not go on like this, honey."

Julie looked over to Abram. "Keep a good hold on this one. Let her rest and let her wounds heal before bringing her into the house." Julie turned to head back into the house and then paused.

"I fear our dinner guests are in for a bit of a shock. Give me twenty minutes to prepare them."

She looked Trish up and down, and then grinned at Abram.

"This may be just what we needed to drive home the point."

Julie re-entered the house and took her seat at the head of the table.

She looked at each of her guests and gave a deep sigh.

"I'm afraid there was quite a bit more going on outside than just two dogs, fighting."

She had everyone's attention and she slowly re-gained her feet.

"Emma, perhaps it would be best for you to leave the clearing of the table and retire to the kitchen for the time being. I have much to discuss with these people and very little time to do it."

Emma left the dishes she had been gathering and did as she was told.

"How to begin is difficult. I'm going to ask you to keep an open mind. What I have to tell you is difficult to believe, but Hunter will attest to the fact I speak truth. More, very shortly, Abram will be bringing in further evidence that what I'm about to tell you is true."

Julie sat down and leaned back in her chair.

"The truth of the matter is, I am a vampire. I have walked this earth for over two thousand years. My name is not important. What *is* important is that you listen very closely to what I have to say." She took in the shocked faces and watched as Wolf narrowed his eyes. Hunter sat in his chair, a small smile playing around his lips.

"The recent murders have been done by my sire. He's turned only one, which I know of, but believe me when I say, he will turn others. I don't know what he is planning, but I sincerely believe we are heading for a final showdown." She pointed at Damien. "You are a true visionary… a seer. I don't know what part you will play in this, but I am sure it will be an important part. We have a connection, you and I. That connection is in place for a reason."

She then brought her attention to Wolf. "It is my belief that you, too, will be instrumental in whatever is about to happen. We, all of us, have been brought together for a reason. I believe further, that your daughter is in grave danger. Knowing how my sire operates, her very innocence is a big draw for him. He would revel in her destruction. We have much to do and perhaps, a very short time in which to do it."

Everyone sat looking at her. Rachel was the first to react.

"How utterly ridiculous! Vampires! Really! Do you expect us to believe this nonsense?"

"You forget yourself, madam." Julie gritted out.

"I'm forgetting nothing! We're leaving! This is a household of lunatics!" She grabbed Kirsten by the arm, preparing to draw the girl to her feet and rush her from the house.

Abram chose that moment to usher in their uninvited guest.

Trish stood in the room, looking around. She could hear those glorious heartbeats, and her thirst got the better of her. All that lovely blood and she wanted to drink, and drink, and drink.

She would drain all of their feeble bodies dry and not think twice.

Trish was enjoying her thoughts until she heard Kirsten's soft voice.

"Trish? I thought you were dead. Everyone thought you were dead, but here you are."

Trish threw back her head and laughed, revealing her fangs.

"Do I look dead to you, Kirsten? Look at you! Little miss goody two shoes. You have no idea what life is. I could take you somewhere wonderful and dark, but won't."

Trish's look became feral as she wiggled against Abram's restraining hand.

"I could show all of you." She went on. "But my sire wouldn't like it. He chose me, Kirsten! He chose me! He didn't choose you!" Even as the words left her lips, Trish knew it was a lie.

The words of the older woman stuck in her mind. If her sire had turned others, where were they? Had he tricked her?

A war raged inside of her. She began to suspect that she had, indeed, been tricked.

Hunter made a small movement, drawing Trish's attention to him.

She tried to shield her eyes and began hissing like a cornered cat.

At that moment, the front doorbell rang and Abram loosened his grip on her arm, momentarily. She used that small release to shove against him and twist out of his grasp.

Trish made for the far wall and quickly scampered up it to the ceiling and crawled onto it. Inexperienced, she tried to move cautiously, but with deadly intent.

To add to the confusion, the doorbell peeled once again, Rachel began screaming, her hands clenched against her ears.

Kirsten tried to comfort her mother, all the while keeping a wary eye on the creature that, at one time, she loved like a sister.

Wolf gained his feet and drew his gun in one smooth motion.

He glanced over at Damien and found the psychic watching the girl, calmly. He and Steve had also gotten to their feet, and Damien pushed the courtier into a corner and shielded him with his body.

Emma, on her way to answer the door, stopped, her mouth gaping open as she watched the spectacle in the dining room.

The doorbell rang, again, insistently demanding to be answered, and Hunter, sighing, got to his feet and patted Emma on the shoulder.

"It's okay, Emma. Return to the kitchen, and I'll answer the door. Stay in the kitchen until I tell you it's safe to return."

Julie and Abram scaled the wall and had Trish cornered. They exchanged glances and made their way across the ceiling, ready to pounce. They had to get things under control, again.

Trish waited until they almost had her, then let herself drop on top of Rachel, both tumbling to the floor.

Abram and Julie floated down and just as Trish was about to pierce the screaming woman's throat and take a nice big gulp of what she was craving, Abram grabbed her, picked her up, and held her tight against his chest.

At that moment, Hunter sauntered back into the dining room with another large man.

The two stood in the doorway, watching and waiting.

To everyone's relief, Trish went still. The fight went out of her.

She thought about the words the woman had said and knew it was truth.

She was temporary. Her sire had wanted Kirsten, all along.

She thought of her mother and father. Huge tears of blood dripped down her pale cheeks. The pain of betrayal coupled with her grief for her parents was almost too much to deal with.

"End me." She whispered. "Can you end me?" She looked first to Julie and then to Abram.

"If that is what you wish, yes, we can end you. It will be painless and quick." Julie told her.

171

"Then end me now, before I change my mind." She looked over to Kirsten.

"Will you be with me? I won't be afraid if you're with me." Trish sent Kirsten a pleading look.

Kirsten went over to her friend, tears streaming down her cheeks.

"I'll be with you, Trish. I'll be with you." She went to hug the young vampire, but Trish stopped her.

"I don't know if I would have the strength to leave you be. I'm so damned thirsty, and I may harm you. Just be with me at the end." Kirsten nodded.

Rachel sat on the floor, sobbing. Never in her life had she ever been so terrified.

Wolf helped her stand, and her terror turned to anger.

"My big brave cop. My fabulous husband. You would have stood there and done nothing to protect me. You're a feeble excuse of a man. Here's a thought, Wolf. Go into the other room and have a nice big drink. Have several. You're nothing. That beast could have killed me; killed your daughter, and all you could do is stand there with your stupid gun in your hand."

Her anger had the better of her and she didn't care; didn't even hear Kirsten's shocked whisper, "Mom!"

Looking at Trish, she let her disgust show. Rachel boldly walked up to Trish and slapped her. Abram let loose of the girl just enough so the silly woman could see what she was dealing with.

Trish grabbed Rachel by the throat and lifted her effortlessly, off the floor.

"See how strong I am, Rachel? I can break you in two and not break a sweat! I could drain you of every drop of blood in your shriveled-up body, and you couldn't stop me. Don't come near me again!" She tossed Rachel like a rag doll and the woman landed at her ex-husband's feet.

Abram, once again, regained a strong grip on the young vampire, and Trish turned to Wolf.

"My sire has plans for Kirsten. I hope you can protect her. He'll call it a gift. It's not a gift! It's a curse!"

Damien and Steve stood quietly. They were mere onlookers in a play of which they had no part, at least not yet...

Hunter and the stranger walked over. "We will make it painless." Hunter gave Trish a beautiful smile. "This is a glorious thing you're doing." He told her.

Trish tried to nod, but couldn't take her eyes off of Wolf. Slowly, he came around the table and stood directly in front of her.

Ever so gently, he placed his hand on her cheek.

"I'll stay with you, too, Sweetie. I couldn't save you, before, but I can do this for you." He leaned down, and put his lips close to her ear. Not heeding Abram's whisper to have a care, Wolf deliberately took his time.

"Tell your parents hello from me, Sweetie. I love you all, and I'm gonna miss the three of you." With that, he leaned in and kissed her on each cheek and then her forehead.

Rachel sat, quivering in a chair Damien helped her into. Wisely, she kept her mouth shut as the small party, consisting of Hunter, the stranger, Kirsten, Wolf, Abram and Julie escorted the thing that had been Trish from the room.

When they returned, Kirsten was crying as Wolf led her to a chair.

Trish had been ended. It was done sweetly and painlessly.

Now, the returning party had much to discuss, and they couldn't waste a moment.

Julie knew what the others didn't. At the moment of the girl's ending, the sire would have known. He would have felt it. He would not take the thwarting of his plan lightly.

Noticing the stranger standing quietly, Julie raised an eyebrow and turned her questioning gaze to Hunter.

His smile was wide and beautiful.

"Allow me to introduce you to my brother. We call him Gabe."

Chapter 23

Lance felt it. The moment Trish was ended, he felt it, and his rage bubbled up and spewed into his surroundings.

He ranted and raged and raved. Lance let his anger take him where he had never been, before. He didn't have to be told who had ended the little twit.

He knew exactly who was responsible and he promised, during his solitary rant, to get even. If it took another two thousand years, he would have his revenge on her as well as that damned manservant she had turned.

He trashed the shabby apartment he used for his lair, and then, proceeded to race up and down the hall, beating his fists on walls, snapping his teeth is frustration.

The girl was stupid. She had managed to get caught, and they ended her. There was no other explanation.

He had given her a wondrous gift, and she squandered it. He would not waste such a precious thing, again.

He needed to calm down. He needed to think, but first, he needed to feed.

He took himself out into the street and knowing just where to go, made his way under the bridge. It was home to many homeless, and he could find a meal without anyone bothering him.

Lance strolled through the cardboard shelters until he found just what he was looking for.

She had to be at least eighty and so frail, a sharp wind would blow her away. She also had been thoughtful to situate her rough shelter some ways away from the other drifters and homeless. No one would see anything. Perfect.

Her unwashed body didn't bother Lance. He had tasted worse during his long existence. He actually found her smell appealing. It was earthy and raised his hunger another notch.

He fell on her and watched her eyes widen with fear. She struggled pitifully under him, trying to scratch and claw at his face.

He could hear her heart beating, irregularly to be sure, but he needed her fear. It would make her blood so much sweeter.

Finally, when her fear was at its height, he smiled a terrible smile, letting her see his fangs, gleaming in the pale moonlight.

With a low growl, he bit, and taking his time, drank every bit of her blood.

Once finished, he carefully covered her. It wouldn't do for anyone to find her before he was well out of the area. The authorities would chalk her death up to old age and rough living.

Until the time was right and he was ready to make his move, he would have to be careful. His foray into the morgue a few nights ago to retrieve Trish had been sloppy, and he hadn't thought it through. He wouldn't make that mistake, again.

Now satiated, he could begin to think clearly. First, he thought, he would raise a small army. Only four would be necessary, he decided, and he would give them just enough of himself to keep them in thrall. He would not waste his gift on another until he had the pretty blonde in his grasp, and even she, with all of her despicable innocence, would have to earn the gift.

Next, he would study her. She must have parents, and that could be a bother. They would need to be killed. Killed and their bodies hidden.

He couldn't afford any more bodies left lying around for the police to investigate.

Once he had the pretty blonde under his control, he would force his first choice to come to him. Perhaps he would kidnap that housekeeper she was so fond of.

He would watch Julie's house, carefully, and decide how to proceed from whatever he discovered.

Feeling better, he set out to find his first soldier. That wouldn't be too difficult. He knew where the young went.

Julie moved her guests into the sitting room, while Abram and Emma cleaned up the mess.

Hunter and his "brother", Gabe, stood off to one side of the room, talking quietly.

Rachel, shaken, sat on the wide cushions of the sofa gracing the room and looked at her hands. She didn't understand anything, and more, she didn't want to understand.

Wolf sat in a large wing backed chair, staring off into space, lost in his own thoughts.

Kirsten sat next to her mother, trying to console the woman who refused to be consoled.

Damien and Steve sat side by side on another sofa and didn't speak. What, after all, was there to say?

Julie filled large tumblers with fine brandy and served her guests, herself. She would give them a few minutes, and then, talk to them sensibly and calmly. If however, the red-head that was currently in a tizzy continued to panic, Julie would do whatever it was necessary to snap her out of it.

She waited until they all had taken sips of their drinks. Even Kirsten imbibed, needing a little bolstering.

After drinking more than half of her drink, Rachel sighed and sat back against the plush cushions and closed her eyes.

"We need to talk about the things seen here tonight. Let's take care of the practical matter, first. We are going to need to get the body out of here. I'm open to ideas." Julie looked around.

"Gabe and I will deal with this." Hunter told her. "The girl was a pawn, but there was still some good in her. We'll take care of it and she can safely be buried with her family." He flashed a beautiful smile in Julie's direction. "This we're allowed to do."

Julie inclined her head and the two men left the room, intent on their mission.

"Let me be very clear. You all now know what I am. You know what Abram is. If this is discussed in public, you will not be believed. Make no mistake, I will destroy your reputations and not think twice. I want this understood."

Rachel gave a small hysterical laugh. "Who the hell would believe us? I was here and *I* don't believe it."

Julie studied the woman and summed her up quickly. Vain, foolish and headstrong. Rachel liked getting her own way and was shallow enough to not care who she hurt. Even if it meant hurting her own daughter.

She couldn't help but wonder how a woman such as this was rewarded with such a treasure as Kirsten, for the girl had impressed Julie. She impressed the woman a great deal.

"Kirsten, judging by the things your former friend said, you've met my sire. I must know all."

Julie frowned at Rachel, who was still weeping softly and wringing her hands.

"Woman, I suggest you pull yourself together. Your daughter, I suspect, is in a great deal of danger. You will be of no help in keeping her safe if you allow yourself to fall apart like this. You've seen what you've seen. There's no going back, now."

Her words brought on fresh tears, and Julie turned from the woman in disgust, focusing her attention on the poised young woman now trying to comfort her mother.

"Leave her be, Kirsten. Tell me all you remember."

Kirsten described in detail the night at The Club, including the altercation between Trish and herself.

Julie noticed Damien nodding in agreement with everything the girl said, and after Kirsten had nothing more to add, she turned to Damien.

"You seem to know a great deal about this." She told him. When he nodded, she raised an eyebrow at him. Inclining her head, she studied him, intently.

"You 'saw' all of this? Tell me. Did you have a sense that my sire knew you were 'watching'?"

"No, I didn't get that, at all. I don't believe he was aware of my particular gift. But, the vision was chaotic and brutal. More brutal than any I've witnessed, before."

Julie nodded, satisfied. She then turned to Steve.

"And you my fine young designer? What of you?"

Steve gave a careless shrug. "If I was in any sort of danger, Damien would warn me."

Julie gave him a small wry grin. "You have this much faith in your friend, then?" She asked and was awarded with one of Steve's beaming grins, his eyes alight with fun. "Absolutely! He's saved my ass more than once."

The group talked far into the night. At some point, Abram joined them, followed by Emma. She carried in a tray holding a silver coffee pot, delicate cups, saucers, and a plate of small sugar cakes.

"I thought you could use a little fortifying, Miss Julie. Is there anything else?"

Julie smiled. "Perhaps you could prepare an extra room for Hunter's brother."

"Already done, miss. I put him in the room across the hall from Hunter. I thought they'd like to be near to each other."

Julie's smile widened into a grin. "Thank you, Emma. You may retire if you wish. We'll see to ourselves."

Emma inclined her head and hustled from the room. Julie would bet a million dollars that Emma would stay in the kitchen, just in case she was needed. The woman really was a jewel.

During the discourse, Hunter and Gabe returned.

"It's done. She will be buried with the rest of her family."

Julie nodded. She didn't want to admit, even to herself, just how relieved she was.

She didn't know how Hunter and his brother had pulled it off. She was just grateful they had.

"Emma has made up a room for your… brother." She told him.

Leaning back, she studied the two men, now standing side by side.

Gabe matched Hunter in height and build. Both had the same fine hair, curling down to their shoulders, and both radiated a special… something. That something made it painful to look at them for any length of time.

There were subtle differences. Hunter's beautiful eyes were a vivid and intense blue, while Gabe's were deep and piercing green.

To Julie, it was like staring into a peaceful forest pond, and she had to avert her eyes. The gentle humor in those green orbs was too much for her.

Gabe gave her a small bow, and his beautiful, strong mouth turned up at the corners.

"I thank you, sincerely, but I cannot stay. I am only here to deliver a message. However, please thank your housekeeper for me."

Turning to Hunter, he said something in their language. A language Julie didn't recognize. Hunter nodded and walked Gabe out.

Kirsten, watching the interchange between the two, felt sad. She would have liked to talk to the one called Gabe.

Hunter returned and took a seat next to the girl. He beamed his wonderful smile, and Kirsten felt the heat rise in her face. She hated that she blushed so easily.

Hunter took her small hand into his large one and looked directly into her eyes.

"Don't fret, little one. He'll be back." Hunter told her, and Kirsten smiled.

Julie cleared her throat and gained everyone's attention.

"This is what I believe," She began. "I believe my sire is looking for another bride." She looked pointedly at Kirsten. "More, I believe he has made his choice." Turning to Wolf, she shot him a piercing look. "He has chosen your daughter."

"Why?" Wolf interrupted. Julie shrugged. "First, she is beautiful. Second she has the sort of innocence… purity; if you will, that he enjoys corrupting."

She then turned to Rachel. Masking her disgust for the weak woman, she kept her voice calm but firm. "Since Kirsten lives with you, you will have to be most vigilant. You must guard this treasure you are blessed with."

Damien stirred. "Why are you helping us? You are vampire, as is your gentleman servant. What's in it for you?"

Julie grinned. The man was blunt and to the point. She liked that. Her answer would be the same.

"I am helping you solely to help myself. I have walked this earth far too long. I want it to end, but on my terms, not his. And, if I can find a way to end him at the same time, I'll do so."

Wolf drained his glass and got to his feet. He walked over to the small bar and began to reach for the brandy. His hand hovered over the bottle, and then he hesitated, reaching for the carafe with ice water and proceeded to fill his glass.

Julie hid her smile of approval.

"You said we have to protect Kirsten. What would you suggest?" Wolf aimed the question directly at Julie.

Before Julie could answer, Rachel roused herself.

"Obviously, she means we have to pull her out of school. Curtail her activities and make her a virtual prisoner in her own home." She snarled.

Julie shook her head. "Not at all. It's important she continue with her life. He'll be watching her. There are precautions, however. You must be careful of who you let into your home. If something needs repairing, make an appointment, and I will see to it Abram is there." Julie looked over at Kirsten.

"You will be safe enough at school. He won't attack while you are surrounded by people. Do you have any activities we should know about?"

Kirsten shook her head, but before she could answer, her mother barged in again.

"Homecoming is coming up. It's a very important social activity. She needs to go to that. We're going shopping for a dress on Monday." Rachel added.

Before Julie or Kirsten could object, Steve interjected. He had been watching Kirsten all evening and decided he would love to dress her.

This would be a perfect opportunity.

"Actually, I have something that would work. I can bring it over, tomorrow, and we'll see how it fits." Turning to Kirsten, he questioned her on her size and what sort of affair the homecoming would be. Gauging her answers, he was positive he had something that would work quite well.

"You will not travel alone, my fine young designer. He will come at you to get to your psychic friend. So! If you are going to dress our beautiful young friend, Abram shall pick you up at Damien's home and bring you to Kirsten."

She turned to Rachel. A sense of urgency filled her, and she leaned toward the woman.

"It is imperative. You must not allow anyone you do not know into your home."

Rachel resented Julie's high-handed ways.

"I have a life! You can't tell me what to do in my own home!" She snarled.

Wolf slammed his glass down and turned on his ex-wife in a fury.

"Of course not, Rachel. God forbid you should put yourself out to protect Kirsten. It's all about you. It's always *been* about you!" His voice was low and dripped ice.

"You can't talk to me like that, Wolf. She's as much my daughter as yours! We're not married, anymore, and I don't have to put up with this!" Rachel stood and snatched up her bag.

"Kirsten! Let's go!" She was almost to the door when Damien's cool voice penetrated her ire.

"Rachel! You don't have to believe, but everything you've been told tonight is God's own truth. Stop and think. Is your pride worth more than your daughter's life?"

Hunter sat quietly, but a small smile played about his generous and beautiful mouth. Oh, he thought, nicely done.

Rachel sat, again, but she was furious. Somehow, she managed to turn this all on her ex-husband. Her embarrassment in front of the elegant Julie King and the other guests stung. How could she possibly break into this type of life after this mortifying experience? And Rachel wanted this friendship with Julie King. She wanted this lifestyle, and she wanted it desperately.

It also pissed her off when the only person who came to her side was Kirsten. What sort of people were these, not to come to the assistance of an upset woman, she wondered.

Wisely, Rachel held her tongue, but she would vent her spleen at Kirsten as soon as she got her home.

&

The group talked, planned and discussed. Julie warned them what to watch for. Abram interjected occasionally, telling them how best to protect themselves.

Kirsten wished she had a notebook so she could write it all down.

Wolf *did* have a notebook and he was busily jotting everything down.

He never stopped to think what all of this could do to his career. If he lost his job over it, so be it. All that mattered was keeping Kirsten safe.

Damien sat quietly, his head resting on the back of the sofa, his eyes closed. His headache had returned with a vengeance, and he hoped he wouldn't be sick until he was home.

Steven took in Damien's pale face, the closed eyes, and knew his friend was suffering. He was about to call a halt to the impromptu meeting, but Damien's hand on his arm stopped him.

Once, during the discourse, Julie excused herself. Going to her room, she grabbed a packet of blood from her small refrigerator, opened it, poured it into a mug, warmed it and drank it down.

Close proximity to these mortals made her twitchy, and she would have enjoyed ripping Rachel's throat out, just on general principles. To do that, however, would sever the tenacious bond the group formed this night and she didn't want to take that risk. They may prove useful to her.

Hunter remained silent, which was rare for him. He wondered if this time, Julie would finally get it right. Gabe told him this was the time and place. It was now or never.

The party broke up. They agreed to meet at Rachel's home the next afternoon. Abram would pick Steve up and bring him, along with his latest creation, to Kirsten.

From now on, they would all be living in each other's pockets.

Heaven help her, Julie thought, she would be forced to be in close proximity to these mortals and not necessarily on her terms.

Hatred for her sire grew. She vowed she would end him and very soon.

Chapter 24

S unday dawned cloudy, and that fit Kirsten's mood, perfectly. She was still reeling from the dinner party of the night, before. She had a hard time believing the things she had witnessed.

If someone had told her there were vampires roaming about, she would have thought he or she was nuts. But, she had seen it with her own eyes.

She laid in her bed, going over everything in her mind. Julie King was a vampire, as was her rather sexy manservant.

Trish had been turned, and those two other men, Hunter and his brother, had ended her.

There was the psychic guy, and what the hell was he all about, and just why did her Dad trust him?

Kirsten had more questions than answers. Then, add in the fact that her mother had gone totally wacko in front of strangers... well; she just didn't know what to think.

She needed to talk to her Dad. She needed sensible answers, but she knew her mother would never allow him to come to the house. Rachel had been sniping at him all the way home, and Kirsten thought they most likely had gotten into a rather nasty argument after she left the car and went into the house.

Knowing how her mother's mind operated, Kirsten thought it was a pretty safe bet that she was still seething.

Well, she decided, if he can't come to her, then she would go to him.

With some sort of plan in mind, she got up and got dressed, thinking to leave the house before her mother even crawled out of bed.

She quietly closed her bedroom door and was about to make her way to the kitchen. She would leave a note next to the coffee pot so Rachel wouldn't worry.

"Going somewhere, are we?" A familiar voice came from behind her.

"Dad! What are *you* doing here? I thought after last night, mom would have banished you to Siberia or something!"

"That's not a very nice thing to say, young lady." Kirsten spun around and faced both of her parents.

"What's going on, here? What are you doing, here, Dad?"

"Drinking coffee. And you were heading, where?"

Kirsten slid a glance at her mother and decided to be upfront.

"I was planning on seeing you. I need some answers. Sane and sensible answers. I know what I saw last night, but-" She let her voice fade away.

"You're having a hard time believing the unbelievable. That's natural, honey. C'mon. Let's go in the kitchen, sit down and talk about this."

Wolf led the way, not giving her the opportunity to argue. He had enough arguments this morning.

Rachel and Kirsten sat while Wolf snatched up the coffee pot. He topped off his and Rachel's cups and poured a fresh mug for Kirsten.

He took a seat next to his daughter and took one of her small hands into his large. She curled her fingers around his palm and pushed her blonde curls out of her face with the other.

"What do you want to know, kiddo?" He asked.

Kirsten shook her head. "Dad, I don't know where to start. None of this makes sense. I know what I saw last night, but it won't fly for me."

"Just take a deep breath. Sip some coffee and wait for the hit, then just ask me what you need to know."

Kirsten sipped and tried to empty her mind. It would need to be wide open in a situation like this, although she was damned if she knew what the situation *was*.

"Let's start with Damien Crist. Dad, is he really psychic? I thought those kinds of people were proven to be fakes."

Wolf shrugged a beefy shoulder.

"I can only tell you what I know. Yeah, Damien is a true psychic. He's been that way since he was a kid. We've worked together on several cases, and he's always been right on. The thing is, honey, he saw everything that happened that night you and Trish went to The Club and saw everything that followed. He sensed you and I are connected and he called me, right away…or rather, had his friend do it."

Kirsten studied her father, doubt clouding those long, amber eyes.

"You said he'd helped you on several cases. Give me just one; give me something to believe in."

Wolf sipped his coffee and thought back over the years he and Damien had worked together. Finally, he chose a case that had a happy ending. He hoped this danger to his daughter would end in a happy ending, too.

"Okay, do you remember that kid that was snatched about a year ago? Was missing for several hours? We all thought she was probably dead, and rather than hoping for a recovery, we were gearing up to search for a dead body. Damien comes sauntering into the office. By the way, I'm not the only cop he's worked with, so he's pretty well-known. His condition to continue to help us was a promise from the department to keep his name out of the newspapers. He's pretty well known as an architect in this city. He didn't need the bullshit that comes with publicity. Anyway, he walks into the office, sits down at my desk and proceeds to draw out just where the perp was keeping the little girl. Gave us a time-line and told us to move our asses if we wanted to find her alive. When he was done, he sat back, bleeding from his nose and ears. Just little trickles, but that's the side effect of his ability. He also had a mother of a headache. One of our uniforms offered to drive him home, but in spite of being sicker than a dog, he insisted on waiting in the office until we got our hands on that kid. Needless to say, we broke into that hell-hole where the creep had that kid and got her out just in time. He was getting ready to sacrifice her to some hell god."

Kirsten remembered that case. Her parents were still together, and she remembered hearing her Dad come home and tell Rachel, crying the whole time.

"If he gets so sick doing this, why does he continue to do it?" Kirsten asked.

"I asked him that same question. It really does take a lot out of him, so I asked him what was in it for him. His answer knocked me back, a little. He said, 'For some reason, God gave me this ability. He let me survive my injuries and this is the result. I suppose I could use it to play the horses or bet on dog races, but that's not what it's intended for. So, if I can help save even one person, the discomfort is worth it.'"

"But Dad, he's rich. He doesn't have to do this. Everyone in the architect world knows who Damien Crist is. So, he isn't in it for the money. And since he doesn't want any credit, he's not in it for the fame. So, I guess I don't understand why he would put himself through all that pain. There's nothing in it for him."

Wolf shook his head. "No, there's nothing in it for him, except helping us do our jobs. The guy has a big heart, a keen intelligence and a gentle soul. I really like the guy."

Kirsten took a moment to absorb what her father was telling her. It was pretty hard to fathom, but Damien had an impeccable reputation. If her Dad trusted him, then she probably should, as well.

"What about the designer?" Rachel interjected. Wolf noticed she was listening… really listening. That's a first, he thought.

"Ran a check on him. Guy's a genius. He studied under Armani." He watched Rachel raise her eyebrows. "He came home to start his own fashion house. Was supposed to leave for New York for some showing, but is holding up until spring."

"Are they lovers?" Rachel asked, and Wolf shook his head. "Nah, Damien's straight as they come. The designer, Steve Worthington, and

Damien have been friends since they were kids. Damien defended the kid; Steve knew about Damien's ability and protected him when he could. Damien's folks paid for Steve's education. You could say they're brothers under the skin."

Kirsten nodded and absorbed everything she had been told so far. She, herself, was a budding architect, and admired the buildings Damien designed and built. She hoped she could be half as good.

Wolf waited. He knew his daughter; knew she was absorbing the things he told her, so far, and knew she would have more questions. Best to let her ask them in her own time.

"Okay, what about Julie King and that manservant of hers? That's all a little hard to believe."

Wolf nodded. "Yeah, it is, but how can you deny what your own eyes showed you?"

"What do we know about them?" Rachel asked. She, too, was having a hard time reconciling herself to the things she had seen last night.

"You know about as much about her as I do. Damien says she's telling the truth. He also picked up on the fact that she doesn't kill mortals for food, at least not anymore. He also picked up on the fact that she really hates the guy that turned her and Trish and murdered Nate and Michele. But, according to Damien, she's the real deal, and we're going to have to work with that."

"The housekeeper?" Rachel asked and Wolf took a long pull from his coffee mug. "Mortal. Widowed back in the sixties and no family. She's worked for Julie for quite some time, so is probably aware of her employer's proclivities."

"This is so strange, Dad. Where does that Hunter person fit into all of this?" Wolf shook his massive head, his gray hair falling into his eyes. "Can't find anything on him, so he's an unknown quantity, but judging by the way he and his brother took over dealing with Trish, I'd say he's one of the good guys."

"Why are you here, Dad?" She had to ask, although she thought she knew the answer.

"You're my only kiddo," He said, "I'm going to be staying here until we find a way to end this and you are safe. Your mother and I discussed it, last night, after you went to bed. This is the safest and most sensible thing to do, at this point."

Kirsten slid a glance at her mother and was surprised to see a flush on Rachel's face.

"So, you believe all of this?" Kirsten asked, and Rachel nodded.

"Yes, I do. I have to admit it was hard to swallow, but I can't deny the things I saw, either. So, after some discussion, we decided that your dad will be staying with us and taking the guest room."

A warm and fuzzy feeling filled Kirsten. They were going to make an attempt to get along, for her sake. Which brought another question to mind and one she was loathed to ask, but she was as straight forward as her father, and she needed to hear the truth from him.

"Am I really in danger, then?" She whispered. Her eyes, so like his own, bored into Wolf's while she waited for an answer.

His first thought was to lie to her. He didn't want to worry her, but decided it was time for truth as unpleasant and frightening as it could be.

"Yeah, honey. You are. According to Damien, this 'guy' has designs on you. Apparently, you sensed there was something wrong about him and backed away. He went for Trish, and we know how that ended."

Kirsten nodded as tears flooded her eyes. She wasn't afraid for herself but mourned her friend.

"What about your work, Dad?" She asked in a whisper. Wolf shrugged.

"I'm on leave for the time being. You know Jake died, as well, so I'm without a partner." He turned to Rachel, "Did you ever call Alicia?" He asked and Rachel nodded. "I talked to her, yesterday. They are taking Jake back to Florida for burial. She said when she comes back to put the house on the market, she'll arrange for a memorial. She said she'd call you once she got her feet back under her. She also told me to tell you to be careful. Did she know about any of this?"

Wolf shook his head and rubbed his hands over his face. "She only knew what little I knew the night all this went down. She's got great instincts, though."

Kirsten got up, rinsed out her cup and pushed in her chair. "I need to take a shower." She announced and left the kitchen.

Her parents knew she needed time to absorb all of this. Rachel didn't know how she could. It still boggled her own mind. How could Kirsten be anything other than confused?

Kirsten came bombing back into the kitchen. "There's mile long limo pulling up in the drive! This has *got* to be the longest car in history!"

Wolf and Rachel raced to the window and neither was surprised when Abram stepped out of the driver's seat and opened the back door. Julie, Damien, and Steve all piled out and made their way to the front door. Steve carried a garment bag over his shoulder and a case in his hand.

"Oh my God! Mom, they're all here, and Steve must have brought a dress with him. You've got to tell him I'm not going to that stupid dance! How can I?"

Before Rachel could blow her top, Wolf smoothly stepped in.

"Honey, it's really important you just continue on with your life." Kirsten opened her mouth to argue, but he raised a hand, stopping her. "Let me finish. First, Trish wouldn't want you to miss this. You were elected as freshman rep to the court. Second, if this guy, the guy who killed Trish and her parents, if he manages to make you afraid to do the things you would ordinarily do, then he's won. Besides, we sort of have a plan to lure him out."

"I'm bait," Kirsten said in a flat tone. Wolf nodded. "Yes and no. Abram will be there, as well as Julie. They will sniff him out. I'll be lurking nearby, in case he shows. We'll nab him, and Julie will end him. You'll be safe enough."

Kirsten looked rather doubtful. "Honey, I'd never put you in harm's way, you know that."

"You'll be close by?" She peered up at her dad and sighed when he nodded.

"I'll be close by, as well, Kirsten." Rachel added. Kirsten wasn't sure if she felt better about that, or not.

Kirsten sighed and ran a hand through her blonde curls. "I'm going to take a shower. I need a few minutes."

The doorbell pealed, and Rachel hurried over to answer it. She gave a quick glance around to make sure her house was presentable and plastered a smile on her face.

That wasn't difficult. She could see her neighbors ogling the limo and Julie King. She just went up in their estimation, and that just made her whole damn day.

Chapter 25

Lance was busy. First thing, he needed followers and set up to accomplish that goal.

He knew just where to find them, so he headed down to the corner pool hall. Throw-away kids hung out there, looking to see what sort of trouble they could get into.

Anything for a fast buck, but they weren't counting on the kind of trouble walking up the street, toward them.

They quickly surrounded the stylishly dressed man. He looked a little frail, and they figured he'd be an easy mark. They were wrong.

Everything happened so fast, they didn't know what hit them.

He took the ringleader, first. Before the kid could scream, Lance bit and then injected just enough of himself to hold him in *thrall*.

He grabbed the second kid and did the same, again giving just enough to hold him captive.

The third kid thought about running. His eyes widened in terror as he watched his friends thrash around on the ground... as Lance's blood began its nasty work.

The fourth started running after watching Lance rear back, his eyes red and those fearsome fangs flashing under the streetlight.

He heard the pitiful scream and took off. He took three steps and felt Lance's arm around his throat. It felt like steel, and as hard as he tried to squirm out of the man's grip, he was totally helpless.

He felt the bite, and then, felt something coppery going down his throat before the man released him.

Moving easily, Lance placed the four young men into a car he boosted earlier in the day.

Satisfied he now had his soldiers, he could now begin to put his plan into action.

The next thing on his list was finding that pretty blonde vixen that had eluded him. Problem was, he didn't know where she resided, nor where she went to school.

The way he saw it, the only option he had was to send his minion to The Club. That was iffy at best, so to hedge his bets, he'd also send them around to the different colleges.

A girl that pretty and that intelligent had to be in school, and The Club was close to the colleges in the area.

This was something he would have to do for himself. That little trollop proved to him; humans are inept.

Lance didn't like any of his options. It was all hit and misses, but until he could come up with a better idea, it was all he had. He'd have to roll with it.

Rachel took one look out her window at the people arriving, and raced to her bedroom. She dove into her closet, looking for something chic, but homey.

Again, she lamented. If only Wolf would give up this cop business and practice law, she could have the sort of life she is entitled to. Designer clothes would be hanging in her closets with all the accessories. Resentment bubbled up, again, spoiling her fine mood and threatening the uneasy truce she now enjoyed with her ex-husband.

It was his entire fault, of course, that she had to go back to work. She hated her job. She would much rather glide around an art gallery or museum, not slave away in a law office.

She hated watching the wives of the partners stroll in after a charity lunch. They acted as if she didn't exist, just because she was a paralegal.

It was the best she could do. Her education had been in the fine arts. Was it her fault she had to go back to work? Was it her fault she had to take something so totally beneath her? No! It was all Wolf's fault. Why couldn't Kirsten see that?

She tore through her sizeable wardrobe until she found something she thought would be suitable.

Donning gray slacks, and a sapphire blue silk blouse, she slipped her feet into gray mules.

She ran a brush through her hair and added a fine gold chain, earrings and matching bracelet. She included a touch of mascara, and following Julie's example, a bit of pale color to her lips.

All in all, she thought she was turned out okay.

Walking into her living room, she cringed. Kirsten was in her usual pair of ratty jeans, an old black hoody that was grayer than black and her nasty old tennis shoes.

Still, the girl was holding court with their unexpected guests, and Rachel chalked it up to the girl's youth. She probably could and did look good in anything, and she was actually charming the aloof Julie King.

"I don't think it's right for me to go to this dance. Trish isn't here, and it just won't be the same." Kirsten was telling Julie as Rachel walked into the room.

"We've been through this, Kirsten…" Rachel began, but Julie held up a hand, stopping her in mid-sentence.

"If I may." Julie began, and everyone fell quiet. "I believe it most important for you to go. As I explained, if you don't attend, you give my sire more power over you. Then, we have the psychological advantage. He will expect you to stay away. Do the unexpected. You also need to ask yourself one question. Would your friend want you to stay away?"

Kirsten listened, and Rachel felt some resentment messily mixed in with hurt. These were the same things *she* had been saying. Her words fell on deaf ears, and now, here was this strange woman, saying the same things, and Kirsten was listening.

Kirsten sat with her head down, a sure sign she was weighing Julie's words. Finally, she raised her head and gave a small smile.

"Okay then, let's see what you have brought for me to wear. If I'm going, I want to look amazing. Trish would expect that."

Steve reached over and squeezed her hand, and then, got to his feet and walked over to the large garment bag he had hung on the back of the front door when he'd arrived.

Steve pulled out what could only be called a creation. The dull gold material shimmered in the sunlight.

On the hanger, it didn't look like much, but Steve grinned as he handed it to her with orders to, "Put this on and let's see what we've got."

Kirsten came out, and she was breathtaking. The off the shoulder sweetheart neckline emphasized the girl's graceful neck and shoulders. The bodice flowed, showing Kirsten's toned body to perfection, and the softly draped narrow skirt accented excellent legs. She felt, and looked, like a princess.

Steve fussed, pinning the gown here and there, until it fit Kirsten perfectly.

"Hmmm, you'll need something delicate to accessorize this. Nothing too overpowering." He murmured.

Julie walked over and circled the girl in the amazing dress. "I think I have something that will work," She told him. Steve grinned, flashing dimples. "Of course you do." He said.

Julie gave him a playful swat on the arm, surprising Abram. This was a side of his mistress he had never seen prior to this.

Julie waved him over to the side of the living room and they held a hurried conference. He nodded once and dashed out the door.

Rachel, busy making coffee and setting up a pretty tray with her finest cups and saucers along with an attractive display of cookies, saw him leave.

"Is Abram leaving?" She asked Julie. Julie nodded. "He's coming right back. I sent him to fetch me something and to bring Emma here." Turning to Wolf to include him in the conversation, she continued. "I rather thought it would be fun to have a..." She sent Damien a questioning look.

"Cook-out," He supplied and won a rare smile.

"Yes, a cook-out. Emma will know what to bring. Tell me, do you have the necessary equipment?" She asked Wolf, who smiled.

"Ma'am, not only do I have the necessary equipment for barbequing, but it would be a pleasure."

She turned to Rachel. "You don't mind?" Rachel had the impression that it didn't much matter if she minded, or not.

The truth of the matter was, she didn't mind. It would be another feather in her cap to tell the people at work just how she had entertained the enigmatic Julie King.

Those lawyer's wives would be pea green with envy, and that just made Rachel's whole damn day.

Steve, busy pinning and draping his creation, glanced up and saw the smug look dance across Rachel's face. He and Damien exchanged glances, both thinking the same thing. They wondered how long it would take Rachel to get a picture of Julie and herself. They didn't have to wait long.

"Would it be okay if I took some pictures of all of us, together? I mean, can you be photographed?" Rachel could have bit her tongue off. Of course, the woman could be photographed. Hadn't she practically drooled over Julie's pictures in the society columns? She felt like a total fool, but Julie quickly put her at ease.

"I think that would be a fine idea. Something to save for posterity." It was the only reference Julie made to the upcoming battle.

"The only people missing are Hunter and his brother." Kirsten said in a soft voice.

Julie waved that away. "His *brother* didn't stay, and Hunter will pop up, now and again."

Damien had been quiet. The headache that nagged at him, almost constantly, was beginning to undermine his energy. He wondered if something else was happening in his head. Perhaps, he thought, it's time to see a doctor.

Taking out a sketchbook he always carried with him, he started sketching. He quickly penciled Kirsten, and then, added Julie as the woman walked around the girl, making suggestions as Steve worked on the dress Kirsten wore.

Changing to colored pencils, his sketch took on life. It was one of the finest things he had ever done and was pleased with it.

"Whatcha working on there, pal?" Steve asked around a mouthful of pins.

Damien shrugged. "Just a sketch. It's pretty damn good, but nothing earth-shattering," he replied, busily drawing and shading.

For the first time in weeks, he could feel the muscles in his neck relax and the headache began to ease, a little.

Doing this kind of work emptied his mind and eased his soul. All he could do was hope like hell nothing intruded to disturb his newfound peace of mind.

A sharp knock interrupted his thoughts as Abram opened the door and barreled through, followed by Emma.

Abram carried in a large pot and had an ornately decorated case under his arm. Emma was laden with bags that tinkled and jingled as she walked.

"Kitchen?" She asked, and Rachel led the way.

Abram deposited the pot on the stove, and then, made his way to Julie, handing her the case.

"I sent Abram for this. I thought it might go well with the gown." She opened it and everyone crowded around, letting out gasps and oh's and ah's.

"That is absolutely beautiful," Rachel gushed as she studied the delicate gold necklace. The stones, golden Topaz, sparkled and flashed with a life of their own.

"Let's try them and see how it looks." Julie said as she walked over to where Kirsten stood. With her own hands, she fastened the necklace around the girl's slim throat. A throat that just a few centuries ago, Julie would have relished biting into.

My, my, she thought, how far I've come.

She placed the matching earrings in Kirsten ears and watched as the topaz teardrops danced. She then added the bracelet and admired the way the stones circled the girl's delicate wrist.

"I think this works quite well. What's your thought, Steve?" Julie murmured.

"I think it's kick-ass!" Steve said, enthusiastically, bringing a smile to Julie's face.

"This is all wonderful, Miss King. But, I can't possibly wear these. If something happens to them, I'd die... I'd absolutely die." Kirsten said.

Julie gave the girl a sharp look. She had a pretty good bull-shit meter, but this girl was as transparent as a spring. She was utterly without guile, and Julie wondered how she came to be that way, especially with a mother like Rachel. It had to be Wolf's influence.

She studied him, as well. Quiet, but with a busy brain. Lots of thoughts going through that head, Julie thought.

She studied father and daughter and came to a decision. In spite of herself, she was becoming rather fond of the girl, and if she wanted to give her a little something, then why not just do it?

"Actually Kirsten, I'm giving you the jewelry." She raised a hand as Kirsten began to object. "The set is too young for me and not to my taste. It goes well with the dress, and I want you to have them."

Kirsten was stunned speechless, but Rachel didn't have that problem. She saw a lifetime of rubbing elbows with the wealthier citizens of Wisconsin, and Julie would open the doors because of Kirsten.

"Don't be ungrateful, Kirsten!" Rachel began. She tossed Wolf a smug smile as she continued. "You never turn down a gift! You were raised better than that. Just say thank you and leave it at that."

Kirsten's face flushed, and Wolf shook his head.

Rachel really is a manipulative shrew, he thought. The only good thing the woman did was give birth to their daughter, and now, she was going to negate that by using the girl to get what she, Rachel, wanted.

Julie patted Kirsten's hand and moved to join Damien on the sofa.

"Thank you..." Kirsten began, and Julie interrupted her.

"No need for thanks, and please, call me Julie." She sent the girl a small smile. "I do believe we are going to be great friends. We have much in common." Julie told her.

Rachel was beside herself with pleasure. Maybe, life would turn out the way she wanted, after all.

Steve, busily pinning the dress here and there could sense the girl's embarrassment. She was not comfortable as the center of attention, and he thought to ease some of her discomfort while he worked.

"So tell me, Tulip face. Where do you go to school and what are you studying?" He asked around a mouthful of pins.

"University of Wisconsin… Milwaukee," she told him. "I hope to become an architect."

Hearing this, Damien perked up, considerably. "Really. My alma matter and my field." He said with a quick smile. He mentioned a professor, and Kirsten admitted that, yes, she was in one of his classes and no, she didn't like him.

Damien nodded. "He's tough, but you'll learn more from him in one semester than some of the others in the next four or five years."

"Where's your sketchbook, Kirsten?" Wolf asked.

His daughter looked like she wanted to fall through the floor. "It's in the den, Dad, but it's not very good." She gave a small shrug.

Wolf went and fetched it, flipping it open and handed it to Damien. "What do you think, Damien? Is she any good?" There was a definite challenge in Wolf's tone as Damien studied the drawings.

"Actually, these are quite good. A little raw, but the potential is there. You have some good ideas, Kirsten. I'm impressed."

Julie and Damien studied the drawings of buildings Kirsten would like to see built. They studied a drawing for a hospital, a senior center, a housing project and several more.

Damien moved his own sketchpad and took Kirsten's onto his lap. He pointed out several places where improvements could be made, some inaccuracies, and ended up looking the girl straight in the eye.

"You have a talent, Kirsten. I'd be interested in seeing what you do with it." Damien told her.

They kept the conversation light. Everyone in that room knew that, tomorrow, Kirsten would be burying her best friend. They were all aware of what Trish had become; were aware that if they weren't careful, the same fate would befall the young girl now in the room.

She needed time, they knew, and they were hell bent to give it to her.

They were aware of even more. There would be no such thing as closure, especially not for Kirsten. They hoped she would be strong enough to rise above it.

Delicious smells wafted through the air, preceding Emma who walked into the living room and took a seat in a comfortable wing backed chair.

"Almost ready for the grill," she told the room, at large. "Sauce just needs to simmer." Turning to Wolf, she continued. "I'm guessing you will be doing the honors. There are two steaks on a platter. Cook those three minutes on each side, just to sear them. Those will be for Abram and Julie." Seeing Wolf's raised eyebrows, she grinned. "Don't worry. The ribs the rest of us will be having will be fabulous. You won't be disappointed."

Kirsten emerged from her room, the gorgeous dress Steve was making for her draped over her arm. She carried the ornate case in her other hand. She walked up to Wolf and handed it to him.

"Dad, please put this in your safe." Turning to Julie, she leaned over and brushed a soft kiss against the cool cheek, surprising the other woman. "Thank you. I'll treasure them for the rest of my life."

Julie was embarrassed. Never before had anyone shown her affection, with the possible exception of her sons when they were small boys. It just wasn't done.

Julie savagely blinked back the unexpected tears that gathered in her beautiful brown eyes.

She took Kirsten's hand in her own and squeezed it, and their hearts spoke to each other.

Emma blew her nose with a hearty trumpet, making everyone grin. Breaking the emotional scene, just as she intended, she announced her barbeque sauce was ready and the grill better get lit.

Wolf fired up the large grill as Emma produced hefty slabs of ribs. She had enough to feed an army, which was handy, since the doorbell rang and Hunter entered the room as Kirsten opened the door.

In his hands, he carried an immense Angel Food cake and luscious, perfectly ripened strawberries, along with a carton of whipping cream.

"Hello. I hope no one minds if I invite myself." He flashed his engaging grin, and Rachel hurried over to him. He seemed to bring out the best in her.

Seeing the change in his ex-wife, he thought it rather a shame the transformation never lasted long.

During dinner, they kept the conversation light. Damien asked Kirsten if she planned on going on the Boston Tour to check out the beautiful architecture in that city. Before she or Rachel could say a word, Wolf tossed in his two cents.

"If it's important Damien, she'll go."

"Oh yeah, it's damn important, Wolf. That tour can make or break an upcoming architect." Damien told him.

"Sugar pie," Steve zeroed in on Kirsten, as well. "When is this little soiree to take place?" He asked.

"In two weeks," she told him. "I still don't feel right about going, but Denny and I had made plans with a bunch of other kids. Trish was supposed to go, too. I feel bad for Troy. He was her boyfriend, sort of."

Hunter leaned over and bumped her with his shoulder. "I have it on the best authority. Your friend would want you to go. She'd be so angry if you stopped living because of this."

"I know," she whispered. "I'll go and try to have a good time. It's just going to be so weird."

Conversation turned to other subjects, mostly centering around Kirsten and her plans for the future. It kept her mind off tomorrow and Trish's funeral as she began eating; something she hadn't been able to manage prior to this.

The group enjoyed the impromptu dinner party, and after desert, Julie sat back. For now, she was satisfied, but she'd have to hit her stash as soon as she got home.

"It appears we have a small summit. I think we need to talk about my sire, Kirsten's safety, and what we're all going to do to see nothing happens to her."

The wind picked up, and the temperature dropped, so the party moved inside.

They gathered around the dining room table, and Julie took it upon herself to light a candle as the others settled themselves.

"Okay, let's talk." Wolf said, and the spontaneous meeting began.

Chapter 26

M onday dawned wet and windy. Thunder rolled, and lightening sizzled in the air. The nasty weather suited Kirsten's mood. Sunshine would have been wrong. This was just so right.

Today, they would bury her best friend and her mother and dad. Her life, as she had known it, would be over, and there would not and could not be any real closure for her. The very idea of forgetting Trish, Michele, and Nate was ridiculous.

Kirsten stood in the shower and let the tears come. She had cried more, in the past few days, than she had ever cried in her life. She suspected more tears would come.

Stepping from the shower, she could hear voices coming from the direction of the kitchen. She recognized her mother and father's voices and picked up on Abram's unique accented baritone. So, he was here as well, Kirsten thought as she toweled herself dry.

As she dried her hair, she forced herself to think about Abram in her home. It was a welcome thought. Kirsten liked the rather taciturn man. She wanted to think about anything other than the ordeal ahead of her.

She added a touch of pink gloss to her lips, and then, went into her room to dress. She chose a cashmere sweater and skirt of soft plum.

Kirsten knew her mother would have a fit over the fact she wasn't dressed in black, but Kirsten knew Trish wouldn't have liked that. Both girls enjoyed color, and Kirsten knew all too well Trish's thoughts on wearing all black.

"It's stupid, Kirsten," Trish had said after attending a funeral, "It's stupid and morbid. I hope when I die, someone has the good taste to show up in red. Funerals should be a celebration of the person's life. Wearing black and being all morbid and stuff, well, that's just dumb and selfish."

"Well Trish, I'm not wearing red, but I know you loved this outfit, so I'm wearing it," Kirsten whispered.

Abram, with his sensitive hearing heard the defiant whisper and grinned. He slid his eyes over to look at Julie, who had been sitting quietly, the whole time, and saw her hide her own smirk.

Damn, he thought, the girl is getting to both of them.

Kirsten glided into the room and saw her mother's frown as she took in the girl's attire, but, before Rachel could say anything, Julie turned and did her own perusal.

The plum outfit suited the girl and the low-heeled, elegant pumps Kirsten wore were a perfect touch, as was the small black clutch the girl was kneading with nervous fingers.

"How lovely," Julie said with a soft smile. "You need one thing, and I believe I have that one thing to finish off your outfit."

From her purse, she withdrew a small box. Opening it, she removed a small gold pendent. It bore the Star of David, and in each of the points, twinkled a small amethyst. Julie fastened it around Kirsten's neck and stood back.

"Yes, just the thing."

Kirsten looked down at the beautiful and obviously very old piece. Her finger gently touched the stones and looking up, her beautiful amber eyes swam with tears.

"This is beautiful, and I'll make sure to get it back to you." She said.

Julie shook her head. "No, it's yours to keep. I want you to have it."

"You've given me so much," Kirsten whispered, "I don't know if I can ever thank you enough."

Julie squeezed her hand, and still holding it, guided her to a chair. Emma bustled around the kitchen, whipping up food to fortify the three family members.

"I'm making French toast, young lady, and you're going to eat some. Can't have you facing what you have to face, today, on an empty stomach." Emma turned from the stove and pointed at Kirsten with the fork she had been using. "And, don't even think to tell me you're not hungry. You'll sit and eat something. Abram, pour the girl some coffee."

Kirsten flashed a wan smile and looked over at Julie, who had taken a chair across the table.

"Are you going?" Her whisper was like spun silk.

Julie shook her head. "We can't. We can't step on holy ground, but we'll be close by. If my sire is in the area, Abram and I will know it, then maybe, we can end this thing, and you all can go back to a normal life."

Wolf reached over and took her dainty hand in his massive one and held on tight.

"Mom and I will be right there with you, honey. It'll be okay."

Rachel opened her mouth to give Wolf a snide remark, but Julie smoothly interjected before the odious woman could get the words out.

"You'll stand between your parents. We've discussed this, Kirsten. You'll stand between your parents, and your father has arranged for more policemen and women to be placed among the mourners. Abram and I will be close. I promise you. My sire will not get near you."

Julie glanced up at Wolf and received a small nod.

"I talked to the captain, last night. Four youths have gone missing. Officially, I'm not on the case, but there's a reason they think the four missing are connected somehow to Julie's sire. We'll be watching for anyone who doesn't look like they belong."

Kirsten sighed. "Dad, am I ever gonna get my life back?"

Kirsten thought back to the things they discussed, last night, after the spur-of-the-moment barbeque and meeting. She would not be allowed to go out, at night. Shopping would only be allowed with her mother and or dad in attendance. While at school, Abram would be near at hand. The Club was off limits for the time being, but she and her friends would be welcomed at Julie's home or Damien's condo. All would be welcome to use the gym or pool at Damien's place, and Julie had an amazing game room.

All in all, she didn't have room to complain, but she felt a little crowded. Resentment grew, but only toward the one responsible.

Julie's sire was to blame for it all, and she hoped in her heart of hearts that his ending would be slow and painful, especially in light of what he had done to Trish and her parents.

"And what about Hunter? Will he be around?" Kirsten had to ask. She liked it when he was close. He made her feel good, but remembering the discussion, she recalled he had said nothing while a small smile played around his beautiful mouth.

"Hunter pops up at will, Kirsten. We can't know what he will or will not do, but I'm sure he'll be around to see you now and then." Julie sighed, then got to her feet.

They had managed to get food down Kirsten's throat, but now, it was time to leave.

Julie handed Wolf her car keys. "Take my vehicle. It has two doors. Should a problem arise, it would delay things. We'll be right behind you." She whispered, and Wolf nodded.

Getting into their cars, Rachel began to complain.

"I don't understand it, Wolf. Why couldn't we just ride with them?" She looked over at the limo Abram and Julie were riding in and sighed. "I wouldn't mind riding with them."

"We're not riding with them because they can't enter holy ground. They can't enter churches and they can't enter cemeteries. What don't you understand? If we rode with them, we'd have to walk in, and that would put Kirsten in more danger."

Jesus, he thought, there's no end to the woman's avarice. She'd put their only child in danger just to get a taste of luxury, and wasn't that what their whole divorce was about? Rachel wanted money and position, and Wolf believed in serving the public good. It hadn't always been that way, he thought, or maybe he just hadn't seen it. The years of her complaining about their lack of social status and their modest home wore on Wolf. No wonder he drank.

"Mom, not now. Please don't argue with dad, now."

Kirsten's voice was awash with tears, and Rachel snapped her mouth shut. It was a fine day, she decided, when her own daughter censored her. The girl was just like her father, Rachel decided, and it didn't make her happy.

Falling into a mood of self-pity, Rachel kept silent.

They were heading south toward First Baptist when Abram's voice came over the ear bud Wolf had borrowed from the department.

"Watch yourself. You've got a tail. Two of them in a souped-up two thousand Dodge. Two more in a Chevy van."

"Got it," Wolf's voice was terse. So, they were going to try to snatch Kirsten on the way to the funeral. Not going to happen, he thought, it's just not going to happen.

"Hang on!" Wolf's voice was tight. At the same moment, he hit the brake and spun the wheel. Speeding off in the direction from which they came, he watched in the rear view mirror as the Dodge followed suit. The van was attempting to do the same, but found his path blocked by a long, long limousine.

The driver braked, climbed out of the car and made a beeline for the two men now hunkered down in the vehicle.

The thug in the passenger seat made the mistake of thinking he could take the man now charging at him like a raging bull. The next thing the minion knew, his feet were dangling, and his throat was gripped in the hardest hand he ever had the misfortune to run into.

"Leave the girl alone." Abram's voice was a low rumble. To add weight to his words, he allowed his eyes to burn red and flashed his fangs in the thug's direction.

Abram gave the little twerp a good shake. "Do you understand me?"

The would-be kidnapper nodded his head, unable to speak. His friend came around the front of the van and attempted to remove his friend from Abram's grip. It was like clawing at steel. Abram turned and his hand snaked out, grabbing the other youth by the throat.

"That goes for you, too. Go back to your master. Tell him he's failed. Tell him he will *always* fail. Make sure you tell him that, and make sure you tell him who it was who stopped you."

He gave them each another shake, and then, tossed them none too gently as cars began to pull over. Drivers were sticking their heads out of windows, asking what was going on.

Julie stepped from the limo and many were shocked to see the woman they had only seen in the society pages standing next to her car.

"It's nothing. They tried to run us off the road. My driver has the situation well in hand." She sent them all a charming smile.

"Want us to call the cops?" one driver called out.

"No, but thank you. I believe they have learned their lesson for today."

Julie's BMW had speed, but the Dodge was quickly gaining on them. Wolf kept his hands steady on the wheel, but they were cold.

Rachel paled in the passenger seat, as she finally became aware of the danger.

"Wolf, what if they catch us?" She whispered.

He shook his head. "Not gonna happen, Rachel. Just sit tight and hang on."

Kirsten, in the back seat, remained quiet. She, too, knew what was happening, but she trusted her dad. She knew Wolf wouldn't let them get her. He had just said as much.

Wolf, about to make another frantic spin-out, glanced in his mirrors and saw a bright red Jag coming up behind the Dodge. The two in the other car saw it, as well.

The driver of the Jag pulled alongside the Dodge, and Wolf couldn't believe his eyes. Hunter was driving, and judging by the smile on his face, was having the time of his life.

Wolf made his one eighty and could see Hunter crank his wheel into the side of the Dodge. Wolf winced at the sound of screeching metal and saw the Jag T-bone the Dodge, sending it into a ditch.

Wolf raised his hand in thanks, and Hunter gave a quick nod as Hunter strolled up to have a conversation with the driver of the now defunct Dodge.

Hunter leaned into the car through the now broken window. Neither man in the car could get out, and he had a captive audience.

"Hi. How're you doing?" He gave them a sunny smile, and the driver averted his eyes. It was painful to look into those glorious and blazing blue eyes.

"Things seem to have gotten out of hand. I'm going to give you a little friendly advice. Step away from this situation, now, while you still can. The next time you see my face, it won't be quite so pleasant."

He strolled back to his car, now in perfect condition, climbed into the driver's seat, and sped away.

He grinned in satisfaction. Lance, he knew, wouldn't be happy about another failed plan. When would he learn, Hunter wondered. When would either of them learn?

Hunter was tired. He had been away from home for too long. He missed it. He missed being with his brothers. His most fervent wish was that Julie would finally get it right and they *all* could go home.

Wolf pulled into the church parking lot, which was already filling up. Some of the cars were unmarked cruisers, so he knew there would be cops, inside and out. It made him feel mildly better.

They waited until Hunter's gay red Jag pulled in alongside of him and Julie's limo glided to a halt on the street across from the church.

"Looks like some legends are true," Wolf muttered to Hunter and was awarded with a wide grin.

Hunter reached into the car and helped Rachel, and then, Kirsten alight from it. Still holding Kirsten's hand, he gave it a small pat.

"Death isn't the end, Kirsten. Remember that." He told her and she gave him a wan smile. Tears gathered in the corner of her eyes, but she said nothing.

Entering the church, Wolf, Rachel and Kirsten watched as Trish's grandmothers hurried to greet them. Nate's brothers joined the small group, as well, and all engulfed Kirsten in warm hugs.

"I'm so glad you came." Mattie said, holding onto Kirsten's arm with one arm and Nate's mother, Theresa with the other.

"I had to come, granny Mattie," Kirsten said. She slid her eyes past one of Nate's brothers and saw the three coffins lined up at the head of the church.

"We thought it best to have the caskets closed," Theresa said. Her usually warm brown eyes drowned in tears, and her unlined face bore the signs of grief. "The funeral home did their best, but it just didn't look like them. Mattie, my boys, and I went to see them, yesterday. Under the circumstances, closed is better."

One of Nate's brothers touched Wolf on the arm and gave a small jerk with his head. Wolf followed him to the back of the church.

"We know you aren't officially working on this, Wolf, but is there anything you can tell us? Anything for us to hold onto?"

Wolf wanted to give him a soothing lie, but that wouldn't have been right, so he shook his head.

"If they know anything, they're not telling me. I'm too close to this, so they wouldn't keep me in the loop."

The other man nodded. "Yeah, that's what we figured. But, if you hear anything, you'll tell us, right? They'll let you do that much?"

"Yeah, I'll tell you." Wolf turned to rejoin his family, but the man put his hand on Wolf's arm again, delaying him.

"The way we figure it, Kirsten is in danger." Seeing the truth in Wolf's eyes, he nodded. "Figured that, too. Look man, I'll be honest. We all thought Nate lost his mind when he and Michele became friends with you and your ex-wife. Here you are, a Southern gentleman and all, and we are what we are. We never figured you two would or could remain friends. In a way, you didn't. You became family. So, I'm here to tell you… you need help with Kirsten. If she needs anything, you let us know. We'll be happy; hell, more than happy to help out where and when we can. We just wanted you to know that."

Touched, Wolf pulled the grieving man into a fierce one-armed bear hug. "It's good to know," Wolf managed to say, once he got past the huge lump in his throat. "Very good to know."

The services began, and they suited Michele, Nate and Trish. They were dignified and sweet, with an uplifting message.

"Death is not the end," The minister told the mourners, and for once, Wolf believed it.

Hunter, standing in the back of the venerable old church, smiled softly. Hadn't he just said the same thing? It was nice to hear someone else believed it, as well.

Leaving the church, Kirsten's eyes met Julie's, and the girl could see some of her own sorrow mirrored in the vampire's expressive dark eyes.

It was startling for Kirsten to remember that Julie and Abram both were vampires. She felt as if she was living in a horror movie, only the threat was very real, and there would be no commercial breaks.

The services at graveside were poignant, sweet and mercifully short.

Both of Trish's grandmothers looked frail and exhausted. Wolf, watching Mattie especially closely, saw the old woman weave, and his heart broke for her.

She's burying her only child, he thought. How does someone hold up after that kind of loss, he wondered.

Leaving the cemetery, Mattie walked over to Kirsten and hugged her, tightly.

"You come see me, now and then, sweetie. Let me know how you're doing." She reached up and patted Wolf's cheek and hugged Rachel.

Turning away, she took the arm a young man and slowly made her way to the waiting limo provided by the funeral home. She never looked back.

The rest of the mourners dispersed, and somehow, Kirsten, along with her parents, was alone with the three coffins, now waiting to be lowered into the ground.

Kirsten placed her hand on Trish's pristine white one, and slowly, she laid her head on the cover. Wolf knew she needed this moment, and he and Rachel stood close-by, should she need them.

Wolf spied several plainclothes cops, hovering here and there, waiting for Wolf and his family to leave. Every man and woman there knew Kirsten was in some sort of danger. The captain hadn't been real clear on just what, other than to say she was in danger of being kidnapped. So, they waited.

Finally, Kirsten straightened up. Her lovely face was chalky, and her amber eyes were heavy-lidded from crying, but she seemed more at peace.

She reached for Wolf's hand and, then her mother's.

"C'mon. Let's go home."

Chapter 27

L ance glared at the four idiots standing in front of him. Failure! Once again, failure!

"It was an easy task, you fools." Lance's voice was deceptively soft, his demeanor calm. "You had to intercept one young girl. Would you care to explain?"

The four glanced at each other, but remained silent.

"I asked you a question!" Lance roared, and the bravest and more foolish stepped forward.

"It wasn't our fault, Master." Lance liked it when they called him Master. Not this time, though.

"Not your fault? Whose fault was it, then? Mine, perhaps?"

"No, sir, Master. It was the woman and her driver. It was their fault." The thug was whimpering now, terrified of what was to come.

"What woman?" Lance snarled. The soft timbre of his voice was gone. He had a pretty good idea who the woman was. The thug's next words confirmed it.

"Dude! She was a total babe! Long dark hair, big brown eyes and legs up to her ears!" One of the other thugs ventured.

Lance's wrath tore through any illusion. His four thugs saw him for what he was. It was not a pretty sight.

The elegance was gone, as was his sublime features. Now, his skin looked like old leather. His few tendrils of hair coiled tightly to his scalp, a scalp that was dotted with liver- colored spots and scabs.

His teeth were no longer gleaming and white. Rather, they were green, and all of them were pointed, like small daggers. His thin and cracked lips barely covered them.

Lance's breath puffed out in fetid little balls, nauseating the one he now held in a vice-like grip.

He looked at the thug in his grasp and lost all semblance of control.

Lance dug his nails in deep, penetrating the chest cavity of the one now in his clutches.

With a deep growl, he rendered his victim, completely disemboweling him. The stench filled the room as his gut burst, spilling its contents on the floor.

Lance fell on him and began to devour his victim before the young man was dead.

His high-pitched screams tapered off to a whimper, and then, there was nothing.

The three remaining thugs lost control of their bladders.

They wanted to run but knew that was useless. He'd catch them before they got out of the building.

The only recourse they had was to stand by and watch this monster devour their friend.

His blood-lust finally satisfied, he pointed to the remains.

"Get rid of this. Forget the girl. I have another job for you to do." He gave them a slip of paper with an address on it.

"I need you to check this out. I believe this building will be perfect for my needs. Come back here when you are finished."

The thug took the blood-smeared paper from Lance's claw and looked at the address.

"This is the old tannery. I know it. What, exactly, are we looking for?"

Lance sighed. He was saddled with complete fools, but what was a vampire to do? He had to take what he could get.

"Privacy!" He snarled. "This building is for sale. I intend to buy it, but I desire privacy. That's all you need to know."

It would be perfect, and the building would have been his if not for interference. That little twit, Julie, is to blame, he decided. She has resources to try and stop him. Fine, he had resources, as well. She's stupid if she thinks she can stop me, he thought, I'll have my due before this year is out.

Thinking of Julie, it became clear to him. She was gathering a small army of her own. Now, if she would just have cooperated, none of this would be necessary. The deaths, up until now, were her fault, he decided. Still, she was necessary. Only another vampire could survive what was coming, next.

Kirsten remained quiet all the way home. For once, her mother didn't seem to be in the mood to snipe at her father, and while the truce was temporary, she was grateful.

Wolf spied the gay red sport car Hunter drove, waiting for them as they arrived home. In short order, Julie's limo glided to a halt next to the car Wolf was driving.

"Come on in. I'll make coffee." Rachel sang out while unlocking the door.

She could feel the eyes of her neighbors peering out windows, and she reveled in their interest.

Rachel didn't have much use for her neighbors. Solidly middle-class, they didn't have the polish she so desired for herself, but entertaining Julie King, even under these circumstances, was something she could rub their noses in.

Julie, understanding Rachel's avarice, shook her head. The woman just didn't get it. Money doesn't buy class, nor did it buy happiness. Julie had more money than anyone, and she wasn't happy. Why couldn't the odious woman understand that?

Once again, Julie wondered how a woman like this birthed such a sweet girl like Kirsten.

The little group gathered in Rachel's kitchen and waited while Rachel did the honors.

Hunter produced a cake, and Wolf grinned at him. "You have quite the sweet tooth." Wolf observed and Hunter flashed him a wide grin.

"Yes, yes I do."

Kirsten gave him an enormous slice and watched with some amusement as he scooped the first bite into his mouth.

The group sat around the table and spoke of mundane things. They spoke of school, cars, and Kirsten's upcoming dance. Anything to keep her mind off the funerals they just attended.

Kirsten's pale face and red eyes were painful to see. Try as she might, she just couldn't contribute to the conversation, unless asked a direct question.

When the doorbell peeled, she jumped up. "I'll get it." She fled from the kitchen. She would take care of whomever, this way, and then go to her room. She needed a little time to be alone. Needed time to reconcile herself to her loss.

She opened the door to Damien and Steve. The dress designer carried a large bag over his shoulder and a smaller one in his hand.

"Hello, Sugar Plum." Steve kissed her soft cheek as she let them in the house.

"We just wanted to stop in to see how you're doing." Damien explained.

Kirsten didn't know if she should be touched at their thoughtfulness or irritated. She knew full well what was in that bag, but she didn't think she was all that interested.

She swallowed the irritation and kissed both of the men.

"We're in the kitchen. Come on back. I'll get you some coffee. Hunter brought a cake." She gave them a wry grin.

Damien took her hand. "Hold up, Kirsten. I want to talk to you."

She looked up at him, her eyes huge question marks as Steve hung the bags on a closet door and went ahead to join his new friends in the kitchen.

"I know this is a difficult time for you. Steve and I have been friends since forever, so while I can't understand your pain, I know how devastated I would be if something happened to the pain in the ass."

A small giggle bubbled past her lips.

"That being said, and from what I know of you, let me just say this. You're never going to forget her, Kirsten, and a small part of you will always ache for what might have been, and that's okay. Just remember this, though. As long as you remember her; honor her memory, she's not really gone."

Damien honestly didn't know if he helped or made her grief worse, but her pale face and red-rimmed eyes hurt him.

She reached up and kissed his cheek.

"You know something, Damien. You're the first, other than my dad, who acknowledged my grief. Thank you."

He patted her cheek and let her lead him into the kitchen.

"So, let me know when you want to see my creation. I'm so anxious to see you in it, Sweetie Pie." Steve beamed at her as she and Damien made their way to the kitchen, and she smiled back.

The man had more than his share of positive energy, and she couldn't help but feel a little better.

Rachel opened her mouth to make a reply, but Kirsten, tired of her mother's interference, quickly replied.

"Just let me finish my coffee, and then, freshen up a little." She smiled, shyly, "I can't wait to see it, either."

"Was Trish planning on becoming an architect, too?" Damien asked. Kirsten shook her head, making her pretty blonde curls bounce.

"No, she was in pre-med." Kirsten sighed. "She would have made an amazing doctor." She added.

Damien nodded and filed the information away for future reference. He had an idea brewing, but needed some time to work out the details.

Kirsten finally pushed back from the table and gave Steve a small smile. "Time to see how this creation of yours turned out." She said and headed for the living room to retrieve the dress.

"I'll help you." Rachel bounced out of her chair to follow.

Unhappy with the lack of attention shown to her, she fully intended to give her daughter a piece of her mind. Julie, correctly reading the situation, gracefully exited her chair, as well.

"I'm coming, too. I can't wait to see how she looks in it."

That little maneuver left Rachel biting her lip. She wanted to tell

216

Kirsten to stop the dramatics. People die, and that's just how life goes. Julie's interference merely postponed the little chat Rachel planned to have with her daughter, later.

The dress fit like a dream, and it suited her. The softly draped bodice and short capped sleeves showed off her toned arms. The slim skirt accented her legs, and from the small bag, Steve produced strappy, spiked sandals, encrusted with amber crystals.

Julie scooped that glorious mass of blonde curls away from her youthful face, letting the rest fall in a gorgeous cascade.

"I think some amber hair jewelry would work." Julie muttered and then turned to Rachel. "What do you think?" Rachel nodded. On most, the hair jewelry would be too much, but Kirsten could carry it off.

"She'll need a wrap. The nights are getting cold," Rachel added. "I may have something that would work." Getting into the mood, she hustled to her room and came back with a short black cocktail coat. "Let's try this."

Kirsten slipped her arms into the coat, knowing it was one of her mother's prized possessions. She turned to let the two women see, and Julie smiled. "Perfect!" She decreed and let the way out of the bedroom.

The men, sitting in the kitchen took one look and rose to their feet. That was the impact the young girl, now looking so beautiful and so vulnerable, had.

"You look beautiful." Wolf took her small hand in his large one.

Steve walked around her, removing the cocktail coat and examined the dress and the girl wearing it with a critical eye. He thought it was one of the best things he had ever done.

"You look perfect," Steve gushed, "Hell, you *are* perfect! I want to design more for you!" Julie laughed, and his cheeks burned. "I want to design for you, too." he told her, rather sheepishly.

Julie patted his cheeks. "Don't fret, darling. I understand."

Uncomfortable with being the center of attention, Kirsten returned to her room. She carefully removed the dress and placed it back in the bag, hanging it in her closet. It would be safe, there, until Steve and Damien left.

In the privacy of her room, she let the tears flow. Trish would have loved all of this, and it wasn't fair she couldn't be here, sharing all of this. So, she let the tears flow, sobbing harshly.

A soft knock interrupted her, and she sighed. Would these people never leave her alone, she wondered.

Hunter poked his head in. "Hey kiddo. Sorry to interrupt, but I need to talk to you. It's kinda important." He sat on the bed next to her, and took one of her hands in his, rubbing it with his other hand.

"I have a message for you. You'll know who it's from." He said. She wiped her eyes and looked up at him, his sheer essence bringing her comfort.

"What's the message?" She asked.

"Okay, here it is. 'Knock it off, Kirsten. I'm in a better place and having the time of my non-life. Stop with the water works, already. It's a waste of time and won't change a freakin' thing. Get on with your life, and I'll be watching. Love ya, girl. Now, get on with it.'"

It was so typically Trish, Kirsten felt a shiver race up her spine. She could almost hear her friend's voice.

"How did you come by this message, Hunter?" She asked.

Hunter shrugged. "Damien isn't the only one around here with special abilities." He didn't elaborate, and Kirsten didn't delve.

The grieving girl put her head against Hunter's broad shoulder and sighed.

"My life certainly has taken a strange turn," She said. "I'm wondering if I'll ever get it back."

Hunter draped an arm around her shoulder and pulled her close.

"It can't go back the way it was, and it will certainly turn out differently than, perhaps, what you envisioned. But Kirsten, it is *your* life. You make it the very best you can. You will do this, not just for you, but for your lost friend."

She straightened up and blew her nose. "Yeah, if I live long enough." She said with a wry grin.

"Oh, I think you're going to live long enough. You have people looking out for you, and those people are resourceful. Don't underestimate them, or yourself. Now, let's go back in the kitchen before all the cake is gone."

A small laugh escaped from between her lips. She placed her hand in the one he offered, and together, they left her bedroom.

"What's your story, Hunter?" She asked, and he smiled.

"Oh, me? I don't have a story. I'm here to do a job, and do it I will. I'm anxious for this to be over. I miss my home."

"Where is your home?" She asked, and Hunter gave a small laugh.

"Oh, here and there, Kirsten. Here and there."

Wolf looked around as Kirsten and Hunter came back to the kitchen. He thought she looked a little better. Obviously, Hunter and she had talked. Whatever was said obviously did his daughter some good.

Those long golden eyes, so like his daughter's, studied the small group. He could only wonder how they all became friends, for friends is exactly what they were. Only one was missing. Wolf made a decision.

"Let's get Emma and then order pizzas." The idea was unanimously approved, and while Abram left to bring the woman to the house, Wolf called and placed the order.

This was not a meeting. There was no talk of the upcoming war. It was simply a group of friends gathered together for pizza and beer.

He wondered how Julie and Abram would handle having a piece of pie. The idea brought a chuckle to his lips as he left to place the call.

Chapter 28

While they ate, Julie pushed her own considerable power toward Damien. She had an idea, but didn't want to discuss it with the others. This would be for her and Damien to do.

So, they discussed it in their own unique way. She held back, not wanting to make him ill. For the first time, since they met, the architect didn't look so wan; so ill.

Damien could feel Julie searching out his thoughts. Her effort did not bring on the usual headache. This felt warm and soft. It was something else to think about, he decided.

Vampires weren't warm and fuzzy creatures, but that was exactly how he felt as she searched his mind; his thoughts.

"Kirsten, will you be going back to school, tomorrow?"

Rachel asked. Kirsten nodded and then locked eyes with Hunter. "It's what Trish wants."

If her answer was cryptic, no one picked up on it, with one

exception. Hunter beamed at her, pleased.

"I'm sorry I missed the fashion show," Emma offered, helping herself to a slice of pie. Kirsten reached for the older woman's hand and squeezed.

"Then I guess you'll have to come and help me get dressed. We'll have a Dressing Kirsten party." She said with a small laugh.

"You're on!" Emma told her, grinning.

Julie sighed and leaned her head on the back of the sofa. She thought the pizza interesting but didn't think she could handle a steady diet of the spicy food.

Abram flashed a rare smile at her, and she knew he was thinking the same thing.

"If everyone is through eating, I'll wrap up some of this pizza for you all to take home." Kirsten announced as she picked up the boxes. Hunter's smile was wide and charming.

"Don't forget some for me, too." He told her.

Damien and Julie were off in a corner, holding a normal conversation.

"I'll swing by your place and pick you up, tomorrow. Will ten work for you?" She asked.

Damien nodded. "I have to take a look at a building site in the morning, but I'll be home, by then. It won't take me that long." He paused for a moment, studying the floor. "Will she be safe while at school?"

Julie shrugged. "You tell me. He's going to get bolder and slyer."

Damien nodded again. "I think she's going to be okay for a while," he said, then added, "Still I think we all need to be alert. Especially Kirsten and Rachel."

She was punctual. Damien shouldn't have been surprised, but his experience with women taught him they could, and often did, show up in their own time. Not Julie, though. Of course, he thought, she is no ordinary woman.

"I made a couple of calls, this morning," she told him, "to ease our way. I've also got an idea, but it will be up to Rachel if she wants to cooperate or has the desire to cooperate."

Damien looked over at Julie. He thought she looked paler than the day before.

"Are you feeling all right? You look a little peaked." he told her.

She shrugged. "I didn't rest, last night. There are plans to be made, and I wanted to get a jump on them." She sighed, showing fatigue. "First, and this stays between us if you don't mind, I want to invest in Steve's enterprise. He has talent. I spoke with Giorgio, last night. He had such high praise for his protégé. So, I want a piece of his action. Then, this morning, I did some investigating. My sire has purchased a building, two actually. They are secluded and perfect for whatever it is he is planning. We will have to be vigilant. Next, I am beginning to wrap up my business, here. I've stayed too long in this place. My acquaintances are beginning to mention the fact I don't seem to age. That's rather inconsiderate of them, but what can one expect when dealing with mortals." She gave a careless shrug, "So, it's almost time for me to leave. That being said, I want to make sure Kirsten is taken care of, one way or another."

Damien considered her words. "Okay, I'm forced to ask the question. Why?"

"Leave it to you to go straight to the heart of the matter. Why do I care? I don't know. Maybe, if I take an interest in her, this will all end. I do like her, she is a sweet girl, but she is mortal."

Damien grinned at her.

"In other words, you have no idea why you are doing this."

"Not a clue."

They arrived at their destination and were met at the front doors, and then, escorted to the Chancellor's office. Neither were surprised to find the Deans of both schools in attendance, as well.

The meeting lasted less than two hours, and by the end of it, an agreement had been reached. Damien and Julie each wrote out hefty checks to get the ball rolling.

There were handshakes all around, and Julie and Damien were off to their final destination.

"Now we'll see what Rachel is made of." Julie remarked.

They found Rachel at her desk, right next to the receptionist. She may be a paralegal, Damien thought, but her employers see her as little more than a secretary. The thought rankled, a little.

"Hello Rachel." Julie leaned a hip against Rachel's desk and smiled as the other woman's jaw dropped.

"Julie! Damien! What are you doing here?" Out of the corner of her eye, she saw one of the senior partners leave his office and goggle at the two now conversing with her.

"Have a little business to conduct with your bosses." Damien grinned a particularly charming smile. "And, I believe this is one of them, now. But, before we get tied up in a meeting, let us ask you this. Do you like your job, or would you like something a little more?"

Rachel cocked her head, wondering where this was leading. She met Damien's patient gray eyes with a direct stare of her own.

"I like this job. I like dealing with the law, and I love research. Why?"

"You haven't answered the question, Rachel. Would you like more?" Julie interrupted.

Rachel shrugged. "I have a daughter to support. Wolf is great about paying child support and always contributes more than he was ordered to, but I'd like to give her a better life. So, yeah, I'd like more."

The senior partner of the law firm walked up to the trio, giving Rachel a questioning look.

She handled the introductions and allowed a small sour smile to cross her lips. The usually taciturn man was positively falling all over himself. It was almost comical to watch him fawn over Julie and Damien.

As he ushered them into his office, Julie stopped at the door. "Rachel, come join us. This concerns you, as well."

"Oh, there's no need for a paralegal to join us." He said and was smoothly interrupted by Julie's raised hand. Damien decided to let her handle things. He would enjoy the show.

"I said this concerns her." Julie said in her most imperious tone, "Therefore, it's important she join us. If you have objections..." She left the rest unsaid, but the man got the message.

"Of course. Rachel, please?" He was most anxious to please as big fat retainers and fees danced through his head.

The three sat in burgundy leather chairs and faced the partner.

"Now, what is it exactly you want from us?" He asked.

"First of all, we will be hiring you to initiate a scholarship fund. The Patricia Elizabeth Rollings Fund." The partner gave Rachel a questioning look. "The young girl who was murdered, along with her parents." Rachel said softly.

"Oh yes, of course. A tragedy." Julie could tell the man had no idea what they were talking about. It didn't matter. He didn't matter.

Damien, sitting between Julie and Rachel, tensed. The man was oblivious, and Damien wasn't sure he wanted this firm to take care of the business at hand. Julie put a calming hand on his arm.

"Let's play this out." She told him, mind to mind, and knew he got the message when she felt him relax.

"Mister Crist and I have considerable dealings we wish to do with your firm. Of course, there is the scholarship, and if we can come to a mutual agreement, we are prepared to do considerable business with you."

"All right." the partner waited for the other shoe to drop.

"Rachel, here, has worked for you for a considerable time. Is her work satisfactory?"

Confusion crossed the old man's face. Julie's lips tightened. He doesn't know, she thought, he has no idea what his employees are doing.

"I'd have to ask her immediate supervisor," the man began and Julie waved that aside.

"Get him in here." The order was given by someone accustomed to having her way.

The old man felt he had displeased the woman and her companion, somehow, and all of those lovely fees were dancing just out of his reach.

He buzzed the intercom. "Get young Dennis in here." he ordered.

A young man of about thirty came in, looking pale and confused. In all of his years working for the firm, he had never been summoned into the inner sanctum, before. He wondered if this would cost him his job.

"Rachel works under you, does she not?" the partner's tone was gruff.

"Yes, sir, she does." Dennis answered.

"She do a good job?"

Dennis nodded. "Yes sir. She does an excellent job. She seems to have a knack and can do research for any suit in record time."

Julie looked at the old man sitting across from her. She raised an elegant brow at him, and the man's face blanched. A great deal is riding on what happens next, he thought, and to that end tried to make himself more amendable; more reachable.

"Fine. This is what we would like done," Julie began and caught Damien smirk out of the corner of her eye. "You will set up the funds for the purpose mentioned. This is my portfolio. As you can see, it's quite extensive. Mister Crist is also willing to allow you to handle his legal business, as well. Here's the catch. Damien and I will set up funds for Rachel to go back to school." At Rachel's gasp, Julie patted her hand, silently telling the woman to be still. "We will see to it that all of Rachel's expenses, including living expenses and her daughter's expenses, not met by Rachel's ex-husband, will be taken care of by us. Providing Rachel passes the bar, she will be taken on by you, and in the proper amount of time, will make partner. If any of this is unacceptable to you, speak now, and we won't take up any more of your time."

The old man looked from Rachel to Julie and back again.

"There is one provision. We will take her on, but not if she practices criminal law. We don't handle those cases, and her grades must be exemplary. Our attorneys all made law review."

Rachel felt as if her world was spinning. She wasn't sure she liked this new twist to her ordered life. Here she was, in her mid-forties, and now she was going back to school? Could she hack it? So much was riding on her, and she didn't know if she was up to it all.

"We'll talk later, Rachel." Julie murmured to her as she gathered up her things, preparing to leave.

They shook hands all around, and then, Julie and Damien took their leave.

Rachel went back to her desk in a daze. Her world certainly had taken a strange turn. She wanted to put her head down on her desk, but the senior partner was watching. So, she gathered up her files and headed for the library. She had work to do.

Chapter 29

Lance walked around the old abandoned building. The real estate agent, anxious to make a sale, chattered along.

"As you can see, the building is solid. It does need some work, though. Are you thinking of opening a factory?"

"Hmmm," he said.

She ignored his non-committal reply, thinking of the nice commission she'd make if she unloaded this white elephant.

Her incessant chattering began to grate on his nerves. He thought how lovely it would be to just rip out her throat and be done with it, but sadly, he just couldn't do that. Too many people knew she was with him, and he needed to keep a lower profile.

They walked through the office areas, and then, into the bowels of the building. Yes, he thought, this will suit, very well.

Lance flashed a charming smile, and the woman with him blushed. Lance turned away from her and rolled his eyes.

"How much is the building?" He asked, and she named a price.

"Of course, I'll be happy to help you arrange financing through our office." She chirped.

Lance shook his head. "That won't be necessary. I'll be paying cash."

He took another look around and flashed that charming smile, once again. "I believe I will take this. It's perfect for my needs."

So delighted at making the sale, she began to babble. "We can go back to my office, fill out the paperwork, and I'll present to the seller, right away."

There would be no haggling, she thought. He was going to offer full asking price. She couldn't believe her luck. With what she was going to make on this sale, she could almost retire.

Lance took her elbow and guided her out of the old building. Even with his superior control, he thought if he had to spend five more minutes with this chatter-box, he would kill her and be done with it.

He walked her to her car, and then, stepped away from her, motioning to one of his thugs whose name he never bothered to learn. He lowered his voice, so it would not carry to the waiting agent.

"This building will be perfect. I'm going with this twit to write an offer. While I'm doing that, you will gather these materials. December is coming faster than we think, and all must be ready."

Lance turned to her and flashed a cheery smile, masking his contempt for her.

"I will follow you to your office. I'm most anxious to get this settled." he told her.

"Yes! Of course! If you write an offer, I can deliver it, right away."

Lance climbed into his car, another new purchase, and watched through narrow eyes as his minions scrambled to do his bidding.

He took one more glance at the old factory, pleased with his decision. It really was perfect.

Carefully, he pulled out behind the agent. I've missed a kill, but there's always later, he thought.

For now, he had other fish to fry.

Kirsten moved like a shadow through her classes. Hearing condolences from kids who hadn't really known Trish was painful, but thanks to her friends, she managed to get through the day.

Rachel was waiting for her when she got home.

"Kirsten! You are never going to guess what happened to me, today!"

Kirsten had a nagging headache and very little energy, but she tried to show a little enthusiasm for whatever it was that was making her mother so happy.

"What happened?"

"Julie and Damien came to the office today! I can't tell you everything that happened. It's confidential, you know, but before the meeting was over, they strong-armed the senior partner. Oh Kirsten! You should have seen it! I'm going back to school, and if I do well, I'll be able to make partner! Just think! A full partner!"

Kirsten sat down with a thump. "Are you serious? I didn't even know you wanted to go to law school! Mom, if this is what you want, I'm really happy for you."

Another turn of events. Kirsten wondered if her life would ever even out.

Rachel beamed at her daughter, and then, tossed back her hair.

"If you don't mind, I sort of have a date. We're just meeting for drinks, so I won't be late. What a day this has been!"

Kirsten shook her pretty head, then walked over to her mother and gave her a huge hug.

"I don't mind. Actually, I have some homework, but I think I'm going to head over to Damien's. I'd like to use his gym, and I have a couple of questions for him. I should be home by ten."

Kirsten changed into a comfortable pair of jeans and phoned Damien.

"I'd like to use your gym, if it's okay with you," she said, and then paused.

"Something else, Kirsten?" he prompted.

"Yeah, I have a couple of questions about school."

Damien chuckled. "Tell you what. Come on over, I'll give you the code to get up to my house. We'll order something in, answer your questions, and if I can work up the energy, I'll go down with you."

"That sounds great! Can I bring anything?" she asked.

"Nah. Just your books."

She hung up after telling him she'd be there in thirty minutes and after receiving the code for his elevator.

Rachel was positively glowing as she and Kirsten left the house at the same time.

Rachel climbed into her car, and Kirsten climbed into her's. Neither of them saw the thug loitering across the street, hidden behind a large tree.

Smiling to himself, he punched in a number. "Yeah, it's me. I followed her from school. I'm looking at her house, right now, and it looks like the two of them live here, alone... What do you want me to do? She and the mother just left." He listened, gave a silent shrug and climbed into his car and drove away. He never saw Wolf pull into the driveway.

Wolf entered the silent house and walked into the kitchen. Kirsten, before leaving, had the foresight to leave him a note.

"Huh! She's gone over to Damien's." He thought for a moment and then, not wanting to be alone, called Damien and invited himself over.

Climbing back into his car, he wondered what Kirsten would think of his decision. He figured Rachel was going to go through the roof, but that wasn't his concern.

Wolf thought back to his morning. It began with a surprise call from Alicia, his former partner.

"Hey Lish! How're you doing?" He was unprepared for what was coming.

"Hey Wolf. Listen, I just have a few minutes. You know I resigned from the force, but there's a private firm looking for investigators. The money is good, we've got a little more leeway than the average cop, and they hired me. They're looking to open an office in the 'Falls.' You interested?"

Was he interested? He thought back through his long years as a cop. He thought he was doing the right thing, but it cost him his marriage and in some way, his daughter.

Wolf wanted to save the world, but he couldn't even save his best friends. How many victims? How many criminals walked the streets in spite of his best efforts?

It was a lot to think about. Working in Menominee Falls, though, could be a good thing. At this point in his life, quasi-normal hours would be a good thing, too.

He punched in Alicia's number. "Yeah, I'm interested."

She would be in town in a few days. They would talk more, then.

Damien's condo was a hive of activity. Kirsten poured over her books, firing off questions at a slightly amused Damien.

Steve bounced from room to room, gathering materials, draping them on the dress dummy he had resurrected from the good old days and grumbled around a mouthful of pins.

The island of calm in the place was Abram. Wolf was surprised to see him there but kept his poker face on.

"Howdy folks. Got the note from my little girl, here, and thought I'd pop in and see what's shaking."

"Oh, dad!" Kirsten's cheeks reddened. "I had some stuff I didn't quite understand, so Damien was nice enough to tutor me, a little."

Wolf nodded. "So I see." he said with a laugh.

He took a seat next to Abram and raised an eyebrow at him.

"I'm here because Kirsten is here. She spoke with my mistress, earlier, and made noises about getting some questions answered, and then, was planning on using the gym. That room is highly accessible. We thought it a good idea if I came over and kept an eye on things."

"Good thinking." Wolf gave him a contemplative look.

"What's your story, Abram? Other than the fact you're a vampire and devoted to the illustrious Julie King."

Abram shrugged. "I was a soldier from Crete, assigned to the House of Herod. My sole task was defending and protecting the princess when she came to live in the house of her step-father. I think I was the one constant in her short life. Even after she married Philip and bore him two sons, she depended on me. Herod kept them in his palaces. He was smitten with her, you see."

Abram gave a careless shrug. "After her sire turned her, she turned me. She depended on me and even in her un-dead state, she continued to depend on me, so here I am."

"Interesting. My mother would love to talk to you about the good ol' days, but I digress. What's Hunter's story?"

Abram shook his head. "I don't know. I only know he's been around since the very beginning. We don't know what he wants, but he watches my mistress quite closely. She's supposed to do something to end this, but we don't know what. All we know is when she runs into problems and doesn't 'solve' them correctly, he looks incredibly sad and then goes on his merry way until the next time. Julie gave him the name 'Hunter,' though, because he seems to be hunting her for whatever reason."

Damien plopped down on the sofa, next to Abram. If he thought it strange to be entertaining a vampire, it didn't show.

"That daughter of yours, Wolf. She is exceptional."

Wolf grinned. "Yeah, I always thought so. Where is she?"

"Went to change. We're gonna hit the gym, downstairs. Want to join us? I probably have some sweats that would work on you."

Wolf started to decline and then thought better of it.

Steve strolled in and walked over to the coffeepot that never seemed to be empty. Damien glanced over at him and could tell he was in a pissy mood.

"Problems, pal of mine?" he asked. Steve studied the men over the rim of the cup.

"I wanted to expand my collection, a little. Take some of Giorgio's ideas. It's not working, and that just pissed me off."

Damien smiled at his life-long friend. "We're all going to hit the gym with Kirsten. Come with us. Work up a sweat, and maybe, something will come to you."

Steve considered the offer and then tramped into his room to change. "May as well get *something* accomplished," he grumbled to no one in particular. No one felt the need to answer him, either.

While the group did their thing, Abram stood guard near the door. He felt restless. There was a hint of tension in the air, but he couldn't pinpoint the where or the why. He wondered if Julie felt it, too. It would be something to talk to her about after he made sure Kirsten arrived home, safely.

Chapter 30

Halloween arrived, and with it, a nasty storm. Sleet spread its icy wings, turning roads and sidewalks into skating rinks. Trees shed their lovely colors under the onslaught, and the wind cut through even the warmest of coats.

"Quite an end to October," Damien said, and Steve nodded. "We won't be getting many Trick or Treaters, that's for sure. Just the kids in the building?"

Damien shrugged. "Not that many kids, Steve. We bought all that candy for nothing. It'll go to waste."

Steve raised an elegant eyebrow at his friend. "My dear, dear Damien. Chocolate never goes to waste. You really should get into contact with your inner female."

Damien laughed. "Yeah, whatever."

With that, he went back to drawing. Kirsten had brought him another drawing of a Senior Center. It was good. She had talent, but her inexperience showed.

Working quickly, he made notes, pointing out some small errors and clipped them to her work.

"If Kirsten continues to show this kind of enthusiasm, and we all live through whatever is coming, I'm thinking of offering her an internship when the time is right." Damien told Steve.

"I kinda figured that, pal of mine. She's that good?"

"Yeah, she is." Damien turned to Steve and looked at him through patient gray eyes.

"I haven't had a vision for a while. Nothing. It's almost as if someone or something is jamming my channels. That worries me a great deal."

"I've noticed. What about the headaches? Those gone, too?" Steve asked.

"Not really. Just sort of a nagging ache. Some days, it's worse than others. I can't shake the feeling, though, that something big is brewing. It's a gut feeling, Steve, and I have a feeling Kirsten and Wolf are going to be right in the heart of it."

"Maybe, you're jamming yourself, Damien. You've been pushing yourself pretty hard on this newest project, and then, you've taken Kirsten under your wing, too. Add to that the fact you seem to be quite taken with Julie King, and you've got a load to carry. I'm going to make a suggestion." Steve paused and topped off his coffee.

"Don't leave me hanging, here, Stevie. What's the suggestion?"

"Nothing major. Take a day vacation. Put away your toys and drawings. Kick back. Have a beer or two and watch some ESPN. I doubt your young protégé will be showing, today. The weather's too crappy. Maybe, that will unjam you."

Damien began to grin. He really liked that idea.

He settled in making good use of his long, cushy sofa. He pulled a throw down around his shoulders and made himself comfortable.

Steve went about his business, quietly. The dress he wanted to create was finally coming together, and he was pleased.

Dusk crept in, and Steve thought to turn on a lamp, letting the soft glow permeate the room. He wanted Damien to relax, and it looked like it was working.

He leaned over Damien to flip on the lamp, and Damien's hand snaked out, grabbing Steve's wrist in a tight grip.

Steve looked down at Damien and paled. The man's eyes, usually a calm and patient gray were almost black. His lips were twisted into a grimace and sweat beaded on Damien's forehead.

"December thirty-first, Steve! December thirty-first. He has a place. It's an old factory, but I can't tell where. December thirty-first is the date. Whatever has to happen *must* happen on that date! Call Wolf and Julie. They need to know."

Damien sighed and sat up, wiping the blood from his nose. Steve motioned toward his ears as well.

So much for a day vacation, Steve thought. And, it appeared his friend was no longer jammed.

&

Julie hung up the phone and went in search of Abram. As usual, she found him in the kitchen, talking to Emma. She thought it was kind of cute, seeing them together. Cute but ludicrous. A mortal and a vampire? How on earth could they possibly make it work?

"Wolf just phoned," she began and saw Abram tense. "Apparently our friendly psychic just had a vision. He saw an old factory, but didn't see where it was. He got the date of December thirty-first. Whatever is meant to happen will happen on that date. We will have to be more vigilant as the date draws near."

"How can we be more vigilant than we are?" Abram demanded. "That poor girl doesn't have a moment to herself! How long before the stress gets to her?"

"I don't know, Abram!" Julie snapped. She ran her hands through her glossy curls. "Until Damien gets a better handle on what is going to happen and where, we're stuck."

"Your sire hasn't made a move on her since his attempts the day of the funerals." Emma piped in. "Perhaps he's lost interest or found someone else to take her place."

Julie shook her head, her face grim. "That's the thing about my sire. Once he has made a selection, there is no turning him from it."

Hunter sauntered into the kitchen, looking for a slice of peach pie that Emma just made. She slapped his hands away from the pie plate.

"That's for dinner, Hunter!" Emma scolded, making him laugh.

"It's close enough, isn't it Emma?" he asked, and she shook her head.

"Not for another hour. Have some coffee or a Coke, until then." She replied.

"So, I take it our friend had a vision, and judging by your faces, you aren't happy about it." Hunter settled on a chair. "Care to share?"

"It wasn't clear. Not counting the date he was given, we don't know any more than we did, before. December thirty-first was mentioned, along with an abandoned factory that he doesn't recognize and has no idea where it is. It could be anywhere, Hunter. My sire has resources, too. If Kirsten is still his target, he could take her anywhere. So no, we are not happy about it." Julie snapped.

Hunter's smile widened until it lit up his entire face.

"Why princess. You are becoming almost human." he teased.

"There's no need to be insulting, Hunter. I like the girl, I'll admit. She's bright, unspoiled and genuine, although how she came to be that way with that mother of hers, is beyond me." Julie fumed.

Abram glanced at Hunter, and then, looked back at Julie. "So, my question is, do we tell her? Wolf knows, but do we tell Kirsten?"

"That will be his decision, I think." Julie answered. "Personally, I feel it be wise to inform her. She won't be able to let her guard down for a moment." She ran a hand through her hair. "The thing is, she's been through so much. She's under so much stress. I just don't think it wise to add to that. But, again, it will be Wolf's decision."

"Question." Hunter raised a finger. "Why are you so concerned? She's a mere mortal, after all. You never cared about them, before. So, why are you all concerned about this one?"

"Not just 'this one,' Hunter. I've come to care for several." She shook her head. "They have touched me, here." She rested her hand where her heart beat at one time. "Emma and Wolf and Damien and Steven have touched me, but yes, especially this girl. I don't know why."

Hunter stood and walked over to her. He knew she loathed him to touch her, it was painful, but he gently ruffled that incredible mass of black curls.

"Figure it out, Princess, and soon." He advised as we walked away.

For the first time in centuries, Hunter felt real hope. Maybe, this time, she'd get it right.

Chapter 31

October flowed into November. All had been quiet, and Wolf felt forced to issue a reminder, especially to Rachel. "Just because the 'sire' hasn't made his move doesn't mean a thing. The nearer we get to December, the more cautious we will have to be. I spoke to the captain, last week. Unofficially, he told me they've been fishing bodies out of the Milwaukee River. All of them had their throats ripped out and the M.E. is sure they had no blood before they were dumped in the drink. So, while he hasn't made his move on Kirsten, it doesn't mean he's not gonna."

Now, he spoke directly to Rachel, not pulling any punches.

"I'm happy you're seeing someone and happy you've been smart enough to keep him away from the house, but I know you, Rachel. You'll get to the point that you'll want to bring him home. That's fine. Just make sure Kirsten is out of the house for the evening. Other than that, I don't care what you do."

It was gospel truth, Wolf thought, he didn't care what Rachel did.

He supposed it should have bothered him when Kirsten told him Rachel was dating someone. It didn't bother him, one bit.

That's a damn shame, he thought. It should have mattered. They were husband and wife, at one time, and shared a daughter, but the only thing Wolf felt was relief. Maybe now, he could get on with his life, just as Rachel was getting on with her own.

Seeing his words sink in, he knew Rachel was reading him wrong, and he hastened to correct any misconceptions she may harbor.

"I don't care you're seeing someone, Rachel. Personally, I hope he can put up with you for the long haul. The only thing I care about is Kirsten."

He turned to Julie who had been sitting quietly.

"You have a sense of this thing you call your sire. Give me something, anything. What's he doing?"

"Wolf, I wish I knew what to tell you. If you have a hope he's forgotten about Kirsten, crush it! My memories, what you would call dreams, are more vivid. I know he stalked me for a very long time. He has a plan that included me, but if he can't get to me, he'll use Kirsten." Julie sighed, and getting up from her seat, walked over to the small table and poured herself a glass of wine.

Sipping, she studied Wolf over the rim of her glass. "Why did you leave the police department, Wolf?" She asked. She gave Rachel a stern look when the other woman gasped.

Wolf shrugged. "I got a better offer." He glared at Julie. "How did you find out?" he wanted to know. Julie gave him a small smirk.

"Let's just say, I have my sources." She turned from him and studied Damien. "No more visions? Nothing?" she demanded and frowned when he shook his head.

"Nope. Been silent as the grave, err… so to speak." his eyes twinkled at her. "Other than that one little twinkle, I've been getting nothing. I figure when it comes, it'll be a mother and my head will explode, so forgive me if I add that it's something I'm not looking forward to."

Hunter stirred and looked around the room. Everyone was sitting around Damien's livingroom, and he had stretched out on the floor next to Kirsten.

"We are coming to the middle of November. Your time is limited.

There is still a lack of trust among some of you," he looked directly into Rachel's eyes, "and too much pettiness. Unless you are all united, you will fail."

Kirsten's face blanched, and a small groan escaped her lips, while Rachel bristled.

"Not now, mom. Please, don't start." Her amber eyes were painful to see. Fear and hopelessness combined, and Rachel lowered her eyes, closing her mouth with a snap.

Steve and Emma bustled out of the kitchen. "While you talk, you all need to eat something." she pointed at Julie, and then, at Abram. "I wasn't sure if you'd want to have something cooked or your own nourishment. I took the liberty." she gestured to two mugs on a tray. "They're heated." She added.

Abram looked around the room, amazed. No one looked uncomfortable as he took a mug and drank its contents down. All he saw was curiosity. They wondered what Emma and Steve had cooked up.

The mortals in the room gathered around, helped themselves to an excellent pork roast, mashed potatoes, and mixed veggies in a cream sauce. Homemade cranberry sauce was offered.

Julie walked over to Abram and took her own mug, drank it down, and handed it back to him. He carefully rinsed them both out, and then, the duo joined their mortal friends at the buffet.

"Will there be dessert, Emma? You know I have a weakness for your desserts." Hunter said with a wide smile.

"Hush! Would I disappoint you?" she admonished, and he wrapped her in a huge one-armed hug.

"No Emma. You never disappoint me." He kissed her warm cheek, and then, moved away.

"I was thinking, while you folks were having your little meeting," Emma said, "Thanksgiving is in a couple of weeks, so Julie, if you won't mind hosting, I won't mind cooking."

Julie raised an eyebrow at her housekeeper, no, her friend.

"I won't mind," she said, "I don't believe we've ever really celebrated that holiday. It will be fun."

Emma smiled a private smile. She had worked it out in her head. If they celebrated, together, it will take them another step closer to where they needed to be.

Emma knew they would have to be more than friends fighting a common foe. They would have to be family. She hoped, with everything in her, that they would make the transition.

Hunter threw her a wink. If anyone, he thought, could get the stubborn princess on the right track, it would be her erstwhile housekeeper.

Talk drifted from Thanksgiving to the following holiday season.

"I believe we'll have our usual holiday gathering for the neighbors and my charity co-workers, mid-December." Julie mentioned. "You all, of course, will be invited."

She looked at Kirsten and smiled. "Perhaps, you would come the evening before and lend a hand?" It wasn't really a question, but she was trying to be polite.

"Yes, of course. I love spending time with you." Kirsten said.

"I think we should all get together and celebrate on the twenty-fifth, too." Emma piped in. "That is, if no one has plans."

Damien grinned at Emma, making her blush.

"Works for me. We celebrate with my family the night, before. We can do it, here, if you like." he flashed a mischievous smile at Emma. "I have a dining room, too."

Emma dished up Dutch Apple Pie and passed out the plates. She became thoughtful while she worked.

Maybe, she thought, it will be enough if they remain friends. Of course, she would like to see them develop more, but friendship had a lot going for it, too. At least, that was her take on it.

Hunter seemed to be reading her mind because he smiled gently at her and winked.

Satisfied with the excellent meal, the group gathered in Damien's living room. Gently, Damien led the conversation back to their prime concern; keeping Kirsten safe and what exactly they would need to do to destroy Julie's sire.

In another part of town, Lance was feeling quite satisfied. He had, in a matter of days, secured a shelter for himself and his thugs and began to build the item they would need to fulfill his own destiny.

The device they were building had a dual purpose, but he would need the altar of humankind's destruction to be finished.

If he could not bring Julie to heel, then he would secure the innocent blonde. He would turn her and destroy all of that nauseating goodness the girl emanated.

At the appointed time, he would impregnate her and bring about the birth of his son, and then together, the world would be theirs to rule and to feed on.

These things had been promised to him, long ago. He had been patient, but now, his time was coming and no one could stop him. He would not be denied his destiny.

Turning, he gestured to one of his thugs. The young man came close, quaking in terror.

"I'm feeling peckish. Get me a little something to eat." he ordered.

"Yessir! Do you want a kid?" the thug squeaked out

Lance thought about it and then shook his head. "No, I'd prefer a woman. A small one. If you can't find one, then a small man will work just as well."

He moved to his living quarters, which he had furnished, lavishly. He may have to live in this hovel until his time came, but he didn't have to live in squalor.

The thug soon returned, dragging a young woman by the arm.

"Took a little persuasion, sir," the thug explained as Lance perused the woman's bruised face.

"How nice, you didn't manage to kill her before you brought her to me." Lance cuffed the thug on the side of his head, dropping him to his knees.

Wisely, the thug remained silent.

Lance gripped the woman in a vice-like grip and dragged her into the room he designated as a dining room.

"Welcome, my dear." he crooned. "I think it's dinner time."

He reared back and exposed his fangs. His eyes burned red, and before she could scream, he latched onto her throat.

She could hear the sucking noises he made as he drank her blood, and before death came for her, she had completely lost her mind.

Finished, he stepped over her body and out into the room his thugs sat, waiting for him.

"Get rid of that. I'm going out."

He watched as they scrambled to do as ordered, and then, Lance dressed carefully.

The three minions sighed in relief as he left the building. For a short time, they would have a little peace, but only for a short time.

Chapter 32

December flew by. For Kirsten, it was a difficult time. She missed Trish, terribly, but enjoyed spending time with Julie.

It was difficult to remember that Julie was, in reality, over two thousand years old. She certainly did not look her age, Kirsten thought wryly.

Damien was a dream, too. All that buff body and gentle nature, and wasn't he just completely smart, too?

Then, there was Steve. Kirsten absolutely adored him. The dress he made for her to wear to Julie's Holiday bash was out of this world.

"Where did you find that?" So many of Julie's society friends had asked and Kirsten cheerfully pointed them in the right direction.

The black bodice with the sweetheart neckline showed off her youthful neck and shoulders. The silver pouf skirt and snug long sleeves suited her, and Julie loaned her an onyx necklace and earrings.

Kirsten looked youthfully sophisticated, and the look on her dad's face had been fun. He was bravely pained. Somewhere along the line, his little girl had grown up. Wolf felt ancient.

Christmas had been a blast, too. Kirsten still couldn't believe the architect's drawing table Damien had given her. Wolf had given her the tools she would need, and they were all top-notch, from the divider to the compass to the slide rule.

Emma had given her a soft cashmere sweater in a warm gray. Kirsten was touched and amazed that the woman had actually knit it, herself.

Steve designed a suit in a gentle coral, and from Abram, she received a leather briefcase with her initials in gold.

From Rachel, she received another suit, this one in a powerhouse red, and Julie had given her citrine and diamond earrings and a matching bracelet.

The thought of Julie made her smile.

"Come, Kirsten. I shall teach you to dance." Julie had told her the last time they were together, and Kirsten had giggled.

"I know how to dance, Julie." she objected, and Julie laughed. "What you call dancing, I call disgraceful. I will teach you to dance as I once danced for a king."

The lesson turned into a disaster and they both had collapsed in fits of laughter.

"Kirsten, what am I going to do with you?" Julie asked, and Kirsten shrugged.

"Put up with me, I suppose."

Julie pulled one of Kirsten's curls, and then, scooted her out of the studio.

Yes, Julie and Kirsten spent a great deal of time, together, getting to know each other.

Julie's maternal instincts began to warm, and she knew it was the girl's simple goodness which brought about the change.

In the evenings, Rachel had a date; Abram would fetch Kirsten and bring her to Julie's home, and then, waited until she was ready to go home.

Sometimes, Kirsten felt crowded, but she understood. Her life, and possibly her very soul, was at stake, so she didn't balk too much.

New Year's Eve dawned cold and dry.

The group discussed it when they were together, Christmas Eve, and decided to hold their little party at Damien's.

Kirsten was busy getting ready when Rachel came up behind her.

"Would you mind if I don't go? I have a date... the man from the office that I've been seeing. He and I thought we'd have a little party, here. So, if you could make my excuses, I'd be grateful."

Rachel had been seeing this man for some time and seemed happy. She was also looking forward to school starting in January.

Her new life was about to begin, and she was giddy with happiness.

"Sure mom. I'm sure it'll be okay, only why did you wait until the last minute?"

Rachel shrugged a shoulder. "Rex wasn't sure if he would be here, or not. He travels a bit, and he thought he may be out of town. He called this morning, though, and he's here and wants to get together."

"So, when do I get to meet this paragon of masculine charm?" Kirsten teased and was surprised to see Rachel redden.

"Very soon, honey. We're still sort of getting to know each other."

Kirsten hugged Rachel and smiled. "You like him a lot, huh?"

Rachel nodded. "Yeah, I like him, a lot," she said.

"In that case, I hope it all works out for you, and I'll give everyone your apologies and tell them you got a better offer."

"Kirsten! Don't you dare!" and Kirsten laughed.

"Don't worry, mom. Your guilty secret is safe with me." Kirsten finished getting ready and hugged her mother, again.

"I'm gonna take off and see if Damien and Steve need any help."

Rachel looked at her beautiful daughter, dressed in jeans and the sweater Emma made, and wondered how anyone could be so sweet. Rachel, herself, didn't think she had *ever* been that good-hearted and felt a pang of shame.

Shaking it off, she waited until Kirsten pulled out of the driveway. It was early enough in the day, and Kirsten wouldn't be home until the next day, so they felt she would be safe enough.

Rachel walked into her bedroom and prepared herself for her date.

Kirsten knew she should call Abram to come get her, but it wasn't that far to Damien's condo, and it was only just now turning to dusk. Besides, she wanted a little time on her own.

She came bombing in the door and earned a good frown from both Abram and Damien.

"What were you thinking, Kirsten? All you had to do was call, and one of us would have picked you up."

She waved a hand. "I'm here, safe and sound. I think you guys worry, too much. There's been nothing since Trish's funeral. He's lost interest."

Abram scowled at her, and she could see him riding a white horse, dressed in armor, and leading a charge. He was every inch the soldier and one accustomed to giving orders.

A sheepish look stole over her face.

"I'm sorry. I just didn't think."

Abram walked over to her and took her chin in his large, cool hand. "Next time, think!" he ordered.

She smiled and nodded. "Yessir!"

Turning to Damien and Steve, she rubbed her hands together.

"Got my grades. I've made Dean's List. Straight A's!" she chirped and was rewarded with huge hugs all around.

"That's my girl!" Steve exclaimed.

"I couldn't have done it without your help, Damien. You explained things so much better than my stodgy old professors." She put her arms around him and hugged, hard.

He patted her back. "Don't be silly, Kirsten. You have the talent. I just cleared up a few muddy waters. I'm so proud of you. Listen now, I was going to wait, but I think I should tell you now. When the time is right, I'd like you to intern with me. I've accepted others for internship, and we won't have a problem getting you in the program. In the meantime, I'm going to offer you a job for the summer. You'll make some decent money, and you'll get a little experience under your belt, as well."

Kirsten was speechless. When she finally found her voice, all she could manage was a whispered, "Thank you."

The elevator doors glided open, and Wolf emerged into the foyer.

"Where's your mother?" he asked, and Kirsten clapped a hand to her mouth.

"With everything else going on, I almost forgot! Mom sends her apologies, but she won't be here. She has a date." Kirsten rolled her expressive wolf-like eyes and shook her head. "I haven't met the mystery man yet, but he sure has made an impression on mom."

"Yeah? He must have money." Wolf said and then wished he could saw his tongue in half. "Sorry honey. If the guy treats her well, that's good."

Once again, the elevator doors opened into the foyer and Julie and Emma glided into the condo, their hands laden down with food.

"Julie, I actually have food here." Damien told her while relieving her of some of her burden. He glanced over to Steve and Wolf and jerked his head in Emma's direction. The two men hurried over to help.

"Jeez, Emma, what? You were expecting an army or two?" Steve teased, and she swatted him on the arm.

"Some is for now, and some is for after midnight. Now, hush and help me sort out what's what."

Kirsten began fidgeting, patting down her pockets and looking through her purse.

"What's up? You got ants in those very chic pants?" Steve asked.

"I think I left my cell at home. I'm just gonna run over and get it."

Before anyone could move, she raced into the elevator, before her father or friends could stop her.

"Abram!" fear trembled in Julie's voice, and all eyes turned toward her. "Abram! Go after her," she ordered.

His eyes were tortured as he shook his head. "I can't. I can't float down. There are too many people in the street."

Wolf was jabbing at the buttons of the elevator, willing it to return to the condo and bring Kirsten back with it, but as the doors finally slid open the car was empty.

They all piled into the elevator, and Wolf swore as it seemed to inch its way down to the parking garage.

"Dammit! How many times was she told not to *do* this?" he growled. "I'm gonna wring her foolish young neck!" he vowed.

He looked over at Damien. The man's gray eyes were black, and blood seeped from his nose and ears.

"We've got to hurry!" he gasped, trying to stay on his feet. "We've got to hurry!"

Kirsten arrived home and noticed the very nice BMW parked at the curb. "Nice wheels," she murmured as she slid her key into the lock.

"Hey mom! It's just me! Forgot my cell! How am I gonna call you at midnight without my cell!" she sang out.

The words turned to ashes. Sitting in her living room was the creature she had been avoiding, the creature who murdered her friends.

Next to him, on the sofa, was the lifeless body of her mother.

In an instant, Kirsten took in the puncture wounds on her mother's throat. Rachel's lifeless eyes stared up at nothing, and her mother's skin was woefully pale.

Kirsten dashed toward the door, but it was too late. Lance had her by the hair, dragging her back into the living room.

"Hello Kirsten. I've been looking for you," he said in that silky voice. Tears welled up in her eyes as hopelessness welled in her heart.

There was no hope for her. None at all.

Chapter 33

"Oh Jesus no!" Damien groaned. "He's got her. He killed Rachel, and he has her! I can give you directions. It seems I am watching through Kirsten's eyes. Oh God, that kid is terrified. Step on it, Wolf!"

Blood poured from Damien's ears and nose as he slumped against Steve. Wolf ran to the driver's side and looked at Julie and Abram.

Steve was holding his handkerchief to Damien's nose, trying to staunch the flow. He never saw Damien leak this much blood. It horrified him.

"Come on! Get a move on!" Wolf yelled.

"Go ahead! Abram and I will meet you there. Damien will tell you where to go and we shall follow Kirsten's scent! Just *go!*"

Wolf peeled out of the underground parking. Terror for Kirsten riding with spiked hooves up and down his spine.

"Go, Abram! I'll be right behind you."

She took one look at Emma's white and grim face, and her fear

250

jumped another notch. Turning away, Julie used her incredible speed and dashed for home.

If this was going to be done, she thought, than it will be done properly.

She did not stop to think what her own fear meant, and she did not stop to think why it mattered. All she knew is they had to get to Kirsten.

If she would have been a prayerful woman, she would be praying now, but she felt she had lost that right long, long ago. She would depend on Abram and herself.

Lance enjoyed Kirsten's fear. He reveled in it, and he hoped to produce more.

Ever so gently, he licked the side of her neck. He could feel her pulse jump with each flick of his tongue. The sound of her blood rushing through her veins intoxicated him like a fine wine.

Shock wrapped itself around Kirsten, and for the time being, she was insulated from the full horror of everything happening. She could not tear her eyes away from the body of her dead mother, lying almost obscenely on the sofa she had prized so much.

Lance, prolonging the moment, waltzed her around the living room, dipping and swaying. Oh, he was enjoying himself. He had one prize and he rather thought the other would be coming.

His thugs had kept him apprised. His princess and this girl were friendly, but he could not quite figure out why. Mortals were so beneath them. Still, if they were friendly and the princess had genuine feelings for this girl, so much the better.

Everything was working just the way he hoped it would.

So, for now, he could take his time. He played Kirsten as a cat plays a mouse, and when it appeared she would swoon, he jerked her upright, forcing her to stay in the here and now.

Glancing at a clock, however, told him he really should begin that which must begin.

Kirsten watched in horror as his fangs elongated and his eyes burned an unholy red. His smile was more a sneer as he lowered his head to her throat and bit.

Damien swore in silence as he witnessed Kirsten and the vampire. Wisely, he did not tell Wolf. The man was driving, and if Wolf lost control, they would never be able to stop the son-of-a-bitch.

"What do you see, Damien, Dammit!" Wolf demanded and Damien groaned, again. The pain in his head was unlike anything he'd experienced, before.

"Rachel's dead, Wolf. I'm sorry, but Rachel's dead." Damien felt safe enough telling him that much.

"What about Kirsten? Is she still alive?" Wolf asked. His heart beat against his ribs, and the fear for his daughter tasted like copper.

"Yeah Wolf, she's still alive." Damien said. Better not to tell him, yet, that the vampire had bitten her. Better to wait and see.

Next to him, tears streamed down Steve's cheeks, and in the front seat with Wolf, Damien could faintly here Emma cursing under her breath.

A part of him was amused. Who would have thought such a fine lady would know words like that, he thought.

Abram neared Rachel's home and stopped. He sensed the sire would be on the move. Whatever the creature had in mind would not take place, here.

He hung back, watching, using his incredible eyesight. It would be better to wait until Kirsten was taken to the creature's lair.

Cautious, he looked around. The sire would have his thugs, those he had placed in thrall. It would not do if he were taken by surprise.

He wondered what his mistress was doing. He wondered, too, if they would be able to save Kirsten.

Damn these mortals, he thought, and damn him for getting involved. It was better when he felt nothing.

Now, he was in terror for Kirsten. He sensed Rachel was dead. The sire would not allow her to live, but what of Kirsten? The girl touched him, and he did not know if he should be pleased or annoyed. He would think about that, later.

Julie raced into her house and up the stairs. It took a moment for her to find what she needed.

Tearing off her clothes, she prepared herself, using her speed. Time is of the essence, now, she thought. She became aware that Kirsten had been bitten, and she wanted to sob. What if they were too late, she thought. What if this was all for nothing?

Angry, she shook the thought from her mind. It could not be too late. Nor for Kirsten.

Ready now, she raced out of her house and began to move toward the house Rachel and Kirsten shared.

Julie knew Rachel was dead, and she wished she could ask whatever deity there is, but she could not bring herself to do that. She would rely on herself and on Abram.

Lance was careful. He did not want this gem of a girl dead, just more compliant, and he did not want her in thrall. He wanted her aware of everything about to happen to her.

Carefully, he picked her up in his arms and carried her out the door and to his car. Placing her in the passenger seat, he looked around taking care no one could see him.

The street was deserted, and so he let himself into the car and began to drive. This would be a night to remember, he thought.

Abram, hidden, watched as the sire drove away. He followed, hoping his mistress would pick up his scent and follow.

Strong as he was, he would not be able to destroy the creature, alone. He was not sure Julie would be able to do it, but together, they would try.

"Where the hell is Hunter?" he fumed. "He's always around until he's needed."

It took some doing, but he followed Lance to the old factory and watched from the shadows as the creature carried Kirsten into the building.

His heart sank when her head lolled to the side. He could see the two puncture marks in her throat, and he wanted to wail.

"Stay calm," he whispered. "Let us see what we shall see."

Moving cautiously, he began to follow Lance into the building but a large hand on his shoulder stopped him.

Spinning around to meet the threat, his heart almost started beating, again, when he saw who it was.

"Wait for the others, Abram." Hunter said.

"Where the hell have you been?" Abram hissed and Hunter smiled at him as though pleased.

"I had to prepare myself, too." Hunter looked off into the distance and then turned back to Abram. "Ah... Here come the rest of our friends."

Abram turned and watched as Julie came to a graceful halt next to him. Hunter pointed, and Abram could see Wolf and his party pulling in.

"Hail, hail, the gangs all here." Julie said in a snide tone, and Hunter laughed in her face.

She looked him up and down and frowned. "You know, in all of our centuries, together, I have never seen you other than exceptionally turned out. What is this you are wearing?"

Hunter was dressed in a black leather duster, buttoned from throat to ankles.

"Oh, just a little something I found. Do you like it?" he asked and was rewarded with a most unladylike snort. She did not deign to answer him.

Damien stumbled from the car and let his stomach resolve itself on the pavement. He felt as if a thousand demons were doing a tap dance on his brain, and nausea rolled over him in sickening waves.

"Damien, stay in the car. We've got this." Wolf told him, but Damien shook his head and immediately regretted it.

"No, I'm coming in with you. Don't argue with me. I'm too busy being sick."

Wolf sighed. The guy could be so damn stubborn.

Steve came up next to Damien with a Wet-Ones and a can of Coke.

"Here, wipe your face and take a swig of this. You look like shit, Damien, but you being you, you will be coming in with us." Steve slid a glance at Wolf. "He's so stubborn."

Wolf nodded. "Yeah, I noticed."

Damien was rewarded glyph

They went in as a group, as a family, with Julie and Abram leading the way. Abram, his head back, flared his nostrils and picked up Kirsten's scent.

"This way. Move slowly and stay behind us," he warned the others.

Cautious now, they moved, taking great care not to make a sound.

"We need the element of surprise. There's no telling how many he has in thrall." Abram whispered.

Damien looked and felt ill. Abram thought it may have been a mistake to bring him with, but it was too late to send him back, now.

❧

Abram and Wolf exchanged glances. The dim cavernous rooms they moved through were perfect for ambush. Should they be attacked, Damien would be at risk, but Abram shrugged. They wouldn't leave him behind.

Julie walked at their side, alert and on the hunt. She could smell death, as could they all.

"He's been using this place as his lair," she whispered. "Can you smell it?" The men simply nodded.

Steve and Emma struggled to keep Damien on his feet, but he was getting weaker. Flashing in between vision and reality was taking a toll on him.

Hunter brought up the rear, watchful, wondering and hopeful.

Wolf's fear for Kirsten was almost tangible. He alternated between rage and despair.

His child is in danger, and he failed to protect her. Rachel was dead and he had failed her, too.

Abram gave him a sharp elbow in the ribs.

"Thinking like that won't get Kirsten back. You are not alone in this. Keep your mind on the job at hand." Abram admonished him. Wolf nodded.

Moving toward flickering lights, the group spread out as much as they could.

Ahead, Wolf could make out a type of altar, and his heart sank. Kirsten lay on the damn thing and even in the flickering lights, he could see how pale she was.

Holding back the impulse to rush to her, they held back. Waiting to get jumped, and still, when the three thugs rushed them, they were unprepared.

The biggest of the three grabbed Wolf and hit him alongside his head with a tire iron, dropping him to his knees.

The other two went after Damien and Steve. Abram rushed to their defense and grabbed the first of the two he could reach. He could easily snap his neck, but a voice behind him stopped him.

"Kill my man and the girl dies." Lance called out. "Come quietly, or she dies, now."

Now, Julie thought, now is the time.

Julie was eerily calm as she strode forward. She met her sire eye to eye and shrugged off her coat.

"Cain," she said, softly, and because she was watching his face closely, saw the flicker of surprise dance across his features.

"It has been a very long time since anyone called me by name. How did you know?"

Julie shrugged. "I've known almost from the beginning."

"Yes, well, those times are long gone. They thought me dead you know. All these ions I have walked the earth, taking what I wished. No one knew."

Julie went to him and placed her hand gently on his arm. "It must have been difficult for you." she began and his laugh cut her off.

"Difficult? Not at all, my dear. I was free. From the moment Lilith turned me, I was free. Free to do what I wished. Free to take and destroy. Free of the burden of sickening and relentless *love*. It was not difficult, at all." Lance turned to her. "I destroyed her, you know. She was the only being who could destroy me, so I ended her, first," he laughed harshly. "Given a chance I would do it all, again."

"Cain, let the girl go, and I will come to you, willingly." Julie said softly.

"Does she mean so much to you?" he asked. Julie bit her lip. Now it could get tricky. If she said yes, he could kill Kirsten just for the fun of it, and if she said no, he could kill Kirsten just for the hell of it.

"She's mortal, Cain." Julie hedged. "What does she matter to you? Let her go and we can feast on her some other time."

"What you say has merit. You do know what it will cost you if you come to me, do you not?"

Julie nodded. She would birth a monster, and that monster would destroy her. There would be an ending of all she is. Still, if she can buy some time for Kirsten, and Wolf, and all of them, her destruction would be worth it.

Hunter watched her closely, waiting.

Cain loosened the chains holding Kirsten to the altar. Wolf was afraid to breathe. The vampire could change his mind in a flash and still kill her.

Abram wanted to beat his fists against a wall, but as his rage grew he felt a soft arm slip around his waist. Emma stood proudly at his side.

"Just wait, Abram. Don't do anything, just yet. Wait." she whispered to him.

Emma just *knew* Julie had a plan. She would have to be patient and see how this all played out. And, she was prepared. In her coat pocket was a pistol that had belonged to her husband. Before she would let that thing take a bite out of her or any of them, she would kill them all, first. For now, though, she would wait and see.

"I'm going to take my maid and prepare myself, Cain." Julie told him. It occurred to him she did not ask his permission.

"Ask me nice, and I'll think about it." he was toying with her and she knew it. She had to gain the upper hand. Julie had a plan, of sorts. It was haphazard, at best, but it was the best she could think of.

"These things need ritual, Cain. You know that as well as I. Emma! Come with me." She didn't wait for permission.

The two women walked to another room, and Julie grabbed Emma's hand in a frantic grip.

She shrugged the coat from her shoulders, and Emma saw she clutched a small bag.

"Reach inside of this, quickly. There's a small bottle. I can't bear to touch it. Once he has me on that despicable altar, I will look over at you and wink. That is your signal. You will splash the contents of this bottle in his face. Oh, and Emma, try not to get any on me."

While she talked, she readied herself, and Emma could only stare at the transformation.

Julie was dressed in a robe of fine white linen as soft as a cloud. Amethyst twinkled at her throat, ears and fingers. On her wrist, she wore a wide silver cuff bracelet that Emma had never seen, before. The pattern was foreign and exotic and the bracelet was obviously very old.

"Once you splash him, stand back and let Abram take over. He will know what to do. Get Kirsten out of here as soon as you can."

Julie scooped her hair back and held it in place with two diamond clips.

"Okay, I'm ready. Good luck, Emma." she turned to go, then

stopped and wrapped her housekeeper in a tight embrace.

"Thank you, Emma, for all you've done for me. Thank you for all you've been to me. "

Before Emma could answer, Julie stepped back into the room where Cain waited.

"I would ask your indulgence for one more moment." She waited until Cain inclined his head in the smallest of nods.

This was the woman he remembered. She looked exactly as she had the day he turned her, and it pleased him.

She stepped in front of Wolf and silently squeezed his hand. Hoping he would understand, she moved to Steven and gently patted his face. She took Damien's sweaty and pale face in both of her hands, she forced him to look her in the eyes.

"Do not forget me, Damien. I think I could have loved you."

Turning to Abram, she stared into his eyes and waited. He nodded. They had been together for so long, no words were needed.

She met Hunter's eyes and looked into his for as long as she could bear it. He must have read something in her own expressive brown eyes because he suddenly smiled and gave her a small bow.

Turning back, she faced Cain. "Let Kirsten go. You've won. Let her go or this ends now." she gestured toward his thugs. "If you think they could stop me, you are sadly mistaken. Let her go."

He pushed Kirsten toward her father and watched with some satisfaction as the girl crumbled at his feet.

Julie took a quick look at her and could have wept in gratitude. The girl was weak, but he had not put her in thrall. Kirsten would be all right.

Julie took two steps toward Cain when Hunter called out.

"Herodia! Why do you do this?" he asked in a booming voice.

She turned back to him and smiled, her fangs glinting in the dim light.

"I do it for love," she told him and flew at Cain, her lips drawn back in fury as she launched herself at the male vampire.

His complacent smile turned to a leer as he braced himself to meet her attack.

They fought. They clawed and hit and bit at each other, healing as quickly as the damage was inflicted and still, Hunter waited.

Julie, now Herodia, fought with everything in her, but she was losing. She felt herself losing ground and she sobbed in frustration. He would end her, and then Abram, and he would devour those she had come to love.

And still, Hunter waited. There was one thing lacking from her, and he hoped she would find it, soon.

Finally, as her strength was ebbing, as the battle raged between the two, she cried out in a soft voice. "Oh God!"

Hunter smiled and threw back his head. He opened his mouth wide and the sound that issued from his throat was unlike anything heard, before.

To Wolf, it sounded like a thousand voices singing and the force of it drove him to his knees. Damien clasped his head and crumbled in a heap, unconscious.

Abram trembled, pain tearing through him, and he felt as if he were melting from the inside out. He clasped Emma's hand and kissed her knuckles as his strength left him, and he too collapsed.

Steve was crying and cradling Damien's head in his lap while Kirsten twitched and moaned.

Cain's strength ebbed, and just as a clock began to toll midnight, Julie flexed her wrist. A dagger slid into her hand, and she thrust with all of her might, sending the blade into Cain's heart.

No sooner did she pierce the organ, than he disintegrated in a cloud of black dust.

Julie sank to her knees. She felt as if her bones were melting, and she was boiling from the inside out. The pain was unimaginable, and she longed for her own ending. Anything had to be better than this.

Hunter turned to Damien, first, and picking the big man up, he cradled him as a mother would cradle a child.

Finally, Damien opened his eyes and smiled, and Hunter put him back on his feet, before turning to Julie, now gasping in pain.

He crouched down in front of her and waited for her to raise her eyes to his.

"You are not dying, my dear. You are becoming mortal. You've been given another chance. Make the most of it."

He straightened and walked to where Abram was in the throes of his own agony. "It will soon be over, Abram. Well done, faithful servant."

He walked over to Emma and hugged her tightly.

"Emma, I shall miss your pies and cakes. They are heavenly." he told her with a twinkle in his eyes.

"Steven. You have done well. You are a faithful friend and good brother. I have enjoyed you, immensely."

Kirsten looked at Hunter with eyes filled with sadness.

"Kirsten, your path is set. You have been a good daughter and a wonderful friend. You will mourn her, of course, but do not let your mother's death overshadow your happiness in the coming days."

Hunter shed his duster and all could see huge silver wings at his shoulders. He was dressed in gold light armor and carried a massive broadsword.

"Who the hell are you?" Wolf asked while cradling his daughter.

Hunter laughed. "Just call me what others call me. Michael." And he was gone in a beam of light.

Epilogue

They didn't talk about that New Year's Eve. There didn't seem to be a need to.

Damien still had visions but no longer the headaches. Whatever Michael had done to him had a lasting effect. For the first time since he was seven years old, he felt healthy.

Damien and Julie spent a lot of time, together, as did Abram and Emma. By spring, the four were talking weddings.

Kirsten, mourning her mother, threw herself into her school work. While she excelled, she missed Rachel and ,of course, Trish. She remembered Michael's words to her once she was released from the vampire. She supposed she should be grateful he hadn't turned her, but still, she had her bouts of depression.

Wolf, knowing the signs, arranged for her to get some help from a grief counselor and her own good sense and sweet nature didn't let the tragedies overcome her.

The Rollings murders, Rachel's killing, and those at the morgue, were never solved and had been left open. It probably was just as well.

Wolf resigned from the police force, and after Alicia returned to Milwaukee, he signed on to work with her.

"Sometimes, I really miss Hunter, or rather Michael." Julie mentioned to Damien. "He was a nuisance while all of this was going on, but now, I miss him."

Damien lightly fingered her curls. "I wouldn't worry about it too much. I have a feeling he'll show up, one of these days."

Thoughtfully, she sipped her coffee. "Maybe, he will." She agreed.

Damien's cell went off, and Steve's voice bounded over the air.

"I'm a success, Damien! They love me, here!" he crowed.

"What's not to love?" Julie asked, putting her lips close to the receiver. "Congratulations!"

In spite of his success during Spring Fashion Week, Steve promised to be home.

"I can't let my best friends get married without me!" he boomed and brought a smile to both faces.

Wolf walked into the brand new offices of his brand new employer. Alicia perched on a desk with a cup of tea in her hand and grinned at him.

A door opened, and an elegant woman of about fifty sauntered into the office.

Wolf took in the unlined face and the short silver hair. She had a toned and finely muscled body, and it took a minute before he recognized her.

"Velvet Black." He whispered, and her generous mouth broke into a wide smile.

"Welcome, Wolf. You look so shocked. You didn't think I'd sit back on my ass after I left the force, did you? So, welcome. Welcome to Black Velvet Investigations. You'll be working for me."

She handed him a cup of coffee, and Wolf was home.

About the Author

Redemption is Karen Salamone-Jourdan's second book, following Gabriel's Gate.

A product of early Catholic education, and then, the Milwaukee Public school system, she found the joys of reading at an early age.

Since retiring, she has used the time to follow her first love; writing.

She is the mother of two and resides in Ripon, Wisconsin with her cat, SweetPea.

Stay tuned for many more works!